Praise for the Jovian Universe

Captivating science fiction.

> — BlueInk Review (Starred Review)

Kim Catanzarite excels in depicting changing family interactions and relationships against the backdrop of sci-fi events.

> — Midwest Book Review

Irresistible appeal to fans of science fiction — crisp writing, superior storytelling, and intriguing characters.

> — Christian Fernandez, The Book Commentary

A foray into intrigue that's thoroughly steeped in psychological revelation.

> — Diane Donovan, Senior Reviewer MWR

If you love visually stunning sci-fi, you'll enjoy this story. [Her] writing is so cinematic that you feel the majesty and the mayhem—the glorious, the gory, the good, the terrifying—as if you've been thrown into the middle of it yourself.

> — ıdependent Book Review

The Jovian Pentalogy

They Will Be Coming for Us
Jovian Son
Bright Blue Planet
The Moon Children
The Cold Light of Fate

THE
COLD LIGHT
OF
FATE

KIM CATANZARITE

forster
publishing

A LUCY H SOCIETY BOOK

ISBN: 979-8-9912761-2-2 (paperback)

ISBN: 979–8-9912761-1-5 (e-book)

Printed in the United States of America

1 3 5 7 9 10 8 6 4 2

Published by Lucy H Society Books, an imprint of Forster Publishing, United States of America. Distributed by Ingram Book Group, www.ingramcontent.com.

Cover design by Damonza

❀ Formatted with Vellum

For those who live by the Golden Rule

"O fear not in a world like this,
And thou shalt know erelong,
Know how sublime a thing it is
To suffer and be strong."

—Henry Wadsworth Longfellow

The Jovian Universe Year 2051

List of Characters

- Svetlana Peterman: wife of Andrew
- Andrew Jovian: son of Caroline and Edmund
- Evander Peterman: son of Svetlana and Andrew
- Nadia Peterman: wife of Evander, lives in Russia
- Dmitri: eleven-year-old son of Evander and Nadia, newly appointed supreme being
- Natasha: rapidly aging daughter of Evander and Nadia
- Evan: eighteen-year-old daughter of Svetlana and Andrew from the universe without Jovians

Jovian Royalty

- Caroline: aka Queen Jovian, leader of Jovian Earth

- Edmund: husband of Caroline, Jovian co-leader
- Miranda: powerful Jovian, leader of the Mars settlement
- Leo: husband to Miranda, co-leader on Mars
- Dana and John (Peterman): Svetlana's adoptive parents, humanitarians
- Uncle Jimmy: aka James, an enigma, rumored to have been born on Mintaka, a self-proclaimed Jovian
- Aunt Constance: wife of Jimmy
- David: adopted son of Jimmy and Constance, a supreme being who died in Book 4

Others

- Ida Moore: human who bridged the connection between Jovians and NASA in the 1970s, well over one hundred years old
- Dayana: tends the greenhouse at Starbright
- Elara: an extraterrestrial stowaway seeking pinecones for Europa
- Head Leonard: leader of Starbright's security squad and the elite group of Leonard clones
- Fran Vasquez: Andrew and Svetlana's loyal friend and former FBI agent, current co-leader of the Coalition
- Lisa Vasquez: friend to Andrew and Svetlana, former hospital nurse
- Max Vasquez: son of Fran and Lisa, Evander's pilot apprentice, currently a full-fledged space pilot

Chapter 1

Dayana

Some believed she was born of the earth's core.

A burning ball of maternal fire pressed into liquid and streamed through cracks and fissures the way magma flows uphill. So intent was her energy to reach the surface of the Earth that when she met with its tectonic plates, her ferocity slammed into them and shook the ground in every direction.

The day the thing that would become Dayana broke through the rocky crust was the day Pangea cracked into pieces. She entered the living world with a crashing bang and a gasp, desperate for her first breath as if emerging from deep ocean waters.

Exposed, she crawled across the desert, a semisolid creature in search of a riverbed in which to cool. She came to recline in a stream of roiling rapids and spread herself upon the silt. Like an old woman pulling up the covers of her bed, she settled, buried in clay and mud.

Years passed. The yellow light of the sun filtered through the canopy of branches above. Instinctively, the flora (and later the fauna too) sensed Dayana's simmering presence, the life that pervaded the river in which she slept. The long-leaved trees flourished beside her roiling stream. It was there, under the alluvium that she came upon the elements necessary to mold her human body—first her head, heart, and womb, and then all the rest.

Fully formed, Dayana walked out of that river and onto the land, where she greeted her beloved mosses, ferns, and flowers. Trees of all sizes and shapes. Fungi, vines, clover, dandelions. She wandered for years, following the curve of the stream up hills and through forests, across valleys and into the jungle. Finally she reached the cloud forests of Peru and settled there in a stone house with a thatched roof—among the people who lived there—for many hundreds of years.

They called her Pachamama, a mysterious woman who kept to herself, came and went like the wind, and was very much like everyone else, and not at all like everyone else. She never grew old—or died.

Millennia passed before Edmund Jovian met Dayana in Machu Picchu. He introduced her to Starbright International, and she agreed to make it her home. There she slept under a warm blanket of lime-green moss in a plot of soil padding a corner of the greenhouse. Few in the building had spoken to Dayana or so much as saw her face. None had ever witnessed her arrival or departure, because she was always there, slumbering in her peat, stirring with dust particles in the light, or flowing with the oxygen and hydrogen atoms in the fountain's water.

Dayana tended the greenhouse. As Evander once said, she was charged with "ministering to all things '*kingdom plantae*.'" Her presence inspired seeds to shuck their shells and hoist their stalks, to blossom in the morning light and shower in evening dew. She kept watch over the precious, vulnerable seedlings that thrived in her home and across this bright blue planet.

That morning, roused by the gentle fingers of the sun, she rose from her bed of soil. She wore a handwoven shift dress the shade of wheat decorated with beads of turquoise fastened with threads of gold at its hem. The glass walls that rose high above her dark-brown hair invited the sun's warmth, and the damp of birth and death and nourishing ground pervaded the air. As Dayana made her way through plants and potting beds and gurgling fountains, she lent her gentle touch and whispered encouragement to the many juveniles there. "Yes, yes, very good," she said and, "Oh, how lovely you are," bending to touch their maturing bark or to gaze into the spiral of their seed cones.

When she reached the center of the room, she sensed a charge in the air: something cold and promising. She paused before instinct drew her to a small grove of Jack pines. Passing underneath their long-needled branches, she entered a space lively with the babble of water and ice. Ancient aquatic specimens from the Jupiter System clustered within a narrow pool. The *Cryophylla glaciata,* a species found in the oceans of Europa, fed upon saltwater, some of them rising six-feet tall with many arching, seaweedy arms. Dayana approached them and came upon a much smaller creature wedged in between the *Cryophylla* trunks. It was a mostly formless lump in a clay pot set in the middle of the bigger trees like a little penguin chick at the base of the adults that surrounded it.

"Oh, no, no, no, little babe, you don't belong over there," she whispered as she eyed a potting table it should have occupied across the way. Carefully, she pulled the little lump and its pot from the trees that surrounded it. Near-freezing water gurgled over its sides and wet her palms, then streamed down her arms and spilled upon the earthen floor below.

The babe trembled like an amorphous infant struggling to raise its heavy, bowed head. Dayana leaned in close and smiled at the sound of breath in and out, in and out.

"You are waking up," she whispered with delight. The babe opened its tiny knot of a mouth, then two blinking gray wrinkles for eyes, gurgling as if it were greeting its mother for the first time.

"You know what that means, don't you?" Dayana gazed upward, beyond the glass rooftop above, into the place where the atmosphere meets the exosphere and merges with the beyond.

"She must be on her way."

Chapter 2

Natasha

Natasha knew she wouldn't receive the red-carpet treatment when she, Svetlana, and Svetlana's teenaged daughter, Evan, time-tripped to Great-grandmother's Jovian Universe, but she hadn't expected to be thrown into a cell and locked up, either.

Whether by marriage or DNA, all three of them were Jovians, for goodness sake!

While two giant Leonards dressed in black security squad uniforms pulled Svetlana in one direction, the metal-headed one had taken Natasha in one rough hand and gripped Evan in the other, and escorted the two of them into the tubes. He threw them in a room that measured no bigger than an average walk-in closet and left them there.

Similar to a train's sleeping compartment, two cots flanked a wooden tabletop bridged in between. There were no windows to see out of, no pictures to look at; the walls donned the dull white common to pages found in old hard-cover books. The metal sliding door opposite stood thick and enduring, futuristic compared to its surroundings. She and Evan would not escape using brute force alone.

"Are they just going to leave us here?" Evan practically shouted, though at this close proximity, she could have mouthed the words and Natasha would have understood.

Reclined on one of the beds, Natasha wished to be alone—no offense to Evan. The time trip they'd taken from Svetlana's universe (a world without Jovians) to this one had left Natasha out of sorts the same way it had the first time she moved through decades and universes, with her father, Evander.

They'd both been sick that time too, him more than her.

The nausea Natasha could handle, but the mind-numbing lack of energy was another thing altogether. It came with an irritable mood, which she did her best to conceal while Evan, rattled by her introduction to the ever-babbling Jovian oneness, filled their shared compartment with an aggravating run of nervous chatter.

"This is so awful!" Evan complained for the umpteenth time. "It's like hundreds of people talking at once. I can't even hear myself think."

Natasha wanted to tell her to stop talking, but that would be rude. Instead she said, "It's not hundreds of people talking at once, it's *hundreds of thousands* of people talking at once. It'll get better, I promise."

Because Evan, only eighteen years old, had grown up in a universe without natives of Jupiter, this was her first experience with what it meant to be a Jovian in the Jovian world—to be part of the oneness, the Jovian means of tele-pathic communication, whether she liked it or not. It would take some time for her to become accustomed to the intellectual turbulence that came with the ability to hear the thoughts and verbal expressions of every living Jovian in the cosmos. And for this, Natasha empathized.

But it wasn't the end of the world by any means.

"Be patient," she told Evan. "You'll learn how to tie it up and push it away so it becomes a murmur in the background instead of . . . whatever clamor you're experiencing at the moment."

Evan met Natasha's gaze with a doubtful frown. Her short hair with the long, side-swooping bangs sprawled in a disheveled manner. "Are you sure? 'Cause this is really bad." She dropped her chin and chewed her bottom lip as if she might cry.

Natasha, who was part Jovian and therefore not "big" on emotion, didn't want Evan to think she didn't care, so she responded with a gentle tone of the sort she remembered her mother using when she or Dmitri, her older brother, used to complain. This was done purposefully, as her natural responses were always on the far-less-gentle and more matter-of-fact side.

"We only arrived an hour ago," she said. "Give it time."

"Feels like longer," the teenager persisted.

"I'm sure it does. Rest a bit while I figure out what we should do next." Natasha patted the cot beside hers before allowing her heavy head to sink into the thin pillow. She hoped Evan would do the same.

She didn't.

"Don't take this the wrong way," Evan said, squinting as if that's what she needed to do in order to express herself, "but you look different . . . from when we left home, I mean, when we left *my* home." Evan spoke at an exaggerated volume as if she were competing with the hum of a train engine. "You don't look bad or anything.

You're as pretty as ever, it's just that you, uh, seem a little older."

Natasha had not yet checked a mirror, and frankly didn't want to.

"That's normal for you," Evan said. "Isn't it? That's what you told me, but I just wondered, do you *feel* okay?"

"It is normal for a time trip to age me, and, no, I don't feel great," Natasha said, rubbing her temples. "But it's nothing to worry about. Just sit," she said, patting the cot again. "Rest."

With reluctance, Evan plunked upon the empty bed and lay back. As soon as it seemed she might settle, however, she jolted upright again. "My mom must be worried sick about us," she said. "Where do you think they took her? She and Caroline have a long history of not getting along. Do you think Caroline will hurt—"

Natasha's comm chimed. A clear, high-pitched ping.

She pulled it from her thigh-side pocket. A text from Max Vasquez crossed the screen: "Are you OK? Did you make it home? Would be great to talk. Whenever you can. Call me. When you're not busy or whatever. I'm in transit."

"Who is it?" Evan shouted. "Is it my mom? Does she have a phone?"

Natasha clicked off her comm and replaced it in her pocket. "No, it's someone else. A friend."

"Can they help us get out of here?"

"No. He's traveling right now."

Max was a nice guy that she knew. The son of Fran and Lisa Vasquez. He became her father's pilot apprentice when Evander invited him on the trip to pick her up on Mintaka, the place Uncle Jimmy had brought her to have her heart surgery. They had traveled together for a short time, and now, every so often, Max reached out to ask how she and Evander were doing.

No doubt he'd heard the news of her father's death. He'd loved Evander, she knew, and he probably wanted to commiserate with her in sadness . . . but she really didn't want to face all of that at the moment, and that's why she hadn't replied to his messages.

It was not the time to mourn. She needed to deal with the situation at hand—she had to free Evan from this cell. The fate of the planet depended on it.

Stretched on her back on the cot, she lay her arm across her forehead, determined to think. If only she had the energy to deal with this. She closed her eyes and took a breath. To her dismay, her heart sped up and then tripped and quivered awkwardly. Or maybe she'd only imagined it. Too much worry about a potential problem could bring about phantom flutters. Her father had told her that many times. She had been worried about her heart since the doctors on Mintaka told her it would not serve her well on Earth.

And here she was, spending more time on Earth.

Whether she imagined a problem or not, she didn't have the luxury of time. She needed to play her part, to give this Earth a fighting chance, and then she could leave.

If she survived—which she might not.

Maybe she shouldn't have come.

But she had to. She had to bring Evan here. There'd been no choice about that.

Besides, she wanted to be the one to tell her mother, Nadia, the news about Evander, the story of how he had passed. The idea that her mom would never see her dad again brought on another swell of queasiness, and Natasha held back a gag. If time traveling was this bad for her, it must have been awful when her father did it at his advanced age. But he knew of the danger he'd put himself in. As old as he was when they left Io, as predisposed to aging as he was, he knew a time trip might be his end, and yet he'd still taken it.

Natasha never should have let him.

But she understood that he longed to set things right between himself and his mother, that he'd wanted to apologize to Svetlana for something she hadn't even known he'd done. His penchant for honesty was maddening.

And that was his way: always opting to do the right thing, no matter how difficult.

"I've found you." The playful voice had broken through the murmur of the oneness with startling clarity and volume.

Natasha gasped, then answered internally. "Dmitri?"

"I have been waiting for your return," her brother said as if he stood right in front of her.

"It's so good to hear your voice." She pushed her legs over the side of the cot and sat up as she continued to speak to him in her mind. "I'm sorry it's been so long since I left. I meant to come back sooner. So much has happened." The question of whether he knew their father had died would have jumped out of its seat, had it been a seated thing, but she wouldn't let it, not yet. "And now I'm stuck—"

"In a holding cell inside Starbright International," he said.

"Yes." She smiled a little at his preciseness. "Great-grandmother's Leonard locked us up. I'm not sure why."

"Someone is with you," Dmitri said. "Is it Svetlana's daughter?"

"Yes, her name is Evan."

"The Lost Sister," he said, impressing Natasha with his knowledge. "I can see everything if I try."

With a vibrating hum, the heavy door to the cell slid open.

Evan, who'd been resting upon her side on the cot, lifted her head, her long, loose bangs cascading across her eyes. She swiped them away. "The door," she shouted, unaware of the conversation that just passed between Natasha and Dmitri. "Oh my God, it just opened. Should we go?"

"Come to the astronomical observatory," Dmitri said through the oneness. "I'll lead the way."

"My brother opened it." Natasha explained as she stood. "We're going to see him."

Chapter 3

Max

"It will take a while to get to Earth," Max said, studying the control board and taking a quick look out the main viewport. "A few days at least, and that's only if I can find the right wormhole."

The creature sitting beside him in the copilot's chair literally glowed. Silvery white like a frosted January morning, her light seemed to both absorb and shine from the surface of her skin. That is, if *skin* was what covered the glossy surface of her body. Max really had no clue.

Frankly, her light made it difficult to decipher her more-detailed features even at this close proximity. He couldn't tell if she had hair, for instance, or colored irises, but he could see that she held his tiny pinecone in the careful cup she made of her thick fingers, as if it meant as much to her as it did to him.

The pinecone was his prized possession, given by his father just before Max left Earth five give-or-take years ago (to this day he didn't know precisely how long he'd been gone). He could see that Elara was petite, smaller than the average human female. And once, when she stood directly in front of him, he recognized cheek mounds and a pointed chin as well as two elongated eyes and a small nose. He could see even without full clarity that she was cute. Maybe even adorable. But definitely blurry.

Looking at her for more than a few seconds overwhelmed his vision and made his eyes water.

"I have relayed your message, and Elara gave her approval using language of hands," said Syndi, the *Orion Sparrow*'s AI system.

Syndi sounded about as average as a woman could. Her voice wasn't too high or low, too animated or bland. She maintained a confident tone even when she made social miscues that were no fault of her own.

"Good to know," Max said.

He focused on the keyboard and continued to program their trip, careful to correctly key in the coordinates for the nearest wormhole. He hoped Elara would find something she could eat in the galley, so she wouldn't consider taking a bite out of him. Then again, she didn't seem the carnivorous type, and as a human being *he* actually was carnivorous—or at least he had the potential to be—so if she wasn't worried about him, should he worry about her?

So far, Elara seemed nice enough. Sweet, though he'd only known her for a matter of days. She'd come upon him at a bad moment, in the midst of a breakdown that began when he learned of the loss of his mentor and friend Evander Peterman—best president the country had ever known. While Max bawled like a baby, Elara had approached with concern that seemed to radiate in cool waves that entered and soothed his inflamed insides.

She'd told him to "trust the universe." She'd actually spoken the word *universe*—momentarily forgoing the language of hands—which itself was pretty amazing considering she probably never even heard English before meeting him.

He hated to tell her, but it would be a long time before he started clicking and popping in her native tongue, whatever it may be. Learning languages wasn't his thing. Nothing about school ever had been his thing, but here he was, the pilot of a stowaway from Europa (one of Jupiter's moons), with the help of Syndi, his Syndicate 1330 AI companion, communicating without much trouble.

"Elara asks if you will take her to the seeds when we arrive at our destination," Syndi said.

Elara had hopped aboard his ship when he wasn't looking because she desired a trip to Earth, where the seeds she wanted to plant on her frosty, mostly barren moon could be found. Max understood why she'd taken the risk. If Earth was as cold and barren as Europa, he'd want to make some changes too. And who knows, maybe her people ate pine trees or pinecones, made soup from them, or wanted to build their homes out of them. Maybe forests once covered Europa, but Elara's people had eaten them all.

Could that be? Would pine trees even grow there, in its saltwater crust? He didn't ask questions. Better to assume she knew what she was doing.

"Tell her not to worry," he instructed Syndi. "As I said before, I will make sure she gets the pinecones." He intended to leave it at that but then realized he better elaborate. "But that's not the only reason I'm going to Earth. And she knows this because we've already discussed it—a few times. I have several things I need to take care of when I get home."

He finished charting the course for their journey. "Syndi, in your most kind and understanding voice, please tell her to be patient and not to worry. I don't want her to get upset."

"You have chosen this voice for me," Syndi said. "If you would like to select another, you can visit settings on your console."

"I know," Max said. "I was joking. Just say it nicely, is what I mean."

The day the powers that be made a Syndicate that could joke would be the day the mental health of pilots truly improved.

"A joke is a short story that someone recites to cause amusement or laughter," Syndi said.

"You are correct. As usual."

"What you said was not a joke, sir."

"Technically no, but a joke doesn't have to be a story. It *can* be a story, but it doesn't have to be one. It might be a particular way of saying something or even a tone of voice."

"That is interesting," she said.

"You don't feel amusement, I know," he said. "You've told me before."

"That is correct. But I am programmed to seek to understand and to serve."

"Okay, well, once again, we'll have to agree that the joke went over your head and be done with it."

"I do not have a head for a joke to go over, sir."

Ugh. This was why the Syndicates were not loved by pilots across the universe: They always wanted to have the last word.

"Okay. Whatever," Max muttered. "Moving on. Please tell my passenger not to worry."

"I already did," said Syndi.

If Syndi were human, he might assume she'd been short with him. But sometimes that was him reading into a situation that did not actually exist, as all humans did from time to time.

Regardless, he wanted Elara to know that he had other things to do when they reached his home planet. Priority one: He needed to see his parents. It had been possibly five years since he'd been home, and they no doubt missed him like crazy. Second, he wanted to reconnect with Natasha, wherever she may be. He prayed he'd reach home before she took off again. Third—

A short stream of clicks and utterances met his ears—Elara was speaking her native tongue.

Syndi followed with: "Elara says she will help you."

"Help me what?" Max asked. "Get the seeds?"

"She says, 'My people need the trees.'"

"Yes, I know you do—*she* does. The seeds will grow into trees. It will take a while, though. You know that, right? Syndi, does Elara know it takes time to grow a tree?"

"Elara says, 'We need the trees.'"

"Your people need them," he said with a nod. "I understand."

"Elara says, 'And yours too,'" Syndi added.

"Uh, well, yeah." Sitting back firmly in his pilot's seat, Max swiveled to face his "guest" head-on, her silvery light so glossy, he was tempted to slide his fingers across her cheek or some other part of her just to know what it felt like. Not for any romantic reason, obviously. Just because she looked so damn smooth.

"That's true," he finally said. "Earth does need trees. They're vital to our environment. You and I can't take all the seeds. We have to leave some. Many, actually. Most of them." He paused for a second. "But I can still get a lot for you, so don't worry. You didn't want to take them all, did you?"

Elara reached out with one hand, touching him with

the widest of her three fat-but-still-smooth-and-glossy fingers.

"We will leave some," Syndi interpreted. Then Elara patted the uppermost center of his chest in a gesture of reassurance.

The hair on Max's arms rose. Why did this conversation worry him? How many pinecones did she want to transport to Europa? No matter what, she could only take as many as he could comfortably fit in the cargo bay of the *Sparrow*, and for this reason, he wouldn't stress over it too much.

More worrisome was the question of how he was going to explain Elara's presence to everyone—or even anyone—back home. He didn't look forward to revealing that he'd befriended a stowaway and allowed her free roam of his ship. His father would probably flip out and insist they lock her up—which could not happen, unless they wanted to risk learning which defense mechanisms came naturally to her. Every extraterrestrial came with a set of defense mechanisms, and frankly Max would rather not know which ones she kept locked and loaded.

In the best-case scenario, he'd leave her safely inside the *Sparrow* while he went about his two to three days of business, visiting family and collecting pinecones and whatever other seeds Elara's people might find useful. The ship was a perfectly comfortable place for an extended stay—he'd lived in it for years—so she could easily spend two to three days there by herself.

Then again, if she had some ulterior motive . . . if she, for instance, wanted to bust out of there while he was gone and hide out in a cave on Earth for the rest of her life, he doubted he'd be able to stop her. Clearly she was smart—and brave. During his twenty-minute visit to Europa, she'd found a way onto his ship without him knowing. She'd left her home millions of miles away to travel with a complete stranger. Should he be worried?

No. They'd had many talks about pinecones. That's what she wanted. That's why she was here. He was sure of it.

Chapter 4

Svetlana

How much time had passed since the menacing pair of brutes closed Svetlana into this cell? She rubbed her forehead and glanced around the room in search of a clock. She'd sat on the queen-size mattress, with its fluffy French blue comforter and white bed skirt, long enough. Why was her cell a bedroom, anyway? Was this the Jovians' odd way of making her comfortable, of treating her like a guest? Maybe it was their attempt to trick her into believing she wasn't a prisoner of whoever headed up Starbright at this point.

When she'd first arrived, Svetlana had rifled through all of the drawers in the room, from the nightstand to the dresser, finding nothing useful for escaping a cell. Now she stood and went to the closet, one of those small ones found in centuries-old homes. She had poked her head in earlier and saw nothing unusual—a hanging bar with both men's and women's suits and heels and belts—no hidden levers or buttons that might unlock a cell door. This time she'd take a closer look.

On the floor, many boxes of shoes lined up in a row.

The shelf above was crowded with more boxes, all of them different sizes and shapes—hat boxes, maybe? She set out to open each one. This would take some time, and that was good because who knew how long they planned to keep her here?

As she went about her work unearthing felt fedoras and straw sunhats wrapped in tissue paper, she considered what had happened when she, Evan, and Natasha first arrived at Starbright. How that huge man in black security-squad garb waited like a grimacing robot for them at the docking station.

One of Great-Grandmother's Leonards, Natasha had said.

Future nightmares would undoubtedly feature him and his half-human, half-mechanical head. And not only that, but the monstrous way he had ripped Evan and Natasha from her grasp and dragged them away.

The Leonards resembled Leo to some degree, a Jovian family royal. The Jovians used the roots of their own names to label their clones. Hence Andrew clones became Drew and Andre and Andy. Miranda became Randi or Mira. And Leo became Leonard. Leo was Miranda's husband—pretend husband, as Svetlana never believed any of them to be married or even in love with each other. The only exception were her adoptive parents, Dana and John Peterman.

Dana and John were the real deal.

The Jovians must have cloned Leo and then pumped the clones full of steroids to make them a lot bigger and stronger. According to what Evander told her, the Jovians weren't nonviolent anymore. A shock, considering Jovian royalty had always prided themselves on their peaceful ways.

She opened a box from the floor and found a pair of sneakers inside. Looking at them halfheartedly, she remembered what one of the Leonards had told her before the door to this bedroom cell closed behind him: "Caroline doesn't live here anymore."

Svetlana couldn't imagine Starbright without Caroline. If Caroline didn't live there, where did she live? And what happened to her? The Queen Jovian wouldn't just walk away from her empire. Was it possible—a spark of excitement shot through Svetlana's veins—that Caroline had died in the eighteen years Svetlana spent in her much-preferred universe without Jovians?

But the lives of Jovian royalty spanned millennia, and Svetlana doubted she could be so lucky.

Surrounded by cardboard boxes, pastel-colored tissue, and men's and women's shoes of all styles, she wondered who ran Starbright if not Caroline? Why would they allow Natasha's ship to dock in Starbright's underground station only to lock them up? What did this new leadership plan to do with her? What would they do with Evan?

Svetlana shoved all the boxes and things back into the closet and closed the door. She didn't want to think about any of this. Obsessing over the safety and whereabouts of one's daughter would not help solve the current situation. She had to be smart. Eventually someone would enter this bedroom-slash-prison cell, and she needed a strategy for when that happened. Getting out of there was the first thing, and finding Evan would be second.

She plunked back down on the bed and picked at a hangnail. Keeping Evan safe would mean flying home to their universe without Jovians. That's what Svetlana really wanted to do, what Evander had promised her she'd be *able* to do. But Natasha's ship had not cooperated. It simply would not start.

The failure had struck Svetlana as inevitable. A voice inside of her actually whispered the word *inevitable*, and that "knowing feeling" had helped her accept the situation: Natasha couldn't program the ship for a time trip, or whatever she'd needed to do. It simply wouldn't let her. It was as if the ship had refused.

And so they were locked up.

Who could help them get out of this place?

Svetlana knew other Jovians in this world, of course. Perhaps Dana and John could help. If they found out what was happening, they would certainly advocate for her. Unlike most Jovian royals, Svetlana's parents actually cared about people. They'd loved and raised her and her adopted sister, Helena, as best as two nonhumans could. Svetlana could count on them if she could only communicate with them.

She glanced around the room in search of . . . food. A bottle of water. *When was the last time I ate someth—*

The sliding door to the room heaved open, and a Leonard in his black security uniform emerged. Svetlana scuttled backward to the headboard, connecting with a gentle thump to the back of her head. This Leonard looked different than the others. Severely pale, almost green in complexion, as if his face had been dipped in a pool of dye. His eyes squinted with red rims, bloodshot all the way through, and his lips were . . . weirdly colorless.

He was odd looking.

Sick looking.

Still, he was wide and tall, his arms like clubs.

The sliding door remained open even after he stepped inside, body armor clanking. There was something off about his gait. A hesitancy. He carried a small tray with a soup-sized bowl and a drink cup beside it. Her dinner? Or maybe lunch?

He approached the dresser that butted up to the side wall. Svetlana waited for him to place the tray there or to say something, but he did neither. He didn't even glance in her direction. Instead, he stumbled on nothing that she could see, lurched forward, and collapsed in a heavy heap. The metal crash of the tray hitting the wood floor sent her shoulders toward her ears.

Expecting the Leonard to scrabble back to his feet, Svetlana didn't offer assistance or even move from where she hunched upon the bed.

The man groaned a raspy exhale, but no signs or sounds of movement followed. What was happening? *Was* he actually sick? Could he be so ill that he just died in front of her? It occurred to her that whatever ailment took him down may be contagious, and she did not want to catch it.

On all fours, she crawled to the bottom of the bed and peered over the side for a closer look. "Hello?" she said softly, not wanting to wake him if he'd passed out for some reason.

His body remained motionless.

Svetlana jumped down, adjusted her unitard, and stepped toward the still-open door. With a quick look back to make sure the Leonard didn't move, she sped into the empty corridor radiating with light so white it was almost silver.

She was free. How? Why? This was too good to be true! She laughed out loud and started to run.

Now, where would Evan be?

Chapter 5

Dmitri

Time and distance no longer applied to him as it once had. All Dmitri had to do was sit on the stool in the center of the astronomical observatory (something he did most hours of every day) and he took off—cerebrally—through the oculus above. His mind connected with the world "out there," and he sped through it without caution.

There was no holding back. Just speeding, speeding, *light*-speeding through space.

In this manner, he traveled amid planets and moons, asteroids, stars both young and old. The velocity at which his consciousness moved defied physics. It was, simply put, magnificent. The ease at which he learned everything about the cosmos—the moon, the sun, the cloudy colored nebulae and black holes—would have baffled his ordinary human mind had he still possessed one. Wormholes, dark matter, giant dust clouds, magnetic fields! All of it was right there, at his fingertips, as if that's where all of those things had always been.

David had granted him this power. This knowledge

and ability. And Dmitri's ordinary human anatomy could not make sense of it—but his Jovian one did.

He understood that the part of him that traveled was universal, untouchable, like a drop of oil spread across an oceanic expanse. But his physical self remained *here*, on Earth. He was still a Jovian hybrid living in his new home at Starbright, a young man sitting upon an ordinary wooden stool. The son of Evander and Nadia Peterman, and brother to Natasha.

Strange was this new cerebral existence, and also completely natural. He was an individual, and he was a network. He listened to every Jovian mind and also spoke internally to just one at a time. He had located and conversed with Great-grandmother, his dead father, and his sister. He was both the thing that connected Jovians to the webbing, the lattice, the fabric that provided the threads—and a user of the thing that connected them.

A human brain *and* a conscious force speeding through the ever-expanding universe.

His cousin, Alexandria, stirred beside him, and he drew back to the here and now. The observatory came to him, or rather he returned to it. The dark, damp stone walls, wide-open oculus, and subtle echoes of physical movement surrounded him. The stool he sat on caught him like a cupped pair of hands.

It was Alexandria who tied him to his home and his physical body. Her function in life had changed when his function in life changed. Alexandria was present when David, the Jovians' former supreme being, transferred his power to Dmitri, and so Alexandria had received some of that power too. She became a necessary part of Dmitri's existence: the part that anchored him to Earth, to his physical self. Because sometimes he ventured so far into the "out there" that the cosmic influences tempted him to let go, to forget who he was on Earth. When that happened, it was as if the part that he knew as himself began to leak away, atom by atom.

Alexandria stopped him from losing himself.

"Losing himself" was what had happened to David, who had recently passed. At Great-grandmother's command, David had ventured so far so often for so long, year upon year, that at some point, he could not find his way back. And there'd been no one there to remind him to.

Dmitri had Alexandria. Whenever he wandered for too long, she took his hand in hers. Instinctively, she knew when to do it. When she took his hand, the warmth of her concern entered through his palm and flashed like a warning in his brain. The pressure of touch on his physical self roused him, drew him back, and reminded him he was still a person. A person who lived in the human realm, in the astronomical observatory at Starbright International.

And so he returned, as he did today, and when he opened his eyes, the sight of Alexandria in his periphery appeared, and he released her hand. Immediately he sensed movement beyond the door to the tube. Natasha was here. He opened the door with his mind. A scuffle upon the observatory floor followed. The hesitant tap of footsteps met with the stone walls.

Natasha whispered, "You're fine. Just stay beside me."

"How do you expect me to act *normal* with all the noise in my head?" Evan complained.

"You don't have to talk. Just stand beside me."

Dmitri and Alexandria greeted Natasha and Evan with their attention.

"Great-grandmother is with the Coalition," he said. After being in the "out there," the sound of his voice was so sudden and physical that he experienced every vibration from his vocal cords to the hairs in his ears. "You will find her in the bunker."

He pictured his great-grandmother, (also known as Caroline or Queen Jovian), in a room with Fran and Lisa Vasquez, Connie, and a dozen other Jovian clones, all of them seated in front of computer screens, speaking into wristcomms, surveying satellite images. The Coalition monitored the planet for any signs of the Moon Children on land and alerted the rest of the world of their whereabouts and likely next attacks.

Natasha gazed at him with the kind of startled shock one cannot keep from reaching their eyes. "You're so . . . different."

An image of his wheelchair came to his mind. The way his body moved and clenched and spasmed prior to obtaining David's power. Back then his words lengthened and contracted depending on the position of his muscles from moment to moment. He sat with that for a second, or even less than a second, but the memory sliced into him with the effortlessness of a razor blade. He missed the boy he'd been only a few days before. He missed his former life.

Alexandria squeezed his hand, thinking he'd drifted into the "out there" again.

He met Natasha's worried frown and raised his brows. Yes, he'd changed, and so had she. The last time he saw her, she had set her dolls in a row and proceeded to feed them tea from tiny plastic teacups. Now she was a woman who might have had her own children, more like their mother than the little girl who'd left Earth for Mintaka.

"Both of us have changed," he said.

Natasha nodded with a wordless hesitance that made him feel, uncomfortably, like a stranger to her.

"Dad and I," she spoke slowly, "when we travel, we grow older. Quite quickly."

He sensed her reluctance to discuss the topic. "Yes, I know," he said and then followed with "Great-grandmother can no longer take her true form. She moved into the bunker with the Coalition because she needed Fran and Connie's help to organize the clones."

Natasha made no reply. Evan, beside her, breathed loudly, as if under duress. Natasha patted her shoulder, told her she was fine.

"You wondered why Great-grandmother left Starbright," he said. "That is why."

It was easier to speak of Jovian things, Earth's problems, than to think of his own childhood, his broken family.

"But the oneness is back," Natasha said. "Can't she—"

"When I took my place, it resumed," he said. "Someone had knotted the threads of the oneness so that the communications couldn't get through. I discovered it was Edmund."

"Great-grandfather? But why—"

"He disagreed with Great-grandmother on the way forward. He believed she'd become too attached to Earth, too protective of it, too fearful of losing it to someone else, so he interfered with her plans to dominate with her army of clones."

"With communications down," Natasha said, "Caroline couldn't control them."

"Yes," he said. "But when I came here and David transferred his power to me, I broke through the obstruction. Untangled the knots." He raised his chin, experiencing a momentary flutter of pride.

With the oneness in working order, Dmitri observed the thoughts of all Jovians, many of them disgruntled, struggling with each other and themselves, Great-grandmother included. She needed the family's support. She was alone and . . . he wasn't sure this was possible, but he came upon what he believed was her weakness. He'd never known her to be weak, but that was what he felt when he sensed her: shades of meekness and frailty.

"And when you say you 'took your place' you mean that your place is here, in this room?" Natasha eyed the observatory walls with a apprehensiveness she couldn't hide. At the moment, due to cloud-covered skies, it resembled a damp basement more than a gateway to the galaxy. Evan, Dmitri noticed, stared at the ground, hunched over and fidgeting.

"On this chair," he said. "My place is on this chair. David passed his power to me. This is where I must stay. For a time, at least."

"I understand," Natasha said with reluctance, or disappointment, maybe. Dmitri peeked into her mind and saw that living in Starbright, shut into this room, was not what she had envisioned for his life. She'd pictured a warm, safe existence under a blanket, in a room with Mother, eating cheese sandwiches and listening to the chime of his collection of antique keys.

He lingered in her mind while she entered the oneness and observed his initial entrance into it. Only the Jovian royals could see the past, and it pleased him that she possessed this skill. She watched the whole spectacle, from beginning to end: the way David's power had lifted his body above the sacred stool while a bolt of pure energy entered and scalded his insides, changing everything.

"I see what happened to you," she said as she placed her hand in the middle of her chest. He sensed her desire to console him and her decision that it would not be appropriate.

"I am what I was meant to be," he said. "How is your heart?"

She straightened, her eyes darting away. "Fine," she said softly.

Beside her, Evan nervously shifted from foot to foot, crossed and then uncrossed her arms over her chest like a person unable to remain still. He entered her mind through the oneness and observed. Confusion surged and roiled within her. In response, she had put up mental dams to slow the flow. But this only caused a tug-of-war that required her full attention. She did not meet Dmitri's eye, overwhelmed as she was.

Dmitri then sensed Natasha wondering how long he'd been there, on the stool, though she didn't ask the question.

With a vacant stare, Alexandria answered: "It has been about a week."

"I haven't yet made it to the outer reaches," he said, not sure why he wanted Natasha to know this. "There's much to learn before I get there."

Whenever he traveled into the great beyond, the void called to him, though instinct told him not to get too close —and Alexandria, so far, had drawn him back before he did.

"When you get there, to the outer reaches, what will happen?" Natasha asked.

"Then I will know what there is to know."

Natasha dipped her chin. "About the Jovians?"

"About the universe we live in."

"Is that possible?" she asked.

"It will take some time," he said, as he considered how to explain. "It's like downloading a computer program. Bit by bit and piece by piece, you come to accept the new information." He pulled his cluster of keys from his lap, the same set he'd carried with him since he was a child. "Remember these?"

"Of course I do," she said with a smile that made him want to smile too.

"They help me focus. With them, I can cut through all of the chatter and find specific individuals. I used them to find you."

Their past life danced through his mind in a burst of color. Time spent in their home in Kirksberg. The garden room and its scent of gardenias that Mother loved. Its peach and light-blue decorations, the natural fibers of the carpeting and blankets. The way Father came home and sat with them whenever he had a free moment. How Natasha, his sweet little sister with the beautiful baby face, brought him an extra blanket or asked if he'd like her to sit with him.

"Can I listen to your keys?" she used to ask.

"Okay," he'd tell her, "but you have to promise to give them back."

And she did. She always did.

He remembered the day funny Uncle Jimmy with the fat tummy and messy hair came to visit. How he made them all laugh with his juggling. And then, when the adults were elsewhere, he led Natasha away.

Her heart was sick, so Dmitri didn't try to stop them. Uncle Jimmy promised to help her. He also promised to bring her back.

"You went to Mintaka?" Dmitri asked.

"I did." She turned her head away before gazing up at the oculus.

"That's good," he said.

Silence. She hid her thoughts from him, put up a wall his mind couldn't get around. He would change the subject. "James says all the inhabitants of Earth must work together."

"Uncle Jimmy?" Natasha asked just as Evan blurted, "Grandpa James?"

"Yes and yes," Dmitri told them, then he focused squarely on Evan. Her aura was mottled and strange. Red and raw. How did "The Prophecy of the Lost Sister" go? *The lost one, like her brother before, possessed mettle and fortitude . . .* He observed Evan's internal battle to reject the oneness. Could this frightened person possess the mettle and fortitude necessary to lead?

"So, we should go to the bunker then?" Natasha interrupted.

"I think that will be best, yes," he said.

"Will you come with us?"

A lapse in the clouds invited a few scattered rays of sun into the room. They tugged at him for attention.

"His eyes, did you see them?" Evan's voice trembled. "They just flashed like mirrors."

"It's too soon for Dmitri to leave his chair," Alexandria said. "He is not free to wander. Sometimes he disappears for hours inside his mind. Don't worry, I keep watch. I keep him safe."

"From what?" Natasha asked sharply. "Is he in danger?"

"You don't have to worry," Alexandria said kindly. "When he goes 'out there,' I always make sure he comes back."

Natasha stared at her brother's caregiver a little too intently for a little too long, which made her look angry. Dmitri saw past her glaring eyes: She worried that she couldn't trust a stranger with her brother's well-being.

"This is Alexandria," he said. "Alexandria is Aunt Helena's daughter."

"Father's cousin," Natasha said, her face softening. "I didn't realize."

"Yes, that is me," Alexandria placed her hand upon her chest. "Evander's cousin."

Natasha's comm beeped but she ignored it. "Evander always spoke fondly of you. I've heard many stories."

"*Spasibo*," Alexandria replied in her native Russian with a slight bob of her head.

A burst of sunlight poured like liquid gold through the oculus. Dmitri threw back his head and reveled in the brilliant gleaming rays that splashed into his mind and encouraged him to take off.

"I must go," he said, struggling to remain in his body. "I am sorry."

Natasha didn't move, but her intention bore into him like pins that fixed him there. "Wait, just one more thing. . . . Do you know about Dad?"

"Father has passed," Dmitri said, fighting to remain in the physical world. It hurt to be there when the light tempted him so. "He and I spoke. He says we will speak again."

"Tell him I miss him," she said, her voice carrying a note of desperation.

"He knows."

"And what about Mom?" she said. "Has anyone told her?"

The question trailed after Dmitri as he sped through the oculus and entered the bright blue sky. In seconds he'd reached the exosphere, and soon passed Mars and then Venus, unable to respond.

"Dmitri cannot leave the observatory, and your mother is not part of the oneness," Alexandria explained. "He has not told her."

"I'll go see her as soon as I can," Natasha said. "I want to speak to her in person."

"You're leaving me?" Evan yelped. "When?"

Natasha's comm beeped again.

"Someone is trying to call you," Alexandria said.

"Yes. I know." Natasha glanced at her comm.

Dmitri's last bit of attention to the here and now showed him a picture of his sister and Max together, floating in a natural pool in a sun-dappled forest. Max took her into his arms and kissed her. Natasha held him tight. Dmitri had never seen such happiness on her face. And because Dmitri saw this, so did Alexandria.

"You should talk to him," Alexandria said.

Evan's panicked voice echoed to the ceiling: "You can't leave me here alone, Natasha."

"It's all right," Natasha said, placing her hands upon Evan's shoulders. "I won't be gone for long."

"Dmitri thinks you should call Max," Alexandria said again.

Dmitri's mind flickered like a screen, and he saw Evan in the greenhouse with Dayana.

"And Evan should go upstairs and visit Dayana," Alexandria said. "Dayana would like to meet you."

Evan opened her eyes wide and wrapped her arms around herself protectively. "I don't know who that is."

"She cares for the plants." Alexandria pointed toward the entrance to the tubes.

"Maybe later," Evan said. "Right now I can hardly hear—or think. The oneness is . . . *unbearable*. Why is there so much going on in my brain? When will it stop?"

"Focus on me," Natasha said, getting in front of Evan so that all she could see was Natasha's face. "Trust me. It will be all right."

In this manner, they began to walk toward the exit.

"She's trying to block the oneness," Dmitri spoke to Alexandria internally. "She needs to let it in."

"It would be best if you let it in, Evan," Alexandria said. "Don't fight it."

Evan breathed jagged gulps of air. "I have no choice but to let it in. It's not giving me a choice."

"Can Dmitri help get us out of the building safely?" Natasha asked.

The door to the tube whooshed open.

"Of course he can," Alexandria said. "He says to please tell Mother he loves her."

Chapter 6

Svetlana

The tubes offered Svetlana the choice to head either up or down. She chose down for no particular reason. The Leonard who'd collapsed in her cell had not followed, and that was something to be thankful for.

Every three to five yards, Svetlana passed a sealed door, realizing that any of them might house her daughter and granddaughter. But she didn't dare pound on them. Didn't want to risk waking some other beast that would only lock her up again—or worse.

The tube seemed to go on forever, but at least it remained silent except for her own footsteps and agitated breaths—until now.

Ahead, it bore to the left and a whispered conversation came to her attention. Sounded like the girls . . . or was it some trick of her mind? Svetlana's abrupt pause squeaked under the soles of her boots.

"You should have warned me before we time traveled," one of them said with obvious aggravation. The other replied, "Even if I had, would it have stopped you?

This is what you're meant to do, *where* you're meant to be."

Svetlana pressed forward, taking pains to conceal the tapping of her footsteps. She picked up speed, soon jogging, nearing the bend in the tube. She held her breath as she peered around the curve.

"Evan!" she shouted. "My God, how is this possible?"

With a surprising amount of desperation, Evan ran to her and grabbed her into a hug. Tears gathered in her desperate eyes. "Oh, no, don't cry," Svetlana said. "What happened? Did one of those brutes hurt you?"

"Nothing happened," Natasha said when Evan failed to answer. "My brother opened the door to our cell not long after they closed us in. Evan's problem is the oneness. It's new to her, and it's overwhelming."

"This world is crazy!" Evan whined.

"I can imagine," Svetlana said patting her back, as if doing so might impart the confidence her daughter needed. "Don't you worry. I'm going to take you home just as soon as I figure out a way."

"But no." Evan pulled back gently and wiped her nose. "We have to be here. That's not what I meant." She rubbed the tears from her face with the sleeve of her unitard.

"We're heading to the bunker," Natasha said with a gesture toward the sealed door at the bottom of the incline. "I'm glad you found us when you did."

Svetlana didn't move. "I didn't know Starbright had a bunker."

"It's more than a mile away. Not so far that we can't walk. The Coalition is there. We'll be safe."

Evan caught up to Natasha and stood beside her. Her way of choosing sides?

A sudden burst of anxiety raced through Svetlana's

veins. "Wait. You want to *leave* Starbright? But we need to stay close to your ship so Evan and I can get back home when the time is right."

"The ship isn't working. Probably because you have to be granted permission to time travel. We're meant to stay," Natasha said. "At least for now."

"Granted permission from who? You never said anything about that." Svetlana did not want to raise her voice, but this was unexpected, to say the least.

"You agreed that we would try again in a couple of days," Natasha said, too calm for Svetlana's liking. "Would you rather stay here, where we'll likely end up back in a cell?"

With restrained impatience, Svetlana lowered her raised shoulders. "What I want is to get back home with my daughter, Natasha. You know that. Evan obviously doesn't feel well and should not have come."

"What she's experiencing will pass," Natasha said. "And we have to get out of Starbright while we can. I'm sure there are a few spaceships at the bunker."

Damn, this kid—young woman—has all the answers. It was both highly respectable and totally aggravating.

"Will any of the ships at the bunker work for us?" Svetlana asked.

"It's possible. We won't know until we try. And I will be trying. I need to see my mother."

"Nadia?" Svetlana said, as if just remembering who Natasha's mother was. "Where is she?"

"She moved back to Russia. But you and Evan should stay at the bunker while I'm gone."

Evan groaned. "So you *are* leaving us!"

Natasha turned to Evan and spoke with kindness and understanding. "I promise it won't be for long. I haven't seen my mother in several years. I was in kindergarten when Uncle Jimmy whisked me away and, as we can all see, I'm quite a bit older now. My mother probably won't even recognize me. She never wanted me to leave Earth, and now that I'm here, I need to see her. I have to tell her —" She stopped short and gazed soft-eyed at Svetlana. "I have to tell her that my father won't be coming back."

Svetlana's breath caught in her throat. Every time she remembered her son was dead she suffered another small death herself.

"Nadia doesn't know he died," Evan said sulkily. "I totally forgot."

"I won't stay long, I promise," Natasha told them.

Evan gave her a quick, unreciprocated hug. "I'm sorry."

Svetlana was sorry as well. She'd forgotten how much this young woman (a mere child if judged by the number of years she'd been alive) balanced on her shoulders.

Natasha gripped Evan's wrist, and the sealed door of the tube began to rise. A red glow emanated from the room beyond, and the hairs on the back of Svetlana's neck stood at attention. She'd seen this harsh red lighting before, in the empty room that led to Starbright's back exit. Before Svetlana could shout, "Make sure it's safe!" the girls stepped through.

Svetlana hovered in the tube's opening, not sure they should leave. This trip to the universe with Jovians was supposed to be simple. If they left Starbright, wouldn't they be asking for trouble, taking a leap into the unknown? What if Natasha were wrong about spaceships being at the bunker? What if they became stuck there with no way out?

The girls turned and gazed at her with questioning expressions.

"I don't see how living in a bunker is going to help us," Svetlana said. "We might as well find a place to hide here.

Maybe the basement? We know for sure that there are more spaceships here."

"You can leave with us," Natasha said, glowing red under the harsh lighting, "or you can stay. It's up to you."

"Mom, you have to come," Evan said. "Please."

"Your friends Fran and Lisa are at the bunker," Natasha added. "They live there."

Evan scowled and looked like she might throw up. "What is that awful smell?"

"Ammonia," Natasha said as her comm beeped. She pulled it from her pocket and checked the screen.

"Ammonia?" Svetlana rushed forward without a second thought.

The tube closed behind her and a wall came over it, making it undetectable. There was no going back.

"The Moon Children must have attacked Starbright," Natasha said. "Remember what my father told you? Earth is currently sustaining a crisis. The Moon Children are a hive mind that fights with poison gas, and this is what it smells like."

Svetlana cringed at the idea. "Yes, I remember."

Red-brown stains marred the floor here and there, and the seriousness of the situation fell upon Svetlana at once. One should remember the plight of an entire planet even when preoccupied with getting back home with her daughter. But she wouldn't reprimand herself too harshly. After all, if they'd been able to turn around and go home immediately, like Evander had promised, the Moon Children and this planet in crisis wouldn't concern her.

"This looks like the aftermath of an attack," Natasha said. "Though the stains appear to be dry."

"I thought the Moon Children only killed clones," Svetlana said.

"They kill everything that's susceptible to ammonia

poisoning," Natasha said, moving toward the exit door. "They've killed many more clones than humans because clones succumb to lower concentrations of the gas than original humans do. The clones are the first to die, in other words. Then the hybrids, then the Jovians and humans. Even the royalty aren't immune to the exposure."

"I didn't know," Svetlana said, thinking, *Maybe Caroline really is dead.*

"My father said Miranda became very sick when they attacked the second Mars launch," Natasha added. "That's what made her want to leave the planet. She went to Mars soon after."

Svetlana had to know: "Is Caroline still alive?"

"We really have to go, Grandmother. I'll fill you in on all of this other stuff later. The only safe places on Earth are underground."

Svetlana nodded. The "grandmother" thing punctured her resolve.

The back exit door opened wide as Svetlana reached them. Natasha muttered, "Thank you, Alexandria," though Svetlana didn't know why. Who was Alexandria? More important, *where* was Alexandria?

"Let's go." Natasha took Evan by the wrist. "Evan will be a lot more comfortable with her mother at her side, so I'm glad, Svetlana, that you've decided to cooperate."

Svetlana was tempted to tell Natasha that of course Evan was more comfortable with her mother at her side. Did Natasha really think Evan would pick her if made to choose between the two of them? Then again, Svetlana couldn't be sure. After all, Evan had planned to time travel with Natasha against Svetlana's will. But that was the rebellious teenager inside of her, wasn't it? Every kid was rebellious to some degree. And Evan had always been strong-willed, which everyone in her life insisted was not a bad thing (until you asked her to take out the garbage or do her homework).

Natasha gestured down the flight of stairs that led to the parking lot, and Svetlana started down.

"Evan and I will always stick together," Svetlana said in her "I'm an adult and I know best" voice. "No matter what. You should know that."

When they reached the ground, Natasha jolted upright, and Svetlana thought she might argue. Instead, she remained stock-still, then drew in a shaky breath and raised her hand to her chest for a worrisome moment. She cleared her throat and then nodded at Svetlana before moving on as if nothing at all had happened. With an inflection of dire warning that made Svetlana regret her decision to leave the safety of the building, Natasha said, "Into the woods, as fast as you can."

Chapter 7

Natasha

As Natasha, Svetlana, and Evan crossed Starbright's parking lot at full speed, Natasha remembered how years ago her mother forbade her to run. One day Natasha was spinning cartwheels across the lawn and the next she wasn't allowed to so much as skip. And now that she was older—twenty-five or so probably (she had yet to see her reflection)—the heavy hand of worry once again slowed her down.

But she couldn't let it. Her heart was fine, she just needed to stop thinking about it. She distracted herself by taking note of the once beautifully landscaped grounds of Starbright burned to a deep-brown crisp, parched and crumbling. This was the devastation her father had described. The work of the Moon Children and their poison. Young pine trees seemed to have been sprayed with fire. The shrubbery that once created green boundaries in perfect lines had shriveled to ash. Piles of deceased foliage gathered here and there like burial mounds, and blackened leaves scraped across the empty parking lot propelled by wintry breezes.

As the women neared the forest of pines beyond the Starbright property line, Natasha caught sight of a torn piece of blood-soaked clothing wedged into a footprint in the mud. She also eyed the occasional oxygen tank, knocked onto its side and left behind like a fallen soldier.

This fight against the noxious Moon Children was real. People had been injured and died. The bodies had been cleared away, but Natasha sensed them as she came upon evidence of the violent attack they'd sustained.

If and when they reached the old farm field without drawing the attention of the Leonards or anyone else who might want to hold or harm them, they would pause.

The field began about a mile outside of Starbright, where the crusty, dead environment reverted to its old, livelier ways. Expanses of flat land with rich, brown soil spread in between swathes of untended weeds, cattails shimmering raggedly in the breeze. The cold air sent all living things into their natural hibernation, as it had in the world without Jovians or Moon Children—except for the pines, which remained as consistently green as ever. The occasional wide-trunked tree wore its rough, gray bark as it should, without scars or burn marks. Each oak and maple was bare and leafless, however, as was normal for the time of year.

"We have to cross the field, and it's longer than it looks. You two okay so far?" Natasha asked.

"I don't like how exposed we'll be," Svetlana said.

"We'll stick to the tree line as much as possible. Come on!"

They set out in single file, soon reaching a barrier of evergreens that divided the two fields. There they stopped a moment to rest.

A small, subtle hill rose on the opposite side of the field ahead.

"Is that it?" Evan asked, puffs of steam emerging from her mouth. "Is that lump the bunker?"

"It must be," Natasha said, and set off again, taking the lead once more.

Their fast pace sped them across the unplanted field. As they neared the mound and continued slightly past it, they found an earthen platform and an unexpected door.

"I'll go in alone," Natasha said. "As a precaution."

"You think it may not be safe?" Svetlana asked.

"I'm sure it will be fine," Natasha said. "Just wait here, behind these bushes, while I check it out."

She reached the door and held up her fist to knock. Before she could, the heavy metal barrier creaked as it swung open, and a short woman dressed in a black military-style jacket appeared.

A young version of Aunt Constance.

"The former president's daughter," the woman declared with a smirk. "You don't see that every day. By all means, come in."

Natasha didn't smile or say hello in response. "I'm not alone."

"We are aware," young Constance said with raised brows. "All of Evander's relatives are welcome here. Even those from another universe."

Natasha nodded and said, "I hoped you would say that."

"I'm Connie." The woman put out her palm, and Natasha reciprocated by placing her hand on top.

"You have Constance's eyes," Natasha said, "and her stature."

"I have her everything," Connie said, and the two of them chuckled.

Connie opened the door as wide as it would go, and Natasha turned around and gestured for Svetlana and

Evan to follow. Svetlana nudged her daughter, still fidgety and preoccupied thanks to the chaos the oneness caused, though she seemed less harried and nervous since their escape from Starbright.

"Is the oneness toning down the way Natasha said it would?" Svetlana asked as they approached.

"No," Evan answered with a scowl. "It's still loud as hell. But sometimes it's more of a hum than a bunch of distracting noise."

"Hopefully there will be someplace for you to lie down," Svetlana said. "Just stay by me. Don't go running off anywhere, okay?"

"Don't worry, Mom. I won't."

"We'll go home as soon as we can," she added.

Wow, Natasha thought, *Svetlana is relentless.*

Evan frowned in Natasha's direction as she stepped inside and threw an eye roll her mother's way. Natasha considered telling Svetlana that as uncomfortable as the oneness was, Evan did not want to leave—but why tell her what she already knew?

Svetlana entered the bunker and stopped beside Natasha on the platform. She was staring at Connie, just an arm's length away. "Who is that person?"

"That's Connie—"

"I *knew* it," Svetlana said. "She's a Jovian clone. She has Aunt Constance's face. Are you sure this place is safe? You said Fran and Lisa would be here."

Natasha cringed internally. Surely Connie heard her and would find her rude. "The Coalition is made up of clones," Natasha whispered through gritted teeth. "Most of them are Jovian. I assumed you knew that."

"I just don't think it's wise—"

"Hey, Fran," Connie shouted. "You better come up here. There's a problem I think you can help with."

Natasha turned to Connie and mouthed the words, "Thank you."

Chapter 8

Svetlana

With gray in his beard scruff, a heavier-set face, and several pounds that never used to be there expanding his middle, Fran looked to be about sixty years old. *Could that be right?* When Svetlana first traveled to the universe without Jovians, she'd arrived in her very pregnant twentysomething body. If she had remained in this world, she'd be in her fifties instead of the fortysomething she actually was.

All this crossed her mind as she hugged Fran hard, experiencing a cluster of feelings that she couldn't even begin to sort. She was back in the Jovian-influenced world, back with Fran in Kirksberg, Pennsylvania, her old hometown. How strange her life was.

When they finally broke from the embrace, tears glistened in Fran's older-man eyes.

"I always hoped I'd see you again," his low voice rumbled, "but I didn't think it would actually happen. Hey," he sought something behind her, as if just then realizing the reunion was incomplete. "Andrew isn't here. He didn't come back with you?"

"No," Svetlana said, "he——"

"I can't believe this—Svetlana is here?" Lisa shouted from the bottom of the staircase. "Well, bring her down, don't just stand there."

Fran gestured to the stairs, and Svetlana took the lead.

Except for the strands of gray in Lisa's dark, plaited hair and a bit of extra padding on her face (and body), Lisa looked the same. She grabbed Svetlana as vigorously as Fran had a moment before, her familiar kindness emanating from her pores.

With the initial shock acknowledged, Svetlana reached for Evan, an arm's length away, and said, "This is my daughter, Evan."

"It's so good to meet you," both Lisa and Fran said at the same time.

Fran gazed at Evan sadly, still wondering about Andrew, probably.

"I'm sorry," Svetlana whispered. "Andrew is not here. He's *gone*."

Fran's face grew long with disappointment, his light-heartedness put on pause. This was the way of the world. Birth and death, happiness and disappointment, no matter what universe you lived in.

"Is Max here?" Svetlana asked, and before either Fran or Lisa could answer, Natasha said, "He's on his way."

Lisa slapped a hand into her chest and looked like she might fall down. "You're kidding. Are you sure? Don't joke with me, now."

Natasha's comm beeped, and she checked the screen. "No, I'm not kidding. He's coming home. Should be here in a couple of days." She paused to tap the screen. "If all goes well."

Fran and Lisa grabbed onto each other and rocked

back and forth with bulging elation. "I told you he'd be back," Lisa said through happy tears.

"I'll believe it when I see it," Fran said, laughing.

"Well, this is great news." Svetlana was glad to be present for this happy moment, to feel some belonging in this "other" world, to be with the people she loved when she lived here. Thank goodness Natasha made her come to the bunker. Maybe they really would find a way back to their comfortable world without Jovians. Surely their friends and this Coalition would be able to point them in the direction of a working spaceship—and whoever she needed to grant them permission.

"Let's sit down," Fran said. "Are you hungry, thirsty?"

He shouted to the twenty or so members of the Coalition who'd been watching the reunion from the outskirts of the spacious circular room. "Come on, gang, we have guests. Let's get some food together."

Then he led the way through the pubspace's busy center, a sort of oval-shaped bar with a large media screen overhead and several smaller ones to either side. Probably the brains of their operation. On the opposite side of the curve, several round tables emerged surrounded by six or eight chairs each. "Sit, sit. You must be tired from your journey." He gestured to an empty table.

Several Jovian clones arrived with trays of water, juice, yogurt, bread, and muffins. It was then Svetlana remembered how hungry she was, how the Leonard who had brought her food failed to complete his task before he'd collapsed.

"Thank you so much," she said, taking an apple and a bottle of water. "We were locked in cells at Starbright, and none of us have eaten for . . . I don't know how long."

The girls opted for the cinnamon-walnut muffins, the sound of water uncapping and glugging down their throats. Natasha was already on her second bottle, and worse, moaning as she drank.

"This is so good," she said with such uncharacteristic enthusiasm that it drew the attention of not only Svetlana but everyone nearby. "You have no idea how much better Earth water is than space water."

"Sorry, we're just so hungry," she added as Evan reached in front of her and grabbed some kind of roll, taking an enormous bite. "We'll be better in a second."

"Is that what they're doing at Starbright these days, Connie?" Fran asked. "Locking people up and starving them?"

Unlike the others, who wore standard-issue black unitards with white piping, Connie wore a black T-shirt and jeans, a military-style jacket, and leather combat boots. Because her brown hair twisted into two braids—one on each side of her head—and she stood at maybe five feet tall, she could have passed for a high school student. Like a high school student, she also had attitude. The kind that implied she wouldn't be afraid to pick a fight with anyone.

"I wouldn't put it past Head Leonard," she said.

"One of those giant men collapsed in front of me after opening the door to my cell," Svetlana added. "That's how I got away. He looked very sick."

"Really," Fran said, musing. "That's odd."

"I could go over there and have a look around, if you like," Connie said, sounding like she would enjoy such a mission.

"Don't bother," Natasha said. "I just asked my brother. He says it's an illness. Something that's happening to the Leonards after their encounters with the Moon Children. A virus of some sort."

Fran sat back and passed Connie and some other Coalition members a frown, as if he'd expected better.

"Well, it's the first I'm hearing of it, and the oneness is flowing, so why don't we have intel on this? We assumed the Moon Children didn't affect the Leonards, did we not?"

"Initially they didn't," Natasha said, crinkling the empty bottle of water in her hands. "No one here would have picked up on it because they are becoming sick very slowly, over time. Some have more immunity than others. Andy's working on a cure, but so far no luck."

"I wonder if Caroline knows," Fran said.

Svetlana stifled a cough at the mention of her mother-in-law's name.

She's alive.

It was then an older woman's voice wafted across the room: "I only found out a little while ago."

Svetlana tried to see to see but couldn't. Word of unexpected guests must have spread through the bunker, and many Coalition members gathered around their table.

"The Leonard who collapsed in Svetlana's room was the first to die."

Svetlana sat up straighter, then leaned in the direction from which the voice had come. It sounded like Caroline. Sort of. The voice wasn't quite right.

The pubspace went silent. Fran and Lisa exchanged a knowing look.

Svetlana whispered, "Who said that? Is that—"

Fran glanced at her, then rapidly averted his eyes.

"Fran, is Caroline here?" Svetlana's whisper erupted like billowing steam from her mouth.

"Uh," he said, and she stood.

There, at the entrance of the room, Svetlana spotted a thin woman, tall and imposing. But wait. She wasn't all that imposing. Somehow she came across as feeble at the same time. Slightly stooped, rounded in the shoulders, a bit too thin. Was it Caroline? If so, her blonde bob had grown to her shoulders, and she wore a butter-yellow sweater and light-blue jeans. Whoever this was didn't look much like the Caroline Jovian Svetlana used to know.

"Caroline lives here," Fran said slowly.

"With all of *you*?" It sounded accusatory, and Svetlana wasn't sure whether she wanted it to or not.

Fran reached out with one hand, his fingers splayed. "Hold on. It's not what you think."

"I think Caroline lives here," Svetlana snapped. "That's what I think."

"I mean that she's different," he whispered. "Not like she used to be."

"If you believe that, then you are a fool." Svetlana pushed her chair back and planted her hands on her hips.

"Mom?" Evan said, alarmed.

Svetlana intended to leave the room, but then she remembered this was not her home. There was no bedroom to which she could retreat in a hot fume and lock the door behind her.

Evan gave her a what-are-you-doing glare.

Svetlana stole a second glance at the place where Caroline had stood, but no one was there anymore.

Fran leaned back in his chair and spoke calmly. "Caroline is helping us fight the Moon Children. We have to band together—Uncle Jimmy even sent a message that said so—and Caroline is crucial in helping the planet survive," he said.

Svetlana lowered into her chair. She had dreaded coming to this universe because she didn't want to face Caroline, to live under Caroline's rule. And here she was, residing under the same roof with the woman who had caused her so much pain. Was this some kind of joke? Sometimes she swore the universe was out to get her.

The desperate look in Fran's eyes begged her to settle down. Svetlana remembered those dark-brown Honest Abe eyes. Fran was good through and through. Which may have been why Caroline managed to gain his trust.

He said, "Let's just—"

"I know it's hard to believe that she's helping," Lisa jumped in, "but she is. You've been away for a long time, Svetlana, and there's a lot you don't know."

"I know more than you think," Svetlana said, regretting the words as soon as they left her mouth. "What I mean is, Evander told me what was happening here."

"Look, you must be tired." Fran tapped her arm, drawing her attention away from Lisa, back to his warm expression. "Let me bring you ladies to your rooms."

"Yes, could we do that, please?" Natasha said, looking even paler than she had when they first landed at Starbright. "I'd love to lie down for a while."

"Great idea," Lisa said, standing. "Everyone else, please get back to work."

As the room broke into movement, Svetlana grabbed Natasha's arm and pulled her close. "You could have warned me Caroline was here."

"You weren't safe at Starbright, and we had to leave," Natasha said. "The Leonards, remember? If I'd told you she was here, you wouldn't have come."

"Yes, I know," Svetlana said. "But we have to be able to trust each other."

Lisa started across the room with Evan beside her.

Natasha didn't stutter when she said, "I have no problem with that. Do you?"

Her honesty blew Svetlana away. "I don't . . . think so?"

"Good," Natasha said. "Then we're good."

Chapter 9

Caroline

Caroline retreated to her sleeping quarters, a room off the beaten path, as humans liked to say. No one would accidentally barge in, short of becoming lost and mistaking it for the door to a broom closet or entrance to a secret tunnel out of the bunker. The room itself was a good-sized space, originally built for two. It was one Caroline had lived in before, with Edmund, back when they maintained the appearance of a unified front. But that was years ago, when they'd first decided to inhabit Earth and agreed on the way forward.

Like all of the spaces in the bunker, the room lacked natural light and unfortunately didn't have an astronomical observatory to assuage Caroline's need for it. Being underground, this was understandable and expected, and it had not bothered her in the past. It bothered her today, however. *Now that I am more human and less Jovian,* she admitted to herself.

She sat upon the end of her bed and stared at the wall in front of her. There were no pictures there. Nothing to occupy her attention save the white trim that rose from baseboard to wainscoting in rectangular simplicity. Trim that formed boxes like this box of a room which currently boxed her in.

Not long ago, when she still possessed all of her Jovian abilities, she traveled the galaxy by way of the oneness. Back then, life on Earth never presented a dull moment. Staring at walls was the equivalent of space travel. Of course, not all Jovians possessed this talent; in fact, few of them did. She pitied the others for this lack in their makeup. And now that that skill had gone by the wayside like so many of her others, she pitied herself.

It was only time, Caroline assumed, before she settled fully into human form and lost the last of her Jovian skills.

Loathe the day, she thought.

She also loathed this new tendency she had for sitting in quiet rooms and sinking into solemnity. This proneness to sulking.

And yet here she was, doing it again. But could she blame herself?

Svetlana's unexpected presence this afternoon had done much to deepen Caroline's melancholy. The mere sight of the woman amplified the stark sting of her aloneness.

She found herself longing for the days she and Edmund shared close, like-minded thoughts and ideas. When it was the two of them at the helm of the world instead of just her—two superior minds grappling with the planet's many challenges. Back then, she'd fulfilled her potential, and he'd helped her do it; his presence gave her the fearlessness needed to make decisions that would in time affect the universe.

But now, when she needed him most, he failed to return. David, the supreme one, was dead, as was her beloved grandson, Evander, the world's most talented negotiator, persuader, engager. Miranda and Leo, her loyal followers, had left her to oversee the colonization of Mars. She was truly alone. And worse, she was lonely.

What could be more human than loneliness?

It was an emotion Caroline always knew existed but had never understood. How could a human possibly feel lonely on a planet overrun with humans?

Now she understood all too well.

She closed her eyes and entered the hum of the oneness, then tried desperately to spin off into the universe like she used to. Alas, it was like flinging herself into a brick wall.

Her consciousness stayed put, in this sedate underground room where she spent much of her time alone while the clones and hybrids and humans, and even some of her own family members, gathered at a safe distance away from her.

Because they liked it better that way.

She observed her hands, the dry skin covering over raised veins, decades showing in her lumpy knuckles. She had hoped to grow stronger when the oneness returned, but it didn't happen; if anything, she grew older and weaker by the day. The time she had spent as a Jovian in human form, she could only assume, had caught up with her. Without the Jovian part of her, she had become just another aged human being.

In spite of this, when Dmitri had taken his place at Starbright and he became the new supreme being, the Jovian chatter reentered Caroline's mind as clearly as before. His ascension had scattered the Moon Children, too, dispersing those that spread across the planet in pockets of deadly fog. But this would not be the end of them. They still congregated in rivers, lakes, and oceans in liquid form, and less often in the forests in their bodily form. As long as their queen lived, they would rise as deadly vapor once again.

Only one Moon Child had to be on Earth in order for infinite Moon Children to be on Earth.

Caroline stood and, without a destination to head toward, she stepped to the opposite side of the room, then turned and headed back to the bed, pacing the way Miranda used to. Miranda had always reminded her of a lioness when she'd done it—a dangerous and strategic animal, plotting some future action—but as Caroline gave it a try, she understood that occupying the body while the mind ran its course helped her to think.

The key is the monarch.

There would be no fixing Earth's problem without addressing the Moon Children's leader, simply because as long as the monarch lived, her hive would live as well. As long as she wanted her hive to attack, they would attack. But who would negotiate with the monarch? Normally Edmund would take care of extraterrestrial relations; hence, the reason they were in this mess.

How could he do this to me? How could he send the Moon Children knowing what they can do to Earth?

She'd fix it. She had to. She was the keeper. Protecting and serving the planet was her job. Though she was no more powerful than a human at this point, she retained one advantage and that was her reputation of authority. Humanity in general deemed her an alien queen, and they feared her. Their president remained at Caroline's beck and call. It was only those who resided in the close quarters of this bunker who knew her true, diminishing state. And they, too, saw her as a danger, an unpredictable entity.

But would the fear of her be enough? Would the humans unify as a race and agree to whatever plan for negotiation she and the monarch came up with? If the

Moon Children decided to claim the surface of the Earth as their own, if they insisted Earth's inhabitants take to their sunless, underground dwellings for good, how would Caroline keep those inhabitants from fighting back with bombs and laser beams? How would she convince them they would never win a battle against the hive, that the only way to assure their survival required them to submit?

Caroline's back smarted. She'd woken with an ache in both hips. Subtle pain, but the kind that persisted, the kind more devoted to her than her own family members were at this point.

She retook her seat at the end of the bed and stared at the wall in front of her.

How could she be the keeper if her human body would soon die? How would she prevent Earth from entering a battle of the sort that would assure a fate as lifeless as Mars and Venus's. If she passed away, who would take this rare gem of a planet into the future? Who would ensure its longevity?

Destruction was upon them, and Caroline feared she would not see this problem resolved. She regretted her past actions, the cold manner in which she'd treated both humans and clones most of all, but she was no longer the person who'd acted so coldly. By becoming human, she'd done penance, had she not? And yet no manner of begging had brought Constance back to reinstate Caroline's natural form. Constance might be her only chance to revert to her Jovian self, and that chance, she knew deep in her most human and vulnerable place, would never arrive.

With little energy to fight the urge to lie down, Caroline gave in to it. Why was she always so tired? She allowed her lids to close as she soaked in the horrible worry and helplessness, the weakness that spread from limb to limb.

She thought of Edmund once more and longed for his companionship.

"Caroline?"

A voice flickered through the oneness like candlelight through darkness.

"Caroline, it's Edmund."

She sat up so quickly a wave of dizziness and an ache in her head followed. As happy as she was to hear Edmund's voice, she hesitated to respond, afraid he may have been eavesdropping on her private thoughts. But that was impossible. Her ability to keep others out remained as steadfast as ever.

"Hello," she said, tamping down the enthusiasm that came with this unexpected meeting.

"We need to talk," he said.

"I agree."

"That's good, good. I'm glad to hear you're open to discussion."

"Dmitri has mended the oneness," she informed him with pride.

"He's a bright one, that boy. I knew he would step up, sooner or later."

"David died trying," she added. "I was there when he parted."

"I'm sure that was difficult for you," he said, but not in the warm or soft way a human would say it. "It's over now. He played his part well."

"Dying in the name of the oneness was David's part?" she asked.

"It was a part *you* gave him—but you shouldn't have. He couldn't mend the oneness on his own. I made sure of that."

She'd been right all along: Edmund had been the one to break the oneness.

"I had to try, Edmund," she said testily. "You *knew* I would try."

"Yes, but you tried for too long, driving him at it again and again," he said without feeling. "You kept at him long after he preferred to give up."

Silence. A tightening knot in her gut. The memory of David's death, how she'd watched him grow empty, how the life clearly syphoned out of him. She felt something else as well. Anger. Was it her own or Edmund's? This was new to her: detecting the concealed emotions of another Jovian. Especially Edmund. Why was she able to do this? Had he changed too? Did he feel more deeply than he used to?

"If you made sure he couldn't fix the oneness, then wasn't it *you* who killed him?" she asked.

She waited before speaking again, but Edmund did not respond, and his wordlessness frightened her. Would he break their connection and disappear again for years on end? She couldn't have that. She didn't want to be alone. She needed him.

"Let's not argue," she said without malice. "The Moon Children are wreaking havoc, and Earth needs our help. You've played with fire, using them as a weapon against me. You know they could bring this planet to its knees. Are our differences of opinion worth the risk of a dead planet on our hands?"

"I did what had to be done to stop you," he said, his voice solemn.

She crossed her arms over her chest. "It was more than you needed to do."

"When I made the proposal to involve the Moon Children, the others agreed."

No. That can't be true.

"Which others? Surely not Miranda or Leo. Not Evander." There was no way Evander agreed to such an overzealous solution. "David remained loyally by my side until the end."

"They all agreed you should be stopped, even if not in the manner I chose to stop you," he clarified.

"I see," she said. "Why the Moon Children, why not some other way?"

"The opportunity was there, and I took it. It worked, Caroline. You were stopped. That's why."

Again, she sensed the heat of anger churning inside him, anger she wanted to assuage.

"Evander didn't like what you were doing," he added, "yet he kept an open mind. Still, you pushed him away instead of making him an ally. Why was that?"

"That's not fair!" Her words spread fractals of light across the oneness. This red-hot flame of defense hadn't asked for permission to flare, and she navigated it as best she could, pulling back the reigns that kept her arsenal of fear and regret and sadness under control. She pressed it down, down, down.

Unfortunately years of built-up emotion collided into the walls of her mind and broke through the other side. She stood up, wringing her hands. "I did not push him away," she said in a loud volume she'd rarely used in her lifetime. "I wanted more than anything for him to understand. But his daughter was ill. James had taken her to Mintaka. It wasn't my fault Evander left."

She'd never unloaded such wrath before, never expressed such anger, and oddly, doing so made her want to cry.

Why does fury make me want to cry?

She'd never shed a tear in the presence of Edmund. But the tangle of regret and frustration threatened to foil whatever attempt she made at keeping them contained.

Edmund remained silent.

"I think you should have stayed with me," Caroline said, her voice trembling as she spoke in a gentler tone. "You could have convinced me to stand down. You could have showed me a better way."

She missed him. Talking to him made her realize that her loneliness had sunken to an abysmal depth. She craved his sympathy and understanding. No one knew her the way he did, the way only he could as an original royal in the Jovian family. And yet, after spending many lifetimes with him, she had not once told him what he meant to her. She wouldn't even tell him now. She couldn't. Fear, that awful human affliction, kept her from doing so.

Human existence is torture!

"You weren't open to negotiation at the time," Edmund said in a competent, steady voice. "As a matter of fact, you made it clear that your decision had been made. Miranda supported you, eager as she was to inherit your attention— and my position. She told you what you wanted to hear, and you stopped listening to me. You must watch her, Caroline. There have been whispers of foul play across the oneness."

"Even if I wasn't open to negotiation, you could have tried to persuade me. I'm not perfect, Edmund. I was never as perfect as I was expected to be. And Miranda has proved to be a sorry replacement for you."

"You were as perfect a Jovian as ever lived," he said. "I understood why you believed yourself invincible, why you felt no need to negotiate."

"I did believe myself to be invincible," she admitted. "I'm not too proud to say I regret that now."

She sensed something earnest in the silence that followed, something weighty and reluctant. As if what

Edmund would say next would be the thing he'd never wanted to say.

"You told me you were the keeper," he said, and the question underneath those words begged for an explanation.

"Yes." The shame crossed her human face like a hot rain as she realized all at once he was telling her what she already knew but did not want to admit. She was *not* the Earth's keeper, as much as she wished herself to be. She had never been the keeper.

"But you agreed with me when I said I was."

"I did."

"Why would you agree with me if you didn't believe it was so?"

He hesitated. "I couldn't say no to you."

"I don't understand. All you had to do was tell me I was wrong."

"And would you have accepted my opinion?"

"Well, I—"

"I knew how badly you wanted it to be so," he said. "I knew you loved Earth as much as a mother loves a child. That was all it was, Caroline. It was love, not duty. But you didn't believe in love. And I couldn't find the strength to tell you no, that you were not the keeper, that what you believed was wrong."

Her breath scraped against the back of her throat where a terrible pain lodged. But she could not cry. Not now. This was what humans meant when they said they were at a loss for words, for she couldn't think a clear thought, could not find one logical statement to utter, one reply that would make any sense.

"I failed you, Caroline," he continued. "I couldn't tell you that someone else held and would always hold the position of keeper. Worse, I couldn't tell you not to clone the Jovian family members or that the small instances of Jovian violence would lead to the kind of world we promised we'd never support, that we'd never sanction.

"And that was wrong," he said. "That was not the part I was supposed to play."

"Oh, Edmund," Caroline said. "I've failed you."

The center of Caroline's chest throbbed with the pain of knowing she'd done something colossally wrong. It became difficult to breathe. What she wouldn't do to go back in time and become invincible again!

"That's why I had to leave," Edmund said sadly. "That's why I had to risk everything to stop you."

How did we get to this place? Caroline's pulse throbbed, veins clotting with regret.

"But maybe all is not lost. I sense a change in you," he added. "Am I wrong about that?"

She revived at this glimmer of hope. "No, you're not wrong." Most likely he knew what was going on inside of her, how far from the "perfect" Jovian she'd come. But he didn't mention it, and she appreciated that.

Instead he said, "What are you going to do about Miranda and Mars? Is what I've heard true?"

"Miranda wanted to build weapons for protection, but I absolutely forbade it," Caroline said. "She won't go against my word. Leo won't let her. And even if she still hopes to build them, she hasn't the means."

Edmund chuckled in an ironic manner, and Caroline wondered if he'd ever laughed before. He must have, but she couldn't remember a time when he had. Why would he laugh like this now?

"I'm glad you're still confident in that vein," he said by way of explanation. "Even if you end up being wrong."

She wasn't wrong. Was she? Would Miranda defy her? Did she have what she needed to build weapons? Would

Miranda try to overtake her? Even after Caroline put her in charge of her own planet? Edmund may have known something he wasn't revealing. Before she could ask, he said, "Caroline, I'm in transit, and I have the Moon Children's monarch with me. She is willing to negotiate if you are."

"Yes. I am willing, I desire negotiation," she said eagerly. She would navigate this situation with Edmund at her side. A surge of relief allowed her to breathe freely once again. All would be well one way or another. "Thank you, Edmund, for making this possible. Please tell her we must find a solution we can agree to. I assume she wants a new home."

"She does. And I will tell her you are prepared to speak with her. We will arrive in a matter of days."

"Good," Caroline said, some of the loneliness lifting from her shoulders. "I'm staying at the bunker. In our old room." It felt strange to say that. Why had she said that?

"Yes, I know."

Of course he knew. He knew and probably didn't care. He was still Jovian. Still limited emotionally and as powerful as ever. Unlike her. Her shoulders slouched, the angst spreading from her mind to her body.

"I hope you and I will have time to talk privately," she said, feeling the need for reassurance. "I have much to tell you."

"That can be arranged."

His answer was cold and business-like, not at all what she wanted from him. She missed him. Didn't he miss her? Didn't he look forward to seeing her again, especially after the conversation they just had?

"What I mean is that I hope you will talk to me, Edmund." She stopped just shy of her voice quivering, and cringed in response. But maybe she shouldn't shy away from this part of herself. Maybe this was who she was. A vulnerable individual who, for the first time in her long, long existence, was being honest with an old friend and fellow leader of the galaxy.

Surely the emotion she'd displayed during this conversation confused Edmund.

"I will talk to you, Caroline. I will look forward to it."

"I'm sorry," she said in a loud burst of desperation, and then she sucked in her breath, unused to making apologies of any kind.

"Yes. Well. We . . . will talk," he said after an awkward pause.

"Very well," she said. "Goodbye, Edmund."

Chapter 10

Svetlana

Svetlana woke to the sound of shower spray in the adjacent bathroom. It took a second before she remembered where she was. The room she slept in was very dark. No windows in a bunker, obviously. Evan or Natasha must have woken before her and now prepared for the day ahead. Svetlana would get up too. She couldn't allow Evan to take off on her own, rebellious child that she'd been of late.

Throwing back the blankets, she sat up and hung her legs over the side of the bed. As she rubbed her face awake, a dim light popped on, just enough to see, not enough to make her squint. It must have detected her movement.

And what is this? A small silver device with a dark, shiny screen clasped like a snug bracelet around her wrist. As she moved her hand toward her face, the screen woke with the time and some other symbols for the weather, the AirQ, and a few other numbers and letters she couldn't decipher. A wristcomm? She'd noticed Fran wore one the night before. *Where did it come from?*

Last night, after Evan went to bed and Natasha announced that she'd be going out to explore the bunker, Fran had visited their suite. He was alone, and he and Svetlana sat on the severely rectangular, brown as dirt (and nearly as hard) couch in the living space. She'd put her feet, clad in her futuristic black boots, upon the spartan square of a coffee table and so had he. They both said how great it was to see each other again, and then they complained of being tired. The conversation seemed loathe to move, so Svetlana shared her topmost concern.

"I'll need a spaceship to get back to the other universe," she said, hoping not to offend him with her eagerness to leave. "Any idea where I can get one?"

"What happened to the one that brought you here?" he'd asked.

"It's in the docking station at Starbright. It isn't working right now, or so Natasha says. She tried everything. Is it true that we need permission to take a time trip?"

"Permission?" He rubbed the top of his head. "From who?"

"Natasha said the ship's not working because we're meant to stay here. But I don't believe that. Spaceships don't think, do they?"

"Got me," he said with a laugh. "I don't know much about them. I've never left the planet, and I want to keep it that way."

This surprised her. "Are you saying that if you had the chance to leave, you wouldn't? The thought of living in a world without Jovians doesn't tempt you?"

"This is my home," he said, his answer arriving far too fast for him to have given it any thought. "People here rely on me."

"The Coalition, of course," she said. "I understand."

An awkward moment of silence hovered between them. Somehow, they'd become people from different worlds.

"Look, I wanted to talk to you about Caroline," he said.

Ah. The reason for this late visit. He needed to make sure she didn't plan to murder Caroline in the middle of the night.

"I know you two have history and not much of it is good, but things have changed since you left. She's on our side now, and she wants to help."

Instead of turning toward Svetlana, he stared at the wall opposite, probably because what he said sounded like a betrayal. "She's not like she used to be," he added.

Maybe she and Fran wouldn't be such close friends anymore. Which was fine. She was going home as soon as the opportunity presented itself anyway.

"I know you don't believe me," Fran said, "but we need her to put the Moon Children attack to rest, and Caroline may be the only one who can do it."

"Oh yes, of course, the ever-powerful Caroline is the *only* one—"

"She's actually lost most of her power," he interrupted.

When Svetlana had caught a glimpse of Caroline in the pubspace, she'd appeared frail. But powerless? That seemed unlikely.

"She did look different," Svetlana said. "Is that really why?"

"She can't take her true form anymore," he said with utter seriousness.

"Her *Jovian* form?" Svetlana considered the implications of that. She remembered when she saw her adoptive mother, Dana, in her true form. The night Dana had fallen out of a tree in the backyard and broken her leg. She'd hidden in the bathroom as she struggled to return from a sleek, black, smooth-as-can-be creature into a human being again. It wasn't pretty.

"What was Caroline like in Jovian form?"

Fran laughed a little. "Tall. Like, six stories tall." His eyes widened with the memory. "And powerful, Svetlana, really powerful. She held a grown man in her hand like he was a kid's toy. It was incredible to see. And everybody saw it. The whole world was broadcasting via satellite."

"Wow," Svetlana said.

"Yeah. That's when the world started calling her Queen Jovian."

"So now that she needs you, she's playing nice, is that right? She's mingling with the leaders of the Coalition because she's like a regular person?"

He exhaled a soundless snort and tipped his head back. "The thing is, very few people know she's less powerful, so she still holds her esteemed position in the world."

"But she's physically like a human? A seventy-something-year-old?"

"To some extent she's human, but she still has the oneness. She's still very much part of the Jovian family. So, yeah, that's what I'm trying to tell you. She's different. She's been through a lot." And then he said tentatively, "So you might want to go a little easy on her, you know?"

Svetlana turned away from him and scoffed. "Really?" she said. Fran obviously didn't know her mother-in-law as well as Svetlana did. Caroline was the queen of the blank stares. The one who never cared about anyone except herself, who didn't shed a tear when her son, Andrew, died. Go easy on her? No, that was not something Svetlana could do.

Plainly, Fran had decided to forgive and forget. Good for him. That was his choice.

She let the topic of conversation go, and she and Fran spoke of less important things until they said goodnight.

And now that Svetlana had slept on her thoughts of Caroline and the possibility of "going easy on her," her stomach twisted at the prospect of joining the queen in the pubspace for breakfast—and possibly lunch and dinner—and countless other times while they shared the safety of the bunker.

Or maybe because Svetlana had arrived, Caroline would go back to Starbright where she belonged. That would be nice.

Svetlana could not wait to go home.

She finger-combed her hair and then located her boots on the floor beside the closet door and put them on. The lighting had gradually brightened, mimicking the rise of the sun. Some real sunshine would have helped her anxious, somewhat sour mood, but she wouldn't complain. At least she and Evan had woken in a safe place. Not everyone on this half-poisoned planet could say the same.

The shower stopped, so Svetlana hurried into the suite's living area and took a seat on the uncomfortable sofa. Apparently the Jovians could send a spaceship to multiple universes, but they couldn't build a cozy piece of furniture. That actually made a lot of sense.

Evan emerged from the bathroom in her unitard with a towel wrapped around her head. "Where's Natasha? Not back yet? Do you think she didn't sleep here last night?" The questions spilled out of her the way they did whenever she was nervous and unsure.

"I don't know, honey. I haven't seen her," Svetlana said, begrudging the fact that Evan cared more about Natasha's whereabouts than anything else. "More important, how are you feeling? Is the oneness more manageable today?"

"Oh, uh, yeah." Evan rubbed her wet hair with the

towel. "I mean, it's still pretty loud but I'm getting used to it. A little bit. I think."

Young people had a wonderful way of claiming two opposite things at the same time.

"But," Evan continued, "I have sort of a bad feeling that won't let me be." She looked at Svetlana as if she should know exactly what that meant.

"What can I tell you?" Svetlana said. "This world is crazy, as you mentioned yesterday. It feels very different from home, and I can't wait to go back."

"No. That's not it," Evan said. She returned to the bathroom and came back with a comb, then proceeded to detangle her long, wet bangs.

"Okay. So, what are you talking about then?"

"Someone's been trying to reach me through the oneness. It might be Dmitri. I can hear them but . . . " She stared at the wall with a squinty-eyed look of insecurity, as if studying an abyss she was thinking about jumping into. "It's like their voice lies under layers of blurry, indecipherable words that never shut the hell up. Maybe my access to the oneness is knotted. I could be missing something important."

Those were sentences Svetlana had never expected to hear coming from her daughter's mouth.

"Whatever it is," Svetlana said, desiring to downplay everything Jovian and especially the oneness, "I'm sure it's not too urgent. If so, whoever was sending the message would find another way to reach you. I mean, everyone here has a wristcomm or one of those futuristic cell phones they carry in their pocket. They could just call you." She lifted her arm. "See? Even I have one. No idea where it came from. When I woke up, there it was, just like our black outfits."

Evan checked her own wrists and found nothing there.

She exhaled a breath of disappointment—the realization that perhaps she wasn't as important to this world as she and Natasha assumed.

"The good thing," Svetlana continued, "is that we're in a safe place, where I can focus on finding a way home."

"Do what you want. I have to go to Starbright," Evan said before replacing the comb and the wet towel back into the bathroom.

"Watch your tone," Svetlana said. "And, no, you don't have to go anywhere."

"I need to talk to Dmitri," she said when she reappeared.

"Just call him. Here, use my wristcomm." Svetlana raised her arm.

Evan glared as if Svetlana had committed an incredibly rude crime.

"We will stay here, both you and I," Svetlana said for good measure. "You said yourself you don't know who's trying to reach you—or even if it's you they're trying to reach."

Evan shifted into an angry, hip-jutting pose. She'd always been a skinny child, and like it or not, she could still pass for a fourteen-year-old.

"Are you forbidding me to go to Starbright?" she asked.

Svetlana hadn't forbidden Evan to go anywhere since she entered junior high. But this was a different time, a different place. "For the moment I am, yes," she said. "There are Leonards at Starbright, and they're so sick they're dying. They may have something that's contagious."

"If they did, we probably would have caught it already," Evan said with a huff.

Svetlana would not give in. "And the ones who aren't

sick are brutes who want to lock you up. Is that what you want?"

"You can't stop me from leaving. I'm eighteen, and I already told you I'm not going back home right away."

"If I find someone to take us home that's exactly what you'll do."

Svetlana allowed Evan a few seconds to respond. When she didn't, she groaned. "Why must you fight me at every turn?"

"Why do you refuse to listen?" Evan shouted. "I have something important to do here. Is that so hard for you to believe?"

"I'm your mother, and I don't have to listen to you when I suspect you're wrong."

Svetlana knew this answer would not go over well, but she had been unable to stop herself. She needed to convince Evan to stay put. "*You* have to listen to me. I do not have to listen to *you*. That's something you've never understood."

"Ugh!" Evan threw back her head and produced a frustrated, double-fisted screech that Svetlana suspected she'd been stifling since the day before. "Which way did Natasha go?"

"Last night? I have no idea."

"Can't blame her for wanting to get away from you." Evan stomped toward the door.

"You can't go to Starbright," Svetlana said in a dire tone.

Evan reached for the doorknob. "You already said that."

"So, where will you go?"

"Away from you."

The door flung back and then slammed closed. Svetlana's bones rattled with the ensuing thud. How embarrassing it was to parent a rebellious teen in a bunker, where the leadership of the Coalition, and possibly even Caroline, would come to see for themselves what little control Svetlana wielded over her own daughter.

The room returned to silence, but not calm. Svetlana's nerves zinged and fizzled with annoyance. No way would she sit alone and fume. She needed to move.

The scent of coffee had wafted in when the door opened. She'd take her chances running into Caroline in the pubspace.

MUCH LIKE A BUSTLING LIBRARY, the pubspace remained quiet yet busy. Workers sat at desks lining the circular perimeter of the space, gathered at tables in groups of three and four, speaking in low tones among themselves. Some of them ate. Others typed without interruption or studied screens showing aerial photos of portions of land and outer space. Svetlana found the Evanders disturbing. That initial, eye-catching, *Oh, he's here*, followed by the realization that it wasn't him, just a young version of the real thing.

The big screen above the bar babbled the news at an imperceptible volume. The coffee smelled like something Svetlana did not want to live without; she approached the nearby station and helped herself.

The young clone named Connie, in her usual black attire and brown braids, spoke with a colleague at her workstation at the bar. Svetlana doubted she'd ever get used to this young version of Aunt Constance with long hair and an aggressive attitude. Uncle Jimmy and Aunt Constance were the first in-laws she'd ever met, in their seventies and looking every decade of it.

It felt like a lifetime ago, but she still remembered that night as clear as could be. She and Andrew had spent ten hours at the ice cream shop together, scooping goodies for attendees of the UFO Festival in downtown Kirksberg. Afterward, he showed her the view of the sky from a park bench that he knew (where they ate *chizsteaks*) and then he took her down a quiet street and kissed her. Their love had felt so urgent back then. So utterly important. The only thing in the world.

But that was long ago. Long enough for most of the Andrew clones to have died off, either from heart failure or at the hands of the Moon Children. Natasha had explained that of all the clones, the Andrews were most susceptible to the Moon Children's poison.

As soon as Svetlana claimed an out-of-the-way seat at a round table beside the far wall, Fran and Lisa entered the pubspace. They waved from afar, passed by the coffee station, and joined her.

"Been a busy morning, have you heard?" Fran asked.

Lisa grabbed his arm. "Before you jump right into business, Fran . . . " She turned to face Svetlana, "How are your rooms? Do you have everything you need?"

"Oh, yes, everything is great. Thank you." Svetlana smiled.

"Great," Lisa said.

"Sorry, yes, how'd you sleep?" Fran asked.

"Pretty good." Svetlana nodded.

Sleeping wasn't the problem. Evan's insolence was.

"If you guys don't mind," Lisa said, "I'm going to head to the kitchen. I need lunch."

"See you later," Fran told her. Then, back to Svetlana, he said, "It's noon-thirty, so I'm guessing you slept better than pretty good."

"Noon—really?" Svetlana laughed as she scanned the area for a clock, finding one on the big screen over the bar.

"I'm sure time-tripping causes some lethal jetlag," he said. "Anyway, something huge happened last night while you caught up on your Z's."

"I guess that would explain the focused atmosphere in here," she said.

"Edmund is on his way, and he's bringing the Moon Children's monarch with him."

"The queen of the moon people?" Svetlana asked with a hint of humor.

"She wants to negotiate with Caroline."

"Oh, well, that's good, right?" Svetlana did not want to be involved and therefore remained as separate and uncaring as one possibly can without crossing the line into rudeness.

"In the best-case scenario, it means Caroline and possibly Edmund will be able to help them decide to leave Earth, to live someplace else. They hate their home on Europa, but the clones are saying they may be willing to go back to Io."

"That's interesting," Svetlana said, hoping it would work out for Fran and Lisa's sake. Then a thought occurred to her, a niggling worry. "But why would they want to leave, now that they know how nice it is here?"

"Yeah, if they can't come to an agreement, and the Moon Children decide to fight for their right to occupy the planet, we're in trouble. They could decimate everything. I mean, we know they're capable," Fran said.

"I really hope it doesn't come to that," she said, once again glad she'd be leaving Jovian Earth soon.

Svetlana sat back and nursed her coffee, which definitely didn't taste as rich as it smelled, and she comforted herself with the notion that these people would eventually help her find a ship able to time travel her back home. The Moon Children weren't her problem. One way or another, she was getting out of here. The sooner, the better.

Caroline appeared in the entrance to the pubspace looking strange . . . *disheveled*. She didn't carry herself like the Caroline Jovian Svetlana had known. Was this her new normal, or was something up? She appeared shaken, lurching ungracefully into the room as if she'd just witnessed something awful. She actually staggered before righting herself, a harried kind of panic widening her eyes as she scanned the pubspace in search of someone or something.

"Connie," she called out.

Connie had been at the perimeter, speaking with a Miranda clone stationed at one of the desks. "Over here," she said, rushing toward Caroline. "What's wrong?"

"Screens up," Caroline commanded the others.

All screens in the pubspace that weren't on before flashed to life. Connie took her position at the bar.

Fran had leaped as soon as Caroline made her entrance. He currently pressed through the maze of tables and chairs. Lisa hadn't yet left the pubspace, and joined the others.

"What have we got?" Fran asked, his game face on.

Svetlana couldn't hear their muted voices, so she, too, moved closer. Not all the way to where they gathered, but to a chair at a nearer table.

"Have you been tracking it?" Caroline asked Connie.

"I just checked five minutes ago. It was on course. Nothing unusual to report."

"Check again."

"Why? What happened?" Connie's fingers flew over the keyboard.

Caroline paled. "You don't feel it?" She clung to the

edge of the bar top as if she'd just been walloped and needed the stability. Whatever she grappled with internally must have been so big that it threatened to take her to the ground.

Connie squinted at her screen. "Wait? Is this real?"

"Yes, it's real." Caroline slumped over the bar and closed her fluttering eyelids.

"What the hell is that?" Fran asked, pointing to Connie's computer screen.

Svetlana focused on the large screen in the near distance. It looked like a flare had been set off in outer space.

"Is it a nascent star or . . . " Fran said.

The image jumped and zapped like a lightning storm over their heads.

"There's been a massive explosion in the asteroid belt," Connie said. "Hang on, I'm trying to link to a better view."

The image began to clarify. Svetlana made out the many broken pieces of a whole that appeared to have shattered. It *was* an explosion. Delayed from the far distance, whatever Caroline sensed or saw or learned had blown up was still in the process of separating. Like a snowball that had hit a wall, the pieces and parts flew in every direction in slow-motion.

Flames, ash, metal. Dust.

Mars loomed large and fiery in the distance. A deep, bright red that Svetlana couldn't help but feel was filled with anger.

"What was it?" she asked. "Was it a satellite or—?" She didn't dare say "space station" or "spaceship" out loud.

No one answered.

Caroline groaned. As she came to, she held the counter

with white-knuckled fingers, her head bowed like the head of a wilted flower.

"Do you know what it is, Caroline?" Lisa asked, placing a hand on the older woman's slight back. She seemed so thin, so . . . breakable.

"It's the *Regal Star*," Caroline said. "Edmund's ship . . . his crew."

The room seemed to draw a unified breath. All went absolutely silent.

"Are you sure?" Fran said.

"It's him," Connie spoke sharply. "I . . . " She grabbed her forehead and struggled to say more. "I feel it. There's no mistaking. Edmund is gone."

"I'm so sorry, Caroline." Lisa huddled around her, draping her arms over the older woman's shoulders the way a relative would.

The way a daughter-in-law would, Svetlana thought.

"Come, sit down." Lisa guided Caroline away from the others. They found chairs at an empty table near the one Svetlana occupied. Caroline didn't speak. She seemed unable, as if absorbing the enormity of what just happened required every last drop of her energy.

There was no way Svetlana could lend her the kind of sympathy Lisa provided, no matter what had just happened. She hoped never to touch Caroline, let alone empathize with her.

And yet Caroline exuded the kind of pain that was palpable. This woman who had not shed a tear at her own son's funeral undoubtedly suffered now. Was it real? It sure looked that way.

"What about the monarch?" Fran said, directing the question to Connie. "Edmund was bringing the monarch here. Who the hell would do this?"

"I could be wrong," Caroline answered, her voice a

higher, weaker octave than usual, "but there's a chance that Miranda may have done it."

Fran joined Caroline and Lisa at the table. He sank into a chair, brow rumpled with confusion. "Are you saying the leadership on Mars has weapons?"

"No," Caroline said. "No, they don't."

"Then how could she have done it, and why would she want to hurt Edmund?"

"Miranda was never granted weapons," Caroline said, "but Dmitri told me she still wanted them, that he saw her on Mars discussing the prospect with Leo." Caroline sat taller, an obvious effort to pull herself together. "There's a small chance she could have had them and hid them from us. She may have done this accidentally, or she may—"

"But it's unlikely, right?" Fran said. "Considering the oneness is up and running. I mean, you would have known. And Jovians don't resort to violence."

"I *should* have known, yes," Caroline said, "but thoughts can be hidden, especially by royals."

"Okay, then tell me why Miranda would do it."

"For power," Caroline said. "Because she always coveted . . . my position," she said so softly Svetlana barely heard her.

This was unbelievable. Not only Caroline's outward display of emotional pain, but the fact that one Jovian royal may have purposefully killed another? They weren't human! They didn't play deadly power games. Had this world changed so much since she'd lived here?

"Maybe it wasn't Miranda," Fran said. "We can't assume. It may not have been weapons at all. I mean, it's possible the ship malfunctioned."

"There has never been an accident of this sort on a Jovian ship before," Caroline stated. "Cold fusion engines do not have the capacity to explode."

"That's true," Connie said. "It's practically impossible. I'm reaching out to Mars via comms to get their take on what happened."

"Okay, okay, maybe there haven't been any accidents with Jovian engines," said Fran, "but surely there must be something else we're missing. Let's not jump to conclusions. And let's not accuse anyone of anything until we know more."

Caroline closed her eyes. She seemed to have sunk into deep despair. She propped her elbows on the table, chin cupped by the palms of her hands.

I know that feeling, Svetlana thought. *Like every second you're alive is a strain, a battle fought just to take your next breath.*

"The signal's not getting through," Connie said. "Probably due to interference from the explosion." She continued to type. "Can anyone reach Miranda or Leo through the oneness? I'm not having any luck."

"Maybe it was the Moon Children," Fran said. "Do they have explosives?"

"They have no need for such weapons," Caroline said.

"Right, because they *are* weapons," Fran said. "But still, could the Moon Children's monarch and Edmund have fought inside the ship, and something caused the explosion that way?"

"That doesn't feel right to me," Connie said when Caroline didn't answer. "If they wanted to kill Edmund and his crew, they could have used their poison. No reason to destroy the ship—which they would need to travel to their destination. They don't have the technology for building ships. Nor do they know how to fly them."

"And they wouldn't risk harming their queen," Caroline added. "If she died, so would they."

As this conversation unfolded, Svetlana remembered how Evan had said she had a bad feeling earlier that morning. Could she have sensed this was going to happen? Where was Evan, anyway? She'd left the bedroom suite to find Natasha but never came out for coffee or something to eat. Then again, it was not unusual for her to skip breakfast. Hopefully she and Natasha were hanging out in the room, avoiding her.

Svetlana stood and though she didn't want to draw attention to herself, she asked the question weighing on her mind. "Has anyone seen Natasha this morning?"

Fran turned his head in her direction. "I think Connie said something about Natasha going to see her mother."

"She did," Connie said without changing her focus.

"Today?"

"Uh, not sure. She may have left last night."

"But Nadia lives in Russia," Svetlana said. "How would Natasha get there?"

Fran shrugged in a way that suggested the answer was obvious. "Isn't she a pilot?"

"Oh . . . of course," Svetlana muttered as she took off, rushing past the Coalition members gathered at the perimeter, desperate to get back to the room she shared with Evan and to hopefully find her there.

She better not have gone to Russia.

The means for going home could present itself at any time, and Evan needed to stay close.

Chapter 11

Evan

When one of the Evander clones told Evan that Natasha had left for Russia, she made the decision to return to Starbright alone. She couldn't stay in the bunker with her mother, who wouldn't listen to reason and only wanted to go back to the universe without Jovians. It sucked that the most stubborn mule she'd ever met also happened to be her mother. If the opportunity arose—if her mother managed to find a spaceship and a willing pilot—Evan didn't want to be bullied into leaving.

The same Evander clone who informed Evan that Natasha had left for Russia observed her for long enough to make her uncomfortable. "What?" Evan finally said.

"I know a way you can get out of here, if that's what you want."

"How did you know—"

"I'm part of the oneness too."

"You can see all of my thoughts," she said. "How embarrassing."

He laughed. "Don't worry about your mom. She has a reputation for being stubborn, and I won't tell her you left. Follow me."

He led Evan down a long, curving corridor that came to a dead end. There a door opened to a staircase that went even deeper into the ground. "This was made to look like the entrance to one of the power panels, but it's not. It's a tunnel that leads straight to Starbright. There are a few entrances that go to the tunnel, or so they say, but this is the only one I've ever found."

"Wow, thank you," Evan said with breathy relief. "This is perfect."

"Take the stairs," he continued. "When you reach the bottom, turn around. You'll see a red switch there. Flick it upward and the panel will unlock. Be sure to lock it behind you."

"I will," she said.

"Okay, be careful. Try not to bump into any Leonards along the way."

Evan's mouth went suddenly dry. "Do you think I will?"

"No," he said with a laugh. "Haven't you heard? They're all sick."

"I did hear that, but what if I meet up with one anyway? What will they do to me?"

"You're Evander's sister," he said with gravity. "They won't do anything to you."

"Oh. Really? That's . . . wow." Questions like autumn leaves blew through her mind.

"Welcome to the family," he said with a wink.

She nodded with embarrassing vigor, flustered by the fact that he knew who she was. All of a sudden it felt like the whole world knew who she was, and if so, there would be no going unnoticed anymore. She certainly wasn't used to that kind of attention. At home, in school, she'd always been the quiet one, as good as invisible.

"Okay, uh, thank you, thanks for your help."

She descended the short set of stairs, flicked the switch, and waited for the heavy panel to slide open. Beyond it, a tunnel unveiled like a dimly lit cave, some historic lighting built into the arch of its low-lying ceiling. If she'd had time, she would have studied it more closely. Instead, she found the button to close the panel, which sounded like a boulder sliding, and swallowed loud enough to cause a small echo.

It's okay to be nervous, she told herself.

As she took the first few steps into her shadowy future, the voices in the oneness quieted to a hum. A gentle, soothing (yes, actually soothing) hum. Changes were happening, and that was good. At least, she hoped it was good.

As she picked up the pace, some newfound energy fed invigorated thoughts. For the first time in a long while, she experienced the verve that comes with freedom. Not only because she had defied her mother's mandate to stay put but because this was what she was meant to do. The powers that be seemed to agree with her, to encourage her and speed her ahead—to peel back the fear she'd been feeling for the past few days and reveal a new layer of courage underneath, courage she hadn't known she had.

Her footsteps tapped out little echoes as she strode ahead. Tap-tap-tap, tap-tap-tap, tap-tap-tap. It was a rhythm she soon found herself adding words to. *Yes, this is right, this is right, this is right!*

After ten minutes or so, her body warmed with the movement, and her thoughts turned to the situations she might face. Hopefully not Leonards. That was the first thing. She knew she'd have to enter the tubes and hopefully she would intuit her way back to the astronomical observatory, where she'd find her unusual relatives, Dmitri and Alexandria.

While she plotted her next moves, the occasional "welcome" popped up through the oneness like a fish jumping through the surface of a lagoon. She wondered who'd uttered it. Maybe it was the Evander clone again? Or maybe it wasn't a message meant for her at all. Maybe Jovians greeted each other with "welcome" in the oneness all the time.

But there it was again, rising above the din of voices. "Welcome, welcome, welcome, Evan."

The utterance of her name startled her to a halt. Her heart pounded. *It's for me.*

As she continued through the tunnel, the *welcomes* appeared more and more often, and soon it became constant, like a song sung in unison. *Welcome, welcome, welcome!* the Jovians sang to her. Their voices sounded odd and otherworldly, like electrified violins.

It was the most beautiful sound she'd ever heard, and tears blurred her vision and warmed her nose.

"Welcome," Dmitri said—it was clearly him this time. She pictured him on his stool beside Alexandria, the sunlight dousing them both in gleaming gold brilliance, and Dmitri's eyes became mirrors that made him look, well, alien.

But Evan wasn't afraid. She was happy to hear from him.

"I'm almost there," she said. "I see a door in the distance."

It opened just as she arrived. Before stepping through, she gazed back into the tunnel one last time, back into the life she came from one last time.

She'd made it to the docking station. From then on, she would be looking forward.

Dmitri said, "We are so glad you are here."

"Me too," she said. She crossed the blue-lighted space, found the next opened door, and entered the fluorescent white of the Starbright tube.

Chapter 12

Natasha

The prior night, Natasha went to Russia.

Deep within the ground, significantly below the bunker's main level, a spare ship of the sort Natasha had never seen before docked. Dmitri had discovered this second-story underground level and its hidden vessel through the oneness and led her to it. Maybe he really would know everything one day.

The silver ship had no name she could decipher and wasn't much bigger than a single-engine plane, a model made for two. It was oblong and had circular windows: three lined up in the front, three in the back, and an escape hatch in the ceiling used for entering and exiting.

As Natasha boarded, she pictured her great-grands zipping around in the 1960s, when they'd first arrived at the bunker. They must have loved its chrome trim and deep-red vinyl interior. Like a luxury car built just for them. Maybe Edmund had built it. He'd been known to design a spaceship or two in his time. None of the ships Natasha had ever seen possessed such antiquated character and early Jovian technology, though she knew the machinery and equipment ranked miles ahead of human knowledge and understanding. The navigational tools echoed those of a modern ship enough for her to figure out how to fly it.

It would take her where she needed to go; that was the important thing.

The only problem being that a vessel like this one did not have the best invisibility features—they were more camouflage than unseeable, relying on old Jovian technology that reflected the surrounding environment—solid ground or nearby shore when taking off, and clouds or blue sky when in flight. Clouds created the best coverage, she knew, as did a moonless night.

She typed in the coordinates of her destination, and the engine thrummed to life. It made a strange vibration of a sound, like the rattling waxed paper membrane of a child's kazoo.

"That's what I'll call you," she said. "*Kazoo.*"

As the ship progressed slowly through the wide-spreading station, it seemed to know what to do.

Once in the air, gravity seemed to drop away. *Kazoo* pointed straight up and threw Natasha into the backrest. Her eyes closed against her will, and in the next second, she became weightless—nearly bodiless—as the ship careened, she assumed, to great heights. She wanted so badly to watch this journey unfold, but she couldn't fight the g-force. All she could do was lay back and wait for the ride to end.

The ship leveled off, becoming horizontal again, and Natasha opened her eyes. The dashboard alerted her of their imminent descent, and the small ship eased into low gear.

Natasha scanned the surroundings for a hill or mountain in the distance, when *Kazoo* suddenly dove toward an obscure opening in the ground. Her stomach flew into her throat and her heart flopped into spasm. She grabbed her chest as the narrow entrance opened to a sizable expanse —like a warren dug by a giant rabbit—and she relaxed as *Kazoo* sped through.

The ship even parked itself.

From the looks of things, no one had visited this place in a very long time. Spider webs glistened in the corners, and bats hung from the ceiling amid the stalactites. Talk about old-fashioned.

She found a man's overcoat in a cabinet behind the captain's seat. It was black wool and stylish, probably Edmund's. Russia winters were frigid. Her unitard might suffice, but neither it nor her e-skin were space grade, and she hated to be cold. She exited *Kazoo* through the hatch and jumped to the ground, then put the coat on. A set of crooked stone steps ascended the side wall and before she reached the top, she'd climbed four or five stories.

A glittering cover of snow made for a pretty picture of the tree-covered hillside. As her breath left her body in steady clouds, the moon vaguely lit her path through a forest with many piles of boulders scattered about.

She pulled up her comm and took note of the route to her mother's home. Upon its screen, she also found new messages from Max:

"Hey, just wanted to say hey. Let me know what you're up to."

"I'm going to keep texting until you write back. Hope you don't mind."

"Getting seriously worried that I haven't heard from you in three days. But don't mind me if you're doing some-thing important—or fun."

"Hello? Are you there? I miss texting with you."

Considering her lack of company and the nerves she

suffered thinking about her mom and the awful news she had to deliver, Natasha wrote back right away. "Going to my mother's. Not too excited about breaking the news."

Just typing the words made her nervous, an emotion she had little experience with.

"I'll go with you, if you think it'll help," Max wrote back.

That's what she liked about him. He jumped right in. Didn't ask where she'd been or why she hadn't written. He simply responded to the situation at hand.

And offering to go with her was pretty impressive. But no, it wouldn't help.

"Thank you," she wrote. "I'm already here."

"And I'm still looking for that wormhole," he wrote. "You sure you're okay?"

He was the only one who had asked. And that was nice. But at the same time, the fact that he cared brought out something vulnerable within her. Something that tugged on her defenses. She reminded herself that she could handle anything; her father had told her so many times.

He may have died, but his words lived inside her and always would, even if she couldn't speak with him the way Dmitri could.

"Yes, I'm okay. Your parents are at the bunker. It's about two miles from Starbright. I'll send a link."

"Thanks! Text me anytime. If you need me. Or just want to talk," Max wrote and then added another "anytime."

She sent him the link and came to the end of the forest. According to her comm, she would walk a mile and a half before arriving at the neighborhood her mother lived in.

As she followed the route to her mother's one-story

cottage, the little girl inside her began to show up. The five-year-old who didn't have a chance to say goodbye to her beloved mommy before Uncle Jimmy whisked her away. She double-checked the address as she approached the front door, then paused to center herself before knocking.

When no one answered, a sudden desperation to see Nadia bunched up in her throat. She moved to the side of the house, ascended the slight incline of the wheelchair ramp, and tried the door there. As the minutes passed, she became more and more desperate to see Nadia, to hug her and convey the news about her father—for them to mourn the loss together.

In that moment, she couldn't think of her mother without thinking of her father. They were two halves that made a whole in her mind. *Two halves of a heart*, she thought, remembering a craft-paper Valentine's card she'd made them when she was in kindergarten.

And now one half of that heart had died, leaving the other half alone.

Her mother failed to come to the door. Natasha set off to the back of the house and discovered a misaligned basement window that unlocked with some vigorous jiggling. Once it was open, Natasha slid into the room. She'd be sure to fix the window before she left.

Crossing the basement, she recognized a plastic box filled with her dolls and other toys. *Mother's mementoes of our past life.* She climbed the stairs and wandered from room to room until she came to the one with a four-poster bed. On the dresser that butted against the far wall, a photo of Nadia and Evander dressed like the world leaders they once were propped beside a second, more casual photo of the family, the four of them grinning for the camera.

They had been happy once.

Childhood memories rose to the forefront of her mind.

She remembered how safe and secure and comfortable it was to be part of a family. The great lengths of time she and Dmitri spent together, often with Mother as well, for they were homeschooled with only each other for company. They lived every day in their home in Kirksberg, away from the public eye. It was close-knit and comfortable, time served with sandwiches and snacks, blankets and dolls, and many telescopes.

She gazed into the past until the sadness arrived like an unexpected riptide, rough and uncaring. The life she once led, no matter how happy it may have been, was no more. It had washed away long ago.

She sat upon the foot of Nadia's bed. How hard would it be to tell her mother that her husband had passed without seeing her one last time, without saying goodbye? And worse, how it was all Natasha's fault. *She* was the reason he'd left their comfortable home. For the first time, Natasha gave in to the all-encompassing sadness of mourning. As it flooded inside, her poor heart rattled and shivered, and she wondered if this would be her last day. If her life would end right here, on her mother's bed.

But then the metal glide of a key entered the front door, and footsteps gently thumped the floor, sloughing the snow from boots. Nadia grumbled, "So cold," and a shiver rode Natasha's spine as she realized they were the first words she'd heard her mother say in more than five years.

She stood, and a whirl of dizziness overtook her, the beating of her heart like a misaligned tire, wobbling and punching the road beneath it. She regained her bearings and exited the bedroom, calling out, "Don't be frightened, Mother. I'm here to see you," as she entered the hall.

"Natasha?" Nadia's shoulder bag dropped to the floor. "You've come back?"

Natasha continued forward until her mother came into view. "Yes, Mother, I've come to see you."

"Oh my gosh—I thought I'd never see you again. Natasha, my baby!"

They ran to each other, closing the gap between them.

The feel of Nadia's embrace boggled Natasha's senses. This average-size woman loomed so extraordinary and large in her memory. Natasha must have five inches on her at least. She pulled back to look upon her mother's face, the same classic features and smooth complexion that made for such beautiful pictures of the president and first lady. Perhaps a little less perfect and regal than the idol in her mind, but beautiful still.

Together they laugh-cried. Natasha had never felt such a surging mix of sorrow and happiness.

"Come here." Her mother took her hand and led her into the kitchen, where they sat in chairs at an old wooden table. "You're so grown up. But it's only been five years. How can this be?"

"I'm sorry," Natasha said, awash in guilt.

"Sorry? Why would you say you're sorry, silly girl," she said. "I've never been so happy to see anyone. I don't care what you look like!"

"Me too," she said, her heart struggling to beat properly.

Her mother gazed at her with sheer awe, as if she were looking upon a masterpiece. "It happens to your father as well. The aging. But you're still my baby, still my little girl. As grown up as you are, I can see little Natasha inside of you. Right here and here." She gestured to her eyes and mouth.

The thing that made Natasha so strong and unemotional, whatever it was, threatened to collapse. For a moment, she couldn't speak, didn't want to move. She didn't want to change anything about this long-awaited reunion, this chance for renewed happiness. But time moved as steadily as a river, and she knew she couldn't remain anchored for long. She'd have to move on from this moment, to say other things. She'd have to inform her mother of—

"Dmitri is not with you?" Nadia asked.

"No," Natasha said, and she sought the view out the window, then drifted over the countertops: her mother's canisters labeled "Tea" and "Coffee." A toaster wearing a cloth cover. A shelf with a few cookbooks. "He . . . couldn't make it."

"But he's safe?" Nadia asked. "He's with Alexandria, and your great-grandmother, in Kirksberg?"

Natasha hesitated before answering. She wasn't used to being afraid to speak the truth. "Yes, that's right."

"I wish he would call. I trust that he's all right, but it's been a few weeks since he ran away. The authorities told me something happened at the airport, that they had him and Alexandria in custody for a short time, but they got away—I can't imagine what happened. The airport police promised to let me know when they found him again. I was afraid he was in trouble, but you're sure he's all right? He must be afraid to call me."

"He's okay, Mom. I just saw him. Please don't worry. Great-grandmother needs him for something urgent. And he still has Alexandria at his side, but the next time I see him, I'll tell him he has to come home."

Nadia's eyes filled with tears. "Thank you, thank you. I'm so glad you're here. It's been awful not hearing any news for so long."

"Please don't worry," Natasha said again.

Nadia eyed her with a sidelong glance. "And your father," she asked, raising a hesitant brow, "where is he?"

It was like a wave crashing over Natasha's head, one that took her down to the sand. She couldn't speak. She turned away, thought about leaving the kitchen, saying she needed the bathroom. She wanted so badly to run. To leave this house. To go back to the bunker and never explain what happened in the other universe.

Her breath raced in and out, and the lightness of the air went straight to her head. Would she hyperventilate? No. She could handle anything. She had to calm down. She was the most capable person her father ever knew.

"Natasha, what is it?" Nadia said, her face falling into a frown as she became unnerved. "You can tell me. Has your father made the decision not to return? It's okay if that's the case. You don't know this, but we spoke before he left, and we, well, we decided that maybe we will live apart. If it turned out that that was best for both of—"

"Oh, Mom," Natasha said, the words gushing like blood from a wound. "He's dead! He's dead, and it's my fault. I'm sorry. I'm so sorry. I never would have let him time travel if I'd known, but it was what he wanted, what he insisted we do."

The admittance shattered Natasha's resolve, and the tears streamed, taking her energy, her strength, and her capacity to fight the sorrow and the pain with them.

Nadia closed her eyes and stoically nodded her head. She may have stopped breathing. Her complexion went as colorless as seafoam.

"Mom, no, don't be strong. Please, I can't be strong anymore," Natasha said, choking out the words. "I know you're devastated. I know you are. So am I. Come here." She took her mother with both hands and pulled her close, smelling her gardenia-scented hair as Nadia collapsed into a sob.

Chapter 13

Fran

The Moon Children should have been dead. Their presence should have become a very fast non-issue when Edmund's spaceship blew up along with his crew and the Moon Children's monarch. *If the monarch dies, they all die.* That's what Fran had been told, and no one, human nor Moon Child, can survive the incinerating kind of explosion that leaves nothing behind but ash.

As far as the Coalition members could tell, however, evidence of the Moon Children could still be seen in foggy satellite images across the globe, in the lacy waterways and spotty, opaque dots that continued to crop up beside them on land. Backing this evidence, two instances of poison gas attacks occurred that afternoon: one in a seaside village in Massachusetts and another outside of Loch Ness in the Scottish Highlands.

"I don't get it," Fran said. "Shouldn't they all be dead?"

Caroline let out a breath and pressed her lips together. "They should be," she answered in the tired way she'd taken to speaking. Each day she sounded a little less enthusiastic—a little less alive, if Fran was being honest.

"Another report just came in," Connie said from her desk at the bar. "An attack that occurred an hour ago killed two Evander clones in the Florida Keys."

"Why is this happening?" Fran hated to add pressure where none was needed, but Caroline was the only one who might know the answer to the question. "Could it take a few days for the hive to die? What don't I know?"

"If the monarch died, it would be immediate," she said.

Her countenance of preoccupation bordered on defeat, and that worried him a lot.

"Okay, so we have to assume she's not dead. Somehow she survived the explosion." He rubbed his chin scruff before sipping his coffee.

Caroline stared blankly across the pubspace.

"Or maybe," Fran said, energized by a new thought, "it's possible that Edmund only *claimed* he had the monarch on his ship, but he actually didn't. Maybe he only wanted you to think he did."

"No," Caroline said. "He didn't lie to me."

"How can you be sure?"

"There was a feeling of," she paused to glance at him, then softly spoke the word *intimacy*. "He wasn't scheming" she went on. "We were of a unified mind. I'm certain of it."

Fran sensed every painful bit of the vulnerability necessary for Caroline to acknowledge this. "Okay, okay, I get that. But hear me out. Maybe there was someone who claimed to be the monarch on his ship, but it wasn't actually the monarch. Whoever it was looked like the monarch—I'm told they're hard to see in their physical form—but it wasn't actually the monarch Edmund honestly thought she was. Do you see what I'm getting at?"

Caroline's brow spiked for a second and then eased back into its resting place. She brought her hands together palm to palm, the tips of her fingers grazing her lips.

"Think about it," Fran continued. "If the monarch dies, they all die, so why would they trust Edmund to safely transport her to Earth? He had betrayed them in the past. He took them to an almost completely frozen moon, a desolate environment, and left them there to fend for themselves. They had no reason to trust him—or any Jovian, really."

"That is true." Caroline's tone hinted at regret.

"They may have sent a decoy and kept the real monarch safe."

"That might make sense," she said. "But why go through the pretense of wanting to negotiate? If they wanted to decimate the Earth, they would have done it already." She paused. "And it's not in their nature to lie."

"But maybe they've changed. Or even evolved after the last incident left them—"

"It's possible but unlikely," Caroline said.

"Everything is possible," he said, feeling the heat of frustration in his chest, "whether it's likely is another thing. I don't think we can discount it. I'm only suggesting they could have put a decoy on the ship and sent the real monarch to Earth another way. That would explain why the Moon Children are still out there, still killing people with their poison gas."

He stopped there. He'd raised his voice and needed a minute to calm down before he crossed a line with Queen Jovian.

Thank God she can no longer take her true form, he thought.

"They could still negotiate if they sent her a different

way," he said in a calmer tone. "That's all I'm saying. It would make sense for safety's sake."

"Yes, I see." Caroline shrugged in an unenthused manner. "The question is, how would she get here? They have no means of traveling long distances on their own."

"Yeah, I haven't figured that part out yet," he said.

Connie interrupted: "Fran you have to see this. It looks like they're on the move again . . . just about everywhere."

"What do you mean, *everywhere*?"

"The fog is spreading. It's showing up across the country. All over the world."

"Has anyone reported an attack?"

"Only the ones I've already told you about," she said.

"Keep an eye on it."

He turned back to Caroline. "What does it mean?"

She wore a strange sort of preoccupation upon her face. Pale and tense. Overwhelm, maybe? Or, no, more like some incident in her mind required all of her attention. "Caroline?"

"Yes," she said, blinking up at him.

"What do you think it means?"

She remained slouched and defeated in her seat. "I have no idea."

Fran worried that Edmund's death might be the straw that would break her already-frail back.

"You should go to your room and rest," he told her. "I've got this, and if I need you or anything happens, I'll come get you, I promise."

Chapter 14

Caroline

Caroline left the pubspace hunched over, feeling sick to her stomach, and moving as slow as a tortoise.

"Caroline? Caroline!" Miranda's voice came through the oneness so distinctly it raised Caroline's blonde roots to full attention. An electric sensation prickled over the whole of her scalp like a warning. "I sense your presence clear as day," Miranda said. "Why aren't you answering me?"

Caroline kept her head down and continued through the corridor, thinking, *Not yet, I need a moment, give me a moment!*

The prospect of retiring to her room, lying on her bed, and plummeting into unconsciousness didn't appeal to Caroline as much as it was a fate she had no choice but to give in to. She needed time to gather her thoughts—and her strength—before dealing with Miranda.

As she neared her bedroom quarters, she craved the dim, mournful light of her overhead sconce, the drab walls, and thin cracks like tiny streams crossing her ceiling. She didn't want to be alone, didn't want to languish in the room she'd hoped to share with Edmund that evening, but she couldn't stand to talk to anyone, either.

I can barely stand to be alive.

A warm stream of tears escaped her eyes and met at her chin before dropping away. She sniffed and wiped her face with her fingers. Was she entirely useless to control her emotions at this point?

"Oh, I see what's going on," Miranda said. "I've caught you at a bad time. No need to deny it. I hear every painful sniffle, though I never thought I'd live to witness it."

Caroline reached the door to her room, opened it, and let it fall closed behind her. She lowered onto the side of the bed as if it were a chair and removed her shoes, then quickly pulled back the comforter and slid under. She sank into the mattress fibers, allowing the softness to hold her aching hips and shoulders.

When she closed her eyes, images of the explosion prickled across her lids like an oncoming headache. The echoes of Edmund's death pummeled her chest and took the oxygen from her body. Over and over again, she felt the devastation of his end.

How awful it is to be human!

"Take your time," Miranda said without gentleness or pity. "I've got all day."

Caroline swallowed her reluctance. "Yes, Miranda," she said dully. "How can I help you?"

"Oh, thank goodness. I thought you might have passed out for a second. You sound as awful as I imagined you would." Miranda did nothing to hide her delight in this observation. "Are you okay? What a dumb question. You can't be okay, your husband just died, and you weren't yourself to begin with, were you?"

Edmund's words from the prior night returned: *You*

must watch Miranda. There have been whispers of foul play across the oneness.

"I'm fine," Caroline said, void of the energy to fake it. "Thank you for your condolences."

"Just when he was returning to you . . . what a tragedy."

Whether Miranda had caused Edmund's death or not, Caroline sensed pleasure in her tone, and with it came a whiff of something else: a thirst for power?

"I've been trying to reach you," Caroline said. "The explosion happened too close to Mars not to worry that your base might be in danger."

"Oh, well, thank you for your concern, but there's no need for it. Edmund's ship wasn't attacked. We're in no danger."

"Are our satellites incorrect? Did the explosion not occur in the interplanetary space between Mars and Jupiter?"

"It did. The tremors of aftershock registered for a full five seconds. But our view of it wasn't but a blip in the sky. I suppose it may have appeared closer from your position," she said. "The outer-limits satellites have never been as precise as they should be."

That was a lie. And Caroline didn't appreciate being lied to.

"I tried to reach you as well," Miranda continued. "The accident must have temporarily shaken the oneness —and other means of communication, of course."

"You think the explosion was an accident?"

"What else could it be?"

"I don't know," Caroline said. "But I'm going to find out."

A moment of silence followed, and Caroline let it lie.

"I'll have Leo send you all of our data and images," Miranda finally said.

"Yes, good." *Why hasn't she done so already?*

"And I'm going to return to Earth, too, to help you regain power since Edmund is gone."

"There's no need for that," Caroline said, every nerve in her body firing at the thought.

"But you're in mourning. You don't have to put on a strong front for me—"

"I don't need help, Miranda. And I haven't lost power."

"Caroline," she said, pausing for a sigh, "we know each other well."

"That may be true."

"And I sense your dwindling strength," Miranda said. "What happened to you, what Constance did to you, I wouldn't wish on any Jovian."

"Nothing happened to me," Caroline said. "Stop this, Miranda. Just stop whatever it is you're doing."

Caroline had never raised her voice to Miranda before, never needed to until now.

"All right. You don't want to talk about it. I under—"

"I am still the queen of this bright blue planet," Caroline said, her voice deep with control. "We all have a part to play, and yours has always been and will always be to support me. Not to know me. Not to make decisions for me. And *never* to tell me what to do."

Caroline saw stars as these angry words absorbed the last of her energy.

"Of course not," Miranda said. "I only want to help you through this very trying time in which your husband has passed. You're more alone than ever. That has to be difficult."

The way she spoke, with such lightness, such enjoyment, festered below Caroline's skin. Her shoulders twitched and an ache ran across her already buzzing head.

"It's no secret that the Moon Children have to be stopped before that beautiful planet of yours turns into something brown and shriveled," Miranda continued. "No one knows better than I how much damage those creatures can do to Jovians—never mind the world at large."

"Yes, well, you can leave that to me," Caroline said, in a breathy, winded manner. "Stay on Mars until I request your assistance."

"I'm not sure that I should," Miranda said. "As we both know, you haven't always responded to harrowing situations in a timely manner."

Caroline stared blankly across the room.

"You saw what the Moon Children did to me," Miranda said. "You saw it, clear as day, and yet you sat there watching from the window of your luxury bus. You watched me suffer and did nothing. After all the years I've served you."

"That's not true," Caroline said, bracing herself with the truth. "I sent the Leonard to save you. Maybe you don't remember, but I do."

"Yes, I remember. Len was his name. Len saved me. Kind of him to do so before the majority of my face burned off."

"But you still have your face, don't you?" Caroline said. "And Andy brought you back to health within a day or two, I believe it was."

"It wasn't only my face, Caroline," she said roughly. "It was the sheer terror of the incident. Have you ever struggled for breath? Have you been so close to death that you can taste it? It's not something easily forgotten."

Caroline swallowed the defensive words that scrabbled up her throat and scratched at the roof of her mouth. "I don't see how that matters right now. You didn't die. Len saved you on my command."

"Uh-huh," she said.

"What do you want, Miranda?"

"I already told you. You're in mourning and I want to help. In your current state of health—or sickness—whatever you want to call it, I would think you'd welcome all the Jovian aid offered to you."

"I have the help I need, thank you. And Mars is your responsibility. Find out what happened to Edmund's ship and report back to me."

A moment as long and wide as the space between Earth and Mars spread between them, cold and vacuous.

"I will be there soon whether you want me or not," Miranda said. "That is what you would do for me if our situations were reversed. Is it not?"

Caroline didn't dare answer.

Chapter 15

Max

The *Orion Sparrow* powered down. Through the windows, the blue, calming light of Starbright's docking station struck Max's optic nerves, and whether it was responsible or Max's pride was, he basked in the good feelings of making it back to Earth alive.

"Home, sweet home, baby!" he said as he unbuckled his safety straps. "Better late than never."

He eased back in the pilot's seat and allowed the many layers of his jovial mood to wash over him: relief and satisfaction and excitement to see his parents; elation for the opportunity to drink fresh water and breathe real, bona fide Earth air. He raised his arms into a stretch. "Hello, air. Hello, trees. Hello, mountains and rivers and . . . and, oh my God, doughnuts and pretzels and *pizza!*" He pulled the device from his nose and placed it upon the console. "Goodbye NOxygen clip. At least for a few days."

"Elara wants to know what is happening," Syndi said. "Why are you making such strange sounds?"

He turned to the copilot beside him, all sparkly and light, and squinted in response to her bright complexion.

"Your expression is frightening Elara, Captain," Syndi said. "Please refrain from showing your teeth."

"I believe you are talking about my smile," he said.

"You are showing your teeth. In *Luna Liberi* culture, that is a hostile action that suggests the intention to do battle."

He closed his mouth. Different cultures, different gestures. Got it.

"Tell her I'm sorry. It's what we call a 'smile.' Something we do when we are happy. Does she know what *happy* is?"

"She accepts your apology." Syndi proceeded to make clicking sounds. "'*Happy*,' Elara says, 'is trees. *Happy* is land. *Happy* is a home with sunlight.'"

"Tell her I agree. Listen, Syndi, I need you to interpret everything I say, and please be as precise as you can."

"Yes, Captain. I have been programmed for precision."

"I know. Tell her I'm going out for a while, and she will have to stay here, on the ship. I'm going to leave, and she can't come with me just yet because it's dangerous for her to be seen. There's no one on Earth like her, and she has to trust me when I say the safest thing will be for her to stay right here, on the *Sparrow*, until I get back."

Syndi followed up with the clicks and sort of guttural sounds she'd been using to communicate with Elara.

"I've told her, Captain."

"And did she respond?"

"No response, sir."

"Okay. Tell her I will return in a short time. Ask her to please take a nap or—"

"Elara is not in a sleeping phase right now."

"Yes, I can see that."

"I have asked if she can sleep, Captain, and she said yes."

"Good," he said.

Done deal.

"She's not used to Earth's atmosphere, and she said if she lies down, she will fall asleep."

"Perfect. Tell her to take the berth in back. Once she does, I'll be on my way, and when I return, I will have some pinecones with me."

Syndi's clicking sounds followed.

"I have told her," the AI said.

"And she agrees?"

The glowing blue-silver being stood and walked toward the back of the ship.

Max rubbed his eyes, which felt numb and watery as they always did when his gaze lingered on her for too long.

"She has reached the berth," Syndi said.

"Okay. If she tries to leave the ship while I'm gone, *do not* open the door."

"I will do as you say, Captain," Syndi said.

He entered the airlock and pressed the button to raise the door. As he walked through the docking station, a saucer-shaped shuttle caught his eye—it may have been the one Natasha used to time travel here. He didn't know why he thought so, but he did. He headed eagerly into the tube and began to jog toward the closed-door dead end. If he'd remembered correctly, it would open to the red room and Starbright's back exit.

"It's good to see you," a voice said out of the blue.

Max spun around, arms raised with fists curled in front of his chest, ready to block an incoming blow.

"I'm sorry to startle you. This is Dmitri, and we are meeting in your mind."

"Meeting in my—" Max gazed warily at the tube's walls. "But I'm not Jovian! How is that even possible?"

"Evander is my father."

Mention of Evander eased Max's worry, though not completely.

"My father has spoken very highly of you," Dmitri added.

"Oh," Max said, his sadness reemerging. "I'm sorry for your loss."

"He is not lost to me, so there is no need for that."

The conversation struck Max as a tad too weird. Good thing traveling in space the past few years had taught him to have an open mind. "That's . . . nice, I just thought—"

"You came to see your family. I can tell you how to reach the bunker."

"Natasha—your sister," Max just realized, "already did that. I think I saw her spaceship. Is she here?"

"Not at the moment. Perhaps soon, though. You've brought Elara."

"Um, yeah, how did you know?"

"She is sleeping?"

"Yes."

"Safe journey," Dmitri said.

The tube opened and Max crossed the threshold into the red room, leaving as quickly as he could through Starbright's back exit. He entered the great outdoors—the air hitting him with a cool and refreshing blast—as he thrilled at being back on Earth. His excitement powered his step and took him down the staircase in a few quick leaps. He darted across the parking lot, feeling so alive and free under the oxygen-rich blue sky. The sun warmed the top of his head and lighted the way into the forest. He dragged his fingers across the bark of old and young trees as he took note of the birdsong playing overhead. As eager as he was to see his parents, he was in no hurry to leave the beauty of the woods.

Life was good.

IT WASN'T long before Max heard footsteps behind his own. He turned, expecting to find a giant black-clad Leonard, but instead saw something light and blurry.

"What? No! You were not supposed to follow me. I thought you were sleeping."

"I woke up," she said. "Elara does not need to sleep today."

All of the air rushed out of his body and his hair stood on end. "Holy crap, you're speaking English?"

She seemed to have frozen; he must have been showing his teeth again.

He shook his head and purposefully closed his mouth. Then he cleared his throat, determined to speak in a calm octave. "When did you learn?" he asked.

"Yesterday," she said.

"You learned an entire language in a day?"

"*Luna Liberi* are linguistic by nature."

A lot smarter than me, apparently, Max thought.

"Syndi helped," she said.

Syndi taught her English and didn't tell me? That figures.

"You are upset. You are showing signs of anger."

"No, no, not at all. Not angry," he said carefully. "I'm just surprised."

"Max showed his teeth a moment ago," she said.

"That's just something that happens from time to time. It isn't meant to be threatening." His jaw clenched, and he rubbed his hand over his chin, letting a moment pass. "Um, I don't suppose you'd be willing to go back to the spaceship and wait for me like I asked you to."

"Elara wants to help."

Her voice was so pleasant. She spoke the way a mother speaks to a young child, with softness and patience. Still, she did not seem the type that would give up without a fight. He couldn't exactly wrestle her to the ground or somehow drag her back to his ship, clicking and screaming.

"Okay, you can come," he said. "But we have to be careful. People have never seen anyone like you. They will freak out. I mean, become upset. And the last thing I want to do is cause a scene. I'm going to see my parents for the first time in several years. A long time, and I don't want them to think I—"

"No one will see me," she assured him.

He looked at her, really stopped to look. It was hard to see her, especially in the light of day. When the sun hit her directly, it was similar to gazing at the glaring surface of water. It would make for a good defense mechanism had she lived on Earth.

They continued to walk, Max a few strides ahead. They took to the perimeter, the fence lines and natural borders, until they reached the flat of the old farm fields. In the distance, prior to the hump that was the bunker, a grove of evergreens emerged.

"A forest," Elara exclaimed and suddenly she was off, flying ahead like a gust of wind. He couldn't tell if she was running on her legs or actually suspended in the air, she was so fast.

When Max caught up to her and the pines, he stopped to lift a pinecone from the ground.

"See?" he said, offering it to her. "The seeds. Just like you asked."

He placed it in the shiny palm of her thick, three-fingered hand, and she made a happy clicking sound.

"I have never seen such a forest. So many trees," she said.

He pulled a nylon drawstring bag from his zippered pocket and gave it to her. "You can go in there. Start gathering the pinecones. I'll come get you when the sun sets. Do you know what I mean by that?"

"I will gather the seeds," she said. "You will come back."

"Wait in the forest until I return. Just don't get lost. I'll be back before sunset, okay? While it's still light out. Understand?"

"I will not become lost," she answered. "Syndi said humans say 'I promise' when they mean what they say. I promise you, Max."

He'd have to talk to Syndi when he returned. He wondered what else the Syndicate 1330 had taught their stowaway while he'd piloted the ship.

"Okay, have fun," he told her with reluctance and a bit of a stomachache starting to manifest. "Just stay out of trouble."

Chapter 16

Natasha

In the morning, after her and her mother's night of tears and woe (Natasha would forevermore remember it that way), she entered the bathroom in need of a long soak. However, before she could fill her mother's clawed-foot tub, she stopped cold in front of the mirror.

Her face. It wasn't right.

Her complexion struck her as so light it had reached a state of translucence. Her lips, too, were thin and colorless. Veins climbed the sides of her skull, winding past her temples like vines growing up the sides of tombstones. Dark rings dug ditches below her eyes, and not in the had-a-couple-of-sleepless-nights way, but with gray ghostly shadows that emphasized the hollows of her skull.

This was not how a young person should look, and all she could think was that her heart was not working properly, not beating the way the rest of her body needed it to. She gave in to the headache that had been brewing, the dizziness that made her feel faint. How long could she survive on this planet? How long before time caught up and put her maladjusted body to rest?

She turned the water on, checked the temperature, and waited for the tub to fill. Then she climbed in, easing into its warmth. The water would calm her unsettled mind. It had always comforted her. When she'd lived in outer space, it was water that she missed most of all. *If I have to die*, she thought, *I wouldn't mind doing so in a pool of water.*

After her bath, she toweled off and put on the robe her mother had lent her. It was only seven o'clock and the new sun came gently through the leafless Russian trees as she made her way into the tiny kitchen. The house was a far cry from what her mother was used to. The former first lady of the most beloved president of the United States once lived in the White House and later in a beautiful, refurbished Kirksberg Colonial. Both had come with a cook, a secret service detail, and an AI assistant named Martin.

Natasha entered the kitchen, bright with a fluorescent light overhead. Remembering her dire complexion, she spun around and swiped the light switch.

Nadia, busy at the stove, slowly turned. "What happened to my light? I need to see if you don't want your French toast to be burned."

Natasha lowered her chin. "I have a headache. Do you mind if we leave it off?" She couldn't let her mother see her white-green complexion and ghastly eyes.

"Oh, I'm sorry you're not feeling well. Maybe you're just hungry. I don't need the light," she said as she flipped a slice of the bread. "Did you sleep well? There's coffee on the counter over here."

"I can't drink coffee. It's not good for my, uh, me."

Nadia finished up at the stove and brought a plate to the table.

"But you are healthy?" she asked, as she set the plate down. "Your heart is well?"

Natasha stared at the dish, avoiding her mother's gaze. "It is."

"What did they do, if you don't mind telling me. Did they . . . fix the problem or give you something new?"

Natasha cringed. She did not intend to have this conversation. "Yes, they gave me—they fixed it. The doctors on Mintaka are geniuses. In the field of medicine, they're miles ahead of humans."

"Good. I am very happy to hear that."

Natasha lifted the small pitcher of syrup and poured it over her French toast.

Nadia went back to the stove and made a second plate of food. When she took a seat, she eyed Natasha skeptically. "You look tired."

"Mm."

"I'm sorry. I don't mean to criticize, I'm just saying." She cut into her breakfast and put a piece in her mouth. "Whatever you have been doing," she said, chewing deliberately, "you must be working too hard. Do you eat well?"

"As well as can be expected," Natasha said.

"What did you eat in outer space? I remember the one time I traveled with Daddy, I was only a teenager, eighteen years old, and I absolutely hated the food. Everything was a green liquid and tasted like leaves, though I will admit it made me feel good inside."

"The green shot," Natasha said with a grimace. "I know it well. There's a yellow one too. Tastes almost as bad. A combination of the two made up many of my meals. And the water was awful. I hated showering in it. It was horrible for my hair."

"Greasy, right?" Nadia said with a giggle.

"Yes!" Natasha cried. "Just . . . gross."

They ate a few more bites of food. Then Nadia put her fork down and wiped her mouth with her napkin. "You know, I never wanted my children to leave Earth."

"Yes, I know. Why was that?"

"Because you are human. Like me. Humans live here. On Earth."

"Ah. But I am Jovian as well, Mother."

Nadia shrugged as she pursed her lips, adding a slight eye roll.

"You don't agree?" Natasha asked.

"You are more human than you are Jovian."

"I guess you could say that, but I *am* part of the oneness."

Nadia pushed her plate away as if she'd lost her appetite. "I was afraid of that."

"Genes work in wondrous ways," Natasha said. She continued to eat, her fork clacking with the bottom of the plate. She thought about how much she loved real food—the sweetness of syrup, the buttery goodness of bread dipped in egg—and soon her breakfast was gone.

"I wanted the doctors on Earth to fix your heart problem," Nadia said. "And then Uncle Jimmy took you away without consulting me or Daddy. It wasn't fair," she said, sucking in her cheeks in a way that made her look as angry as she sounded. "But I suppose it worked out for the best. You are healthy now. They told me the humans would not have been able to, well, do whatever needed to be done. So, in the end, I suppose, there was no choice."

"Yes," Natasha said.

If only I didn't have to worry about it to this day.

"The important thing is you're back. And you will stay with me. It will make up for all the years I wasn't able to take care of you. You owe me," she said, grabbing Natasha's hand and shaking it playfully.

Natasha dreaded this moment. She had to tell her mother that she wouldn't stay. That she had to help the others stand up to the Moon Children. And if she wanted to save herself, she'd have to do it fast.

"You are saying nothing," Nadia said sadly. "You are not going to stay with me?"

"Twenty-year-olds should not live with their parents," Natasha said. "And I am a very independent person, you know that."

"Yes, I know. You always were. Even as a tiny child you insisted on doing everything yourself. And when did you become twenty?"

"That is very kind of you, Mother, but look at me, I'm probably twenty-five by now. My body, at least."

"That is too strange for me to ponder," she said.

"Me too, so let's not."

"Well, I hope you will stay with me for as long as you like," Nadia said. "And I hope Dmitri and Alexandria will come back as well, and we can all be a family again."

"There's nothing I would like more," Natasha said.

It was a wish professed with a clear conscience because it was absolutely true.

Nadia bit her bottom lip, her eyes filling and nose turning pink. "I didn't realize how much I needed to hear that."

"I love you, Mom," Natasha said, going against her best judgment and expressing the desperate-daughter thoughts that threatened to pull her under. "I won't be able to stay with you for long because there's something I must do. But I love you and think of you, always, wherever my life takes me."

"But you'll stay at least a week, I hope," Nadia said, apparently only able to think of the present moment.

"Actually, no, I don't *hope*. As your mother, I *insist*," she said in sad fun.

Natasha wouldn't stay a week, but she couldn't bear to disappoint her. "Just know that whenever I do leave it's because I have to, not because I want to."

Nadia stood and took hold of their sticky, syrup-covered plates. "I understand," she said and carried them stoically to the sink. Then she turned around, her shoulders drooping, head bowed. "I wish you could stay with me forever, but I do understand, and I'm so glad that you are here now."

Chapter 17

Svetlana

Svetlana had been searching the bunker for her daughter for over an hour before giving in to the realization that the shelter that housed them proved to be much bigger than she'd first assumed.

The perimeter of the pubspace with its computer stations and shelving with books and other things also opened to corridors, each leading to living quarters, kitchens, plant-growing facilities, water-filtration compartments. The place, it occurred to her, would make a great space station. Maybe it once had been one. Or maybe this was just a copy of a space station that existed somewhere else in the universe.

That freaked her out a little as she imagined the whole thing uprooting itself from its deep den in the earth and taking off for who knew where. But why would it do that? And why was her mind concocting such imaginative scenarios? Evan was missing! She needed to focus. Surely her rebellious daughter had made friends with some young members of the Coalition and was hanging out, discussing the oneness and other Jovian fascinations somewhere nearby.

Evan had wanted to visit Dmitri at Starbright, but when she found out Natasha left for Russia, what would she have done? She wouldn't go to Starbright by herself, would she? Not with the sick Leonards everywhere. Had she become that bold after hanging out with Natasha for just a few days? No one changes that fast. Plus, the oneness had been driving her crazy. Hopefully it continued to do so and eventually she would come to Svetlana and beg her to take her home, where peace and quiet were plentiful.

Svetlana finished a lap around the bunker and found herself back at the pubspace, where Fran and the others gathered. "Has anyone seen my daughter?" she asked.

Fran raised his head in her direction. "She's still missing?"

"I don't know. It's possible she's made some friends and is—"

"Did you check the library?" he asked. "She seems the type who would like books, and if so, she could get lost in that place."

"She does like books. And I didn't come across the library yet, but I will check it out."

"Before you do, come here for a minute," Fran said.

Svetlana joined him and Lisa beside Connie, seated on a stool in front of her computer screen. At first she didn't notice Caroline sitting on the opposite side of Connie, so unassuming and small-boned, perched on a stool with her back hunched like a branch made to hold up too much snow.

"Caroline was just telling us that Miranda is on her way to Earth," Fran said.

"Oh, is that good or—?" Svetlana spoke like a person who feigned interest because she actually was feigning interest. She would find her daughter and leave soon—and none of this other stuff would be her problem.

"It could be a bad thing," Fran said. "According to Caroline, Miranda might want to take over her position."

Svetlana snuffed the laugh that nearly flew out of her mouth. Jovians were just as susceptible to power struggles as humans were.

"I'm not surprised," she said. "Years ago, I mistook Miranda for a friend and it ended very badly for me. Locked in a tower, as a matter of fact."

"Yeah, I remember," Fran said.

"How will she do it, exactly?" Svetlana asked.

"Do what?"

"Usurp the throne? Will Miranda poison Caroline's food or maybe stab her in the back?"

Fran's face fell into a frown. His eyes darted in Caroline's direction, worried she might have heard. Svetlana didn't care if she had, though it was admittedly a callous thing to say.

"It's a lot more serious than that," Fran said. "If Caroline dies, so does the planet."

That seemed a step too far. Did he actually believe all of life on Earth depended on Caroline's existence?

"I don't understand," Svetlana said.

"Caroline has a special connection to Earth, a synchronous relationship." He leaned in and began to whisper. "I already told you about her weakened state, and at the same time Earth is under attack, suffering serious destruction. In other words, Earth is also in a weakened state. It's not a coincidence."

"Oh," Svetlana said, her brow crumpling with confusion. "But—"

"She's the keeper," he added. "It's a Jovian thing and—"

"Actually, what you're saying isn't true," Connie said paused from typing.

"What isn't true?" Fran asked.

Connie turned her attention to Fran and Svetlana. "She isn't the keeper. Are you, Caroline?"

Caroline stared straight ahead, at no one. A moment of silence passed. "As it turns out, no, I'm not."

"The keeper cares for the planet the way a mother would, in a sense," Connie explained. "Basically the keeper and the Earth are one and the same, only they live in two different bodies. The keeper protects the planet until her end, or its end—whichever comes first. She's basically immortal as long as Earth remains alive."

Caroline pressed her lips together as if steeling herself, then sheepishly turned in Svetlana's direction.

Svetlana looked away.

"Even if I'm not the keeper, I am willing to protect the planet with my life," Caroline said.

"The fact is, there is only one keeper," Connie said, "and it's not Caroline."

Caroline nodded, her face long. "That is true."

"Are you sure?" Fran asked.

"I don't see what the problem is," Svetlana spoke bluntly. "If Caroline wishes to be the Earth's protector, then let her protect it."

"Right," Fran said. "Except she can't take her true form anymore."

"I mean, does it really matter who comes forward to protect the planet?" Svetlana asked in a blunt manner, knowing the sentiment would not be well received—not that she cared. "If Caroline wants to do it, shouldn't we let her?"

"She's not the same person you once knew," Fran said, his voice rising.

Svetlana observed Caroline once again. She recognized sadness and weariness in her hunched stance and watery eyes, for sure. Was she sick as well? Even so, that didn't absolve her of all the awful things she'd done in the past. "Seems okay to me," Svetlana said.

"Come on," Fran said with a scowl. "Would you listen to yourself? You've become—" He cut the thought short and shook his head.

Whatever he'd held back, Svetlana didn't care. She didn't have the patience for this crap. She wanted to find Evan and get the hell home. Caroline had enjoyed her regal position on Earth for years; it was time she paid the price for taking the reins.

"You've been in charge for too long to walk away at this point," Svetlana said, feeling bold and righteous. "So, do what you always wanted to do. Be the keeper or protector or whatever you want to call it. Stop Miranda. Save the planet."

"I wish I could. Maybe if Edmund had made it back. Or if I could convince Leo—"

"Your precious bright blue planet is at stake," Svetlana said with exasperation, her words powered by the frustration that began building when Evander and Natasha arrived on her doorstep in Kecksburg and pulled her and Evan into this world. "You love it, don't you?"

Caroline considered. "It's possible Dmitri could reach out and—"

Svetlana made a fist and thumped the bar top in front of her. "Don't you dare put him in danger," she said. "Not my grandson. You leave him out of it."

"I can't beat Miranda on my own," Caroline said, sitting up straighter, possibly regaining some composure.

Connie, as levelheaded as any Jovian Svetlana had ever met, turned to face Caroline and said, "You told President

Abela you and you alone would defend the planet. You told her that's why you were here."

"That *is* why I'm here," Caroline answered with a huff. "But what Constance did to me changed everything."

"If Constance can give you what you need, get her back here," Svetlana said, thinking it the simple answer to possibly all of their problems. "The oneness is open. Beg her to show you some mercy!"

"Ease up, Svetlana," Fran said.

"Ease up?" Svetlana scowled at him. "Are you serious? She doesn't deserve to be handled gently. Do you not remember how she used Andrew, how she used me and my son? She never had compassion when it came to my family, so do not tell me to ease up."

"This conversation is becoming too heated, is all I'm saying. Take a step back. Please."

The fact that Fran voiced his annoyance with her made her twice as mad.

Then Caroline spoke: "This is not the way it was supposed to be. This isn't the way I foresaw the future unfolding."

Was she kidding? About to boil over, Svetlana redirected her attention with the focus of a laser beam. "Welcome to my world," she told Caroline, each syllable sent to vaporize a portion of her self-pity. "Insecurity. Disappointment. Risk. That's the way of the world. There are no guarantees. None at all. You get what you get."

Svetlana expected the woman to respond with a blank stare or some loud sentiment at least, but all Caroline did was lower her gaze to the ground.

"How much time do we have to prepare before Miranda arrives?" Fran asked.

"Twenty-four hours," Caroline said. "Possibly forty-eight."

Svetlana groaned as she bit her bottom lip so hard she saw red. Of course it couldn't be simple. She couldn't just find Evan and whisk her back to their universe before the trouble began. Why did this always happen to her? Was it destiny? Was her involvement with the Jovian world actually written in the stars the way Uncle Jimmy, that horrible, lovely, hateful, adoring creature claimed it might be?

Destiny was real.

Real and *inevitable*.

She fixed her attention on Caroline and spoke without kindness: "You better come up with a plan."

Chapter 18

Max

As he headed in the direction of the mound that was the bunker, Max paused to check the forest behind him one last time. He wanted to make sure Elara remained there, with the trees and the pinecones, where she promised she'd stay. But he didn't see her, and that may have been because she'd already moved deeper into the grove. All she wanted was to gather her seeds to her heart's content, after all. Not to mention, the glare of sunlight upon her skin—or whatever covered her body—made for some of the most unseeable camouflage available in this solar system.

He continued on, stopping a comfortable thirty or forty yards away from the bunker's entrance, in clear view of the Coalition's surveillance, which he knew already had eyes on him. He didn't want to ruffle feathers, so he'd wait there, a nonthreatening distance away, before they invited him nearer.

Someone stood behind the door. He knew because the metal lever moved just before the door itself opened and a small woman dressed in military-style attire came out. She turned her head and shouted into the bunker, "Hey, Fran, you might want to get up here."

His father was here! Stunned, Max didn't move. This was it. The reunion with Dad. Mom, he guessed, would come later. He took a breath, his shoulders rising, as he braced himself for anything from scoldings for being gone too long to great, swooping hugs for making it back alive.

Metal steps tapped in the distance, and when the man himself arrived, he paused just outside the door to catch his breath. Their gazes came together just before the great Fran Vasquez took off like a sprinter toward him.

His father had grown quite a bit, especially in girth, and his face, while the same in most ways, seemed padded, larger in the cheeks, softer around the chin and forehead. Max was so busy studying him that he forgot to move. When he finally remembered that he should move, he couldn't get his legs to work. He stood there, dumbfounded.

His father grabbed him in what would have made for a really good tackle had he wanted to take Max down. He squeezed Max and choked out the words, "You're back. You're home. I knew you'd come back." When they broke apart, he rubbed Max's buzzcut, similar to the one he used to wear. Now his father's hair was overgrown (for him) and gray around the temples.

"Look at you, all grown up," Fran said. "Like a real man."

That was embarrassing. By that time, a few Coalition members congregated by the door. But maybe they stood far enough away not to hear.

"I'm thirty, Dad. Or . . . older."

"Yeah, I know. Still a kid, but getting there, getting there."

It was nice to see his father grin from ear to ear on his account.

Others came up the steps to watch their reunion, arms crossed over their chests, smiles on their faces. They spilled out around the bunker's entrance and spoke among themselves. Max figured visitors didn't come around too often, and this was fast becoming a special occasion.

"Excuse me, please, sorry," his mother's voice reached him before the sight of her did. She was pushing past anyone who blocked her path. "Max!" she shouted. "That's my son!"

He didn't wait this time. He ran, meeting her halfway.

She, too, had aged a noticeable amount. Bigger body, a few more strands of silver than Max had stored in his memory. But she looked good, and she hugged him with a fierceness he didn't remember her having. For some reason, this made him laugh, and he couldn't stop. He was having trouble catching his breath.

When he glimpsed over his mother's shoulder, he recognized Evander's mother, Svetlana, in the crowd among the clones and hybrids. The short woman who first appeared at the door resembled someone he knew, but he couldn't think of who. And then his mother interrupted his observations by pulling back to study him more closely.

"You're so handsome!" she said. "This piloting thing is obviously working for you."

"Thanks, Ma, I do love it," he said, grinning like a schoolboy who just made his mama proud. *Nothing like visiting your parents to send you back to childhood.*

Once again, she pulled him to her chest, rocking side to side, turning him as she did, in a sort of dance move. "I'm so happy you're back!" she cried.

When he peered over her shoulder this time, he faced the pinewood from which he'd come. A glittery shining thing caught his eye and plucked him out of this happy moment. Elara stood before him, only a few feet away, and disappointment dropped like a bomb into Max's stomach. She was mostly camouflaged in the sunlight, and he was sure no one else would notice her—except that she held a bag in her hand. The bag he'd given her for gathering pinecones was plain to see.

While he worried about Elara, his mother said, "Oh no, Caroline came up all those steps? And no one's helping her. Come with me, Max, I need to—"

His mother released him from her embrace and backed up a step just as the bright, shiny thing that was Elara suddenly multiplied. Standing there, with his mouth open, Max wondered briefly if he was on some kind of drug trip. Elara had become . . . so many. Not duplicates of herself exactly, but dozens of herself with slight variations in size and shape. It had to be some trick of his vision. A hallucination. And it didn't stop there. A literal crowd of bodies grew in front of him, backing toward the tree line of the grove Elara promised to forage for the next few hours. It didn't seem real, this growing wave of individuals, but then Max remembered what happened on Europa: how Syndi had counted three beings and then in the next second, ten and twenty and . . .

The glistening mass quickly became too many to count. They hovered for a moment—not long enough for Max to grasp what might be going on—then began to transform. The figures' heads wobbled and roiled—started to disappear—rising in the form of vapor or steam. The bodies' trunks and limbs soon followed, adding to the wispy cloud that slowly rounded into a glistening fog, one that spread all the way down to the ground the solid beings had been standing on only a moment before.

Max's eyes watered and blurred like they did when he stared at Elara for too long.

And then his father cried, "To the bunker! NOxygen clips! Everybody put your clips on now!" He had used his commanding voice, the one that alerted others of lethal danger.

"Lisa, get back to the bunker and set up for triage," Fran shouted. "Hurry!" Then he said, "Max! What are you doing? Come with me!"

All at once, Max's throat constricted, and his nose filled with a pungent scent of chemicals. *Ammonia.* The air burned going down, from nostrils to lungs. He covered his mouth and breathed through his fingers. Where was his NOxygen clip? Had he really tossed it away without a care? Left it in the *Sparrow*, thinking he'd have no use for it?

Had he traveled all the way home only to die of chemical poisoning?

He doubled over and spit. The air, he noticed, was better lower to the ground.

"Elara, stop this! What are you doing?" he shouted.

"Max, come on, son!" His father squinted at him with confusion.

Within a minute or so a wall of opaque vapor stood just feet away. People everywhere hacked with a viciousness Max had never witnessed before.

His father's meaty hand grabbed his shoulder and pulled. He handed Max a NOxygen clip on the run. "It's the Moon Children," he said. "We have to get underground."

The Moon Children?

The deadly attackers that old, wizened woman named Ida had told Max about last time he visited Mintaka?

But Ida said they lived in water. There was no water here. Elara had made this happen. Not the Moon Children. Elara, who was kind and smart. She just wanted the seeds for her people!

I brought her here. I made this happen. What have I done?

The journey to the bunker was maybe twenty-five yards, but it may as well have been a mile.

"No fog this morning," Fran muttered as he grappled with the problem on the fly. "How'd they arrive so quickly? No water, no steam. This doesn't make sense."

Max and Fran came to the first victim sprawled on the ground. Fran wedged his arms under the woman's armpits, and Max helped him raise her to her feet. Her skin flamed bright red as if she'd spent hours unprotected in the sun.

"Take her and get to the bunker," Fran pointed.

"What? No. Where are you going?"

"Go," he demanded. "I'm gonna help the ones who are still alive."

"Then so am I," Max said just as unshakably.

The woman roused and was able to throw her arm across Max's shoulders. Together they staggered the rest of the way to the bunker's entrance. Max handed her off to some Coalition members and turned back. By this time, the least-affected people had made their way inside and only a few of most affected remained on their feet.

The fog of swirling menace progressed inch by slow inch. Ailing clones fell to the ground, desperate for breath; even those who wore NOxygen clips passed out. Max lifted a choking Evander clone to standing and walked him to the safety of the bunker's entrance, then turned back and went for a hybrid whose scalded face had peeled so badly Max experienced a rush of dizziness when he first saw her.

The charred scent of burned flesh penetrated his NOxygen clip, but he didn't smell ammonia. Max felt all right as far as his strength went. Unaffected as of yet. Humans possessed some immunity the Jovians didn't have.

He remembered Ida saying so when he'd met her on Mintaka.

Just another minute and the fog would be upon them.

To Max's left, Fran busied himself with two of the injured at once: a man and a woman still standing but not for long. Max hesitated, not knowing whether he should help his father or the Evander clone struggling to remain standing to his right.

"I got these two," Fran said. "Go, help him!"

But there was no time.

"It's here!" Max shouted. "Dad!"

Fran and the two clones dropped to their stomachs. "Cover your face," he shouted. "Hold your breath!"

Max hit the ground and pulled his e-skin up high on the back of his neck. He wrapped his arms around his head as best he could and pressed his cheek firmly to the ground. Then he closed his eyes. The fog crept over him like a torch flame licking his exposed places while he held his breath and counted the passing seconds. Every once in a while, something like a hand or finger grazed across his back, and at one point, he swore someone's foot stepped on his shoulder. This was not ordinary fog, and sometimes things on Earth were even weirder than in outer space. When he'd counted to one hundred, he squinted up with a clear view of the sky above.

The fog had passed. It headed into the forest that lay beyond the bunker. Max finally drew in a breath of air. It reeked even with the NOxygen clip filtering the toxins. He needed to spit. He might throw up.

"Max! You okay?"

His father was already up with the Miranda clone's arm slung across his back, lugging her toward the bunker. The man he'd tried to help before the fog passed over them lay on the ground, unmoving, a few steps behind. "Get inside," his dad shouted.

Max remembered the Evander clone he'd wanted to help. He scanned the area. There he was, wavering more than before and heading in the wrong direction. Max stood, a bout of dizziness threatening to take him down. He picked up the pace as the Evander stumbled and fell face down in a heap. As Max neared, four legs came into view when there should only have been two.

"What the?" he muttered.

A woman, one of her hands red and swollen, lay underneath the clone. Max couldn't see her upper body or face. What he could see of her was small and thin boned. Especially in comparison to the tall Evander that covered her like a human blanket. Max really hoped they were alive, but neither was moving, so he braced himself.

Had the Evander been escorting the woman when he passed out? Or maybe he'd found her on the ground. From the look of their position, it could have been either. No way would she have been strong enough to free herself from his unconscious body, had she been awake. Or maybe the impact or the poison gas had knocked them both out.

She was light haired, that much Max could see. Her arm pressed into the earth like the wing of a dead bird, and her jeans were soiled at the knees. What he could see of her top half, was mottled with blood. But was it her own? Hard to tell.

Max rolled the Evander off the woman and onto his back. He then carefully pulled the woman by her shoulders and turned her until she lay face up. She'd suffered some horrible face burns that made him turn away.

He placed a hand under the Evander's nose, hoping to feel a soft stream of air, but felt nothing. The woman's labored breaths rattled through the blood oozing from her nostrils. Her bottom lip had split, too, and her cheekbones appeared to have been scratched by feral claws. She needed medical help right away. Stitches to stop the bleeding, and probably a lot more.

He took hold of her with as gentle a grip as he could and carried her the way he would a sleeping child—one arm under her shoulders, one under her knees.

"You're okay," he told her. "I've got you."

She couldn't have weighed but a hundred pounds.

"Thank you, Max," she uttered wearily, a sickly rasp in her throat.

He hesitated in step. He knew her voice. Years ago, before Max became a pilot, he and his father had worked for her at Starbright. It was Caroline. This little old woman with blood in her hair and a third-degree burn and split, oozing cheeks was Queen Jovian? That didn't make sense. How had this happened? He picked up speed as he neared the bunker's entrance.

A woman opened the door for them and muttered, "Holy hell." Then shouted, "Fran, Lisa! Emergency!"

"Go straight down," she directed Max. "You'll find an empty table as you round the bend. Careful on the stairs."

Max descended the steep incline and hastened once he reached flat ground, not stopping until he came to an empty tabletop surrounded by Coalition members, two of them his parents.

"It's Caroline," he said as he placed her upon the table, sorry for every groan of pain she released.

"Oh my God, Fran," Lisa said, the tears instantly appearing. "I thought she was one of the first to make it back inside. I didn't see her out there, so I assumed she was already safe. This is my fault. How could I let this happen?"

"Mom, don't, it's not your fault." Max took a step back

and gazed worriedly at his mother and then Caroline. "She looks so different from what I remember."

"She is," Fran said, his brow scrunching as if the sight of her caused him pain.

Lisa grabbed the small black monitor from the med kit and checked the older woman's vitals.

As Caroline lay upon the table, her breathing accelerated and became labored. She raised her arms and pushed away a clone who tried to place an oxygen mask over her mouth. "Pod," Caroline said.

"She wants a pod," Fran shouted to the others. "Someone call Andy over at—"

"I already have," Connie shouted. "He's not in a position to leave Starbright at this time."

Fran growled. "Damn it, tell him it's urgent."

"He has a situation on his hands, if you'll recall," Connie said. "There are about seven people running Starbright currently and five of them are dying."

"Fine. I'll go over there and get it myself," Fran said.

Max didn't hesitate when he said, "I'll come with you."

Caroline coughed and tried to raise her head. With eyes half opened and lips quivering, she reached for Fran, who hovered over her. "Past my bedroom," she coughed the words, "there's a door . . . a staircase." She collapsed, her chest heaving.

With that, his father took off and a couple of others raced after him.

Max would have followed, but Caroline met his eye, and he couldn't turn away. She raised her head once again, the blood sliding across her cheeks and dripping down her neck faster than his mother could blot it. Her watery eyes widened, unseeing and sick, as she struggled to breathe. "Hurry," she said.

Chapter 19

Fran

From the safety of the bunker, the Coalition watched satellite footage of the Moon Children spinning up like whirlwinds over the waterways they had been existing in and floating across the land to form bird's-eye images that resembled a quilted blanket.

To Fran's chagrin, the fog persisted and spread as the day wore on. The monarch's presence must have roused her hive from dormancy. Dmitri had dispersed these cloud patches when he took his place in the observatory, and it seemed the monarch had brought them back together.

Just how powerful is this thing? Fran wondered.

Reports of poison gas attacks trickled in from countries far and wide. Lands across the globe burned as a result of the ammonia gas, humans of all kinds suffered injury and ran panicked in the streets, and clones died horrific, bloody deaths. Some original humans died as well.

The only individuals who remained unscathed were those who found safety in underground dwellings: subway systems and tunnels transformed into community shelters, the basements of homes, natural caves, and bunkers homeowners had built in their own backyards. Presently these people waited for news and instruction.

Meanwhile the Coalition continued to notify every town, every region that may be under attack. They set the catastrophe scale to "high alert" and instructed all people who hadn't yet done so to move underground.

Connie, with Fran and Lisa beside her, had been trying to reach President Annalise Abela via video call for several hours without success. Finally, the call went through, and her image appeared on the computer screen. The president, with her dark hair pulled into a severe bun, was as good as seated in the Coalition's busy pubspace. In unison, both Fran and Connie sat up straighter on their stools. And, as planned, Lisa hopped to the ground and motioned for nearby Coalition members to give them space and silence as she cleared the surrounding area.

"There have been fifty-two attacks reported in the U.S., and more happening every hour," the president said, her hands clasped in a business-like manner. "Please tell me there's relief in sight."

"I'm sorry, we can't do that," Connie said. "The best you can do is instruct your people to move underground. Hopefully, we'll have something better to offer soon."

"And what about Caroline?" Abela asked. "She personally promised me she'd handle the Moon Children."

"And she will," Fran said, with confidence. "She's working on it. I assure you."

"She usually calls me herself."

"Yes, I know, Madame President," Fran said, buying himself an extra couple of seconds to conjure a decent reply. "I apologize for her absence, but she's unreachable at the moment."

He knew how lame that sounded, but it was the best he could do to prevent further ruffling of the commander in chief's feathers. The leader of the United States needed to retain confidence in the Jovian family and their ability to protect the rest of the world against this alien attacker. If this relationship should crumble, he hated to think what kind of chaos might result.

"But she's here," the president said, "on the planet, right?"

"Oh, yes," Connie said. "Absolutely."

"She's acutely aware of our situation?" Abela prodded further, her brow rising in question.

"Not only is she aware," Fran said, "she's spending *all* her time on it."

The president paused for a moment, just long enough to reach some satisfied internal conclusion. "Please tell her to make a move soon. Modern society has basically ceased to exist at this point. Countries have limited communications with their people and with other nations. We're all at a standstill. No one knows how to proceed. The generals want to set their armies loose, but even they admit doing so probably wouldn't do any good against such a changeable enemy. We don't know how to fend off these creatures."

Her lips came together in a bloodless line.

"Understood," Fran said. "Tell the leaders to get their people underground. Hold your course until further notice."

The image of the president froze for a few seconds before the computer screen blinked out.

"We lost her," Connie said, her fingers working the keyboard. "Fires have wiped out a lot of the towers. Communication is difficult, as the president just said."

"We have no more to tell her, so it's probably for the best," Fran said. "We need to get Andy over here, so he can check Caroline out."

"There's nothing he can do for her," Connie said with

a bluntness Fran didn't like. "And I told you before, he's working on a cure for the Leonards and handling the lab by himself. Head Leonard saved his life in an attack that happened last week, so he's dedicated."

"Even if Caroline might be dying?" Fran cursed, unable to keep a lid on his anger.

"If she is, it's not my fault," Connie snapped.

"I know. It just sounds like you don't care."

"I'm Jovian." She didn't flinch as she stared into his eyes. "I care in my own way."

He stared back, well acquainted with the Jovians' baffling unemotional poise, even in the midst of dire situations.

Across the pubspace, Max occupied a chair at a table by himself, a mug of coffee steaming in front of him, untouched.

"Sorry," Fran told Connie, "I'm human and I need a minute to regroup."

"Yes, you do," she answered.

He nodded. The stakes were too high, and not knowing how to solve the problem raised his damn blood pressure.

The screen above the central bar displayed an overhead view of Pennsylvania. The land appeared blackened in places. Half alive, half dead.

Like Caroline, he thought, *who lay half alive, half dead in her pod.*

He couldn't stop thinking of how she said that if she died, the Earth would die too. And at the moment the Earth was in really bad shape, and Caroline was fighting for her life in the pod.

Connie told them Caroline wasn't the keeper—and Caroline had agreed—so what did any of it mean? Was it just another coincidence? Fran didn't think so, but he also didn't care it if was. He would not let Caroline die. Not when the stakes were so high. He didn't know why he still believed she and Earth were inextricably connected—some weird fear, he supposed—or maybe it was just intuition.

His slow walk across the pubspace led him to Max. He didn't bother to sit before he said, "So tell me again what you think happened out there."

"I *know* what happened," Max said. "I saw it with my own eyes, and I don't appreciate you commanding me to get in the corner and be quiet like I'm ten years old instead of a grown-ass man."

Thrown by Max's strong response, Fran pulled back his defenses and spoke clearly and calmly. "That's fair, but let me explain it this way: My son arrives at the bunker, and there's immediately a deadly attack. How are *they*," he gestured to the members of the Coalition milling about, "supposed to trust you? Do you see how much better it would be for your information to come from me, should I deem any of it of value?"

"Oh, yeah, I guess that makes sense," Max said, easing back with resignation.

"So, please, tell me what you have to say." Fran lowered into the seat opposite Max. "The sooner I hear this, the better."

Max explained how it was he came to bring Elara to Earth. How she didn't speak English at first but learned in a day, how she called herself one of the *Luna Liberi*. He explained that he'd heard about the Moon Children from Fran's very old colleague, Ida, but didn't know Elara was one of them.

"If she actually is," Max said, "which I can't believe, because she has been so nice and, actually, *gentle*. Definitely not a killer."

"Not a killer?" Fran said, following with a laugh that

rose above the din. "That's an insult to the six people who died outside this bunker today. Not to mention the eight others who may be fatally injured, and countless others across the world who are succumbing and have succumbed over the past year."

Max lowered his eyes. "I mean, I don't get it. All she wanted was to come here and gather pinecones, seeds to plant on her planet. Is that so bad? Maybe what happened was a coincidence. Maybe she arrived and the Moon Children attacked at the same time."

"But you said you *saw her* become a crowd of hundreds. You saw her become the hive."

"Yeah, I know, but I might have been hallucinating. It crossed my mind that—"

"You were *not* hallucinating," Fran said angrily. "That's how the Moon Children work. That's what a hive mind is. Besides, did you do anything that would cause you to hallucinate?" Fran's brow threatened to lift right off his forehead.

"No, but when you're in outer space, weird stuff sometimes happens, and you find out why later. I'm just saying."

"Well, you're on Earth now, not in outer space. And I know exactly who did this. It was the Moon Children. No doubt in my mind. You and I agree that what we saw was the hive, so I'm going to take it a step further and say that it sounds like your friend Elara is their monarch."

Max seemed to crumple with confusion. "No, that can't be right."

"I'm pretty sure it is."

Max shook his head and then abruptly froze. His light brown complexion became paper white.

"What just happened?" Fran said.

"I don't know. I thought of something. Whenever Elara referred to the beings on Europa, she called them 'my people.' I thought she meant it in the general sense, but she may have meant it literally. Like, in the she's-their-ruler sense."

"That's probably right." Fran sat back and propped a foot on the opposite knee. "Edmund thought he was traveling with the monarch, bringing her here to negotiate with Caroline, but then his ship blew up—"

Max twitched at this news. "Wait, Edmund's ship *blew up*—but that doesn't make sense."

"It did. And no one knows how it happened. But if the monarch had been on board, all of the Moon Children on Earth would have disappeared. End of story. But they didn't. And I think it's because the monarch wasn't on that ship. She was on *yours*. How or why she was on yours, I'd love to know."

Max swallowed, then cleared his throat. "She was on mine because I told her I would bring back a bunch of, uh, seeds she could plant on her planet. It's a long story, but suffice it to say, some of her people saw the pinecone you gave me when I left Earth and—"

"Get out of here! You still have that thing?"

"Of course I do," Max said with a shy glance up. "It's my prized possession. But, um, when her people saw it, they told me they wanted it. They wanted lots of them."

"Okay, so they want to plant trees on their planet."

"It's a moon, actually," Max said. "Europa, and it's about as uninhabitable as a home can get. You can't blame Elara for wanting a better place for her people to live. Years ago, Edmund abandoned them there, from what I've heard. He tricked Elara into going there as a way to get them off Io, their native home. That's not cool."

"I can't believe you've been to Europa," Fran said. "I remember you talking about it when you were a little kid."

"Well, I finally got there. And that's where Elara

hopped on my ship. I didn't even know she was on board until I reached Io."

Why would Max visit an uninhabitable moon?

"Question," Fran said. "If there's nothing on Europa, why did you go there to begin with?"

"Oh," Max slunk low in the chair. "That was a, um, mistake."

"You landed on Europa by mistake?"

"It's easier to do than you think!" Max said forcefully.

Fran did his best to put out the laugh that kindled inside him. Only Max could land on the wrong moon. But, hell, anyone could make a mistake.

"Look," Max's expression drooped with the sadness of disappointment, "it's the first time I've come home in years, and something like this has already happened and I feel like a colossal failure, so please don't laugh at me."

"No, no, I wouldn't," Fran said, steeling his expression. "What happened is no laughing matter."

"What are we going to do?" Max asked.

"Not sure yet, but I wonder if your good relationship with Elara might come in handy down the road."

"I won't trick her into being captured, if that's what you mean."

Fran grimaced. "You know me better than that."

Max chewed a fingernail. "If I ever see her again," he added, "which I probably won't."

Fran stood. He turned to the rest of those congregated in the pubspace, some of them sitting, some standing. "If I can have your attention." He raised his hand, and the crowd settled, the quiet emerged. "It's been a tough day, to say the least. And I know we've all worked hard. But we can't sit back. The Moon Children are on the move, and Miranda may be on the way. Because Caroline is recovering in a pod, we have no way of knowing what Miranda will do or how she'll attempt to do it. If she was responsible for what happened to Edmund's ship, she is armed. What her plan is, we can only guess. Let's prepare for the worst and hope for the best.

"If anyone needs me, I'll be stationed with Connie, handling the fallout of this incident. Please—"

"I'd also like to say that my daughter, Evan, is missing."

Svetlana, who had just entered the room, took this opportunity to broadcast her own announcement.

"If anyone spoke to her this morning or knows where she may have gone, please let me know," she added.

"Okay, everybody," Fran said, clapping his hands. "Back to work."

He stepped up to the bar, where Svetlana stood beside Connie.

"Connie, would you mind reaching out to Dmitri about Evan? He may be able to help," he said.

Connie shook her head. "Dmitri hasn't communicated with anyone since yesterday afternoon."

Fran sighed with frustration. "What's up with that? Is the oneness out again?"

"Not this time," she said. "I had a read on him last night, and I believe he's 'out there.'"

"Out there?" Svetlana asked.

"As in, out in the great beyond. 'Speeding the cosmos,' we Jovians call it."

Sometimes Fran was glad to be an ordinary human with both feet, and his head, on Earth. "Well, can we reach anyone at Starbright who might know where Evan is?"

"I'll check it out," Connie said.

Svetlana smiled at him. "Thanks, Fran."

Chapter 20

Miranda

Ever since the day she joined the three thousand or so good citizens the Jovians shipped to the red planet via the Starbright-NASA Mars project, Miranda had chosen to take her Jovian form. This was not only for reasons of intimidation and good leadership but also because the Jovian physique fared far better on Mars than the human one did. The saucer-shaped *Umbra Alaris,* (Miranda's spaceship), however, had been built to suit human-sized bodies, much smaller than Jovian royalty, and so Miranda, who stood at ten glossy black feet tall, had transformed into her human form before boarding.

When she exited the Mars space habitat, Miranda had told Leo goodbye, thwarting his final attempt to change her mind with a curt wave of her hand. At the docking station, she had entered the *Umbra* and strapped herself into the pilot's chair. With the new power booster Leo had engineered, the vehicle would arrive on Earth in less than twenty-four hours.

At present, with only four of those hours left to travel, Miranda gazed through the viewport at the blue-green planet spotted with hazy white clouds, half in shadow and half in light. Her expression fell into one of reverent awe.

Soon it would be hers.

EIGHT MINUTES BEFORE LANDING, the *Umbra* entered Earth's atmosphere and Miranda gasped at the force of deceleration and its sudden intense pressure and sweat-inducing heat. The violent shaking would not have affected her Jovian body, but this fragile collection of human skin and bones pressed into the seat as if flattened by a giant's palm. She fought to withstand the thrust, producing groaning sounds while she squeezed her eyes tight.

A minute later, the force let go, and Miranda wheezed, drawing deep, heaving breaths like she had the day the Moon Children left her choking and bloody.

This would be the last time she'd occupy her human form. When she reached Caroline's chambers, she would metamorphose into her Jovian self for all to see. Caroline wouldn't be able to stop her. It was about time Earth's population accepted her people and their sovereignty. In all the millennia Jovians had occupied the planet, only Caroline had dared break the sacred rule that forbid showing their extraterrestrial form. Caroline had revealed her stunning six-story self just one time, and then, like a mouse scuttling back into its hole, never did it again.

Miranda wouldn't scuttle or hide.

She would be the one humankind would bow to.

The *Umbra* touched down and taxied to the center of the docking station. Miranda exited the ship and paused to observe her surroundings. Had all activity and production come to a standstill? The place ticked with disuse, and the lack of security alarmed her. She crossed the vast, blue-lighted area without encountering a being of any kind. At the entrance to the tube, she showed the scanner her human eyes, and it allowed her access. As she followed the tube to Caroline's chambers, Dmitri attempted to enter her mind through the oneness, but she pushed him out. He was a neonate and no match for her.

Her human retinas would not get her into Caroline's private room. Instead she settled into a meditative state and began her physical transformation right there, in the tube. The change started in her extremities, her hands and feet tingled and then blackened, the conversion spreading like a fire lapping over her spine, rising up her neck—a twitch of sublime pain as it entered her skull—the center of her body coming alive with power, finally spreading to her arms and legs.

With the change complete, an unexpected euphoria washed over her, one of wholeness and satisfaction.

Without making a sound—not so much as a grunt or groan—she slid her mutable fingers into the entry's seal and applied brute strength to peel the door back.

Well, that was easy, she thought, and stepped inside. A reflection in the wall screen above the dresser showed her long-legged form, slim and shining, simple and sleek. She stopped in front of it to admire herself. She was, in a word, *gorgeous.*

She strode through the main room into the smaller dressing area. There. The human-size desk against the wall, a square seat tucked underneath and a lighted, oval-shaped mirror on top. The place Caroline observed her human features and bobbed hair. All the time she spent perfecting her appearance. Maybe, it occurred to Miranda, Caroline *wanted* to be one of them.

A thin drawer spanned the width of the desk and opened to a collection of jewelry. Caroline had never admitted to her deep affection for her gemstones—only a human would adore colored rocks—but her admiration of them had been obvious to Miranda. As obvious as the weakness that overtook Caroline now.

The collection of gems made for a pretty, impractical display. A faceted array of red and green, yellow, amber, every color imaginable. The deep-blue stone the size of a postage stamp awaited her arrival. Lovely, but Miranda still didn't see the point.

She sought Caroline's mind through the oneness and found it dormant. Why this would be, she didn't know. Caroline was human the last time Miranda spoke to her. Human, not dead.

Dormancy could indicate suspension in a pod, which would mean something had struck Caroline down— injured her or caused illness. And if so, that would only make it easier for Miranda to put her out of her misery.

Miranda pulled the blue sapphire ring from its pillowed bed and fitted it on her shiny black finger. Stretching out her long, lean arm, she feigned to admire the stone the way a human would. The chamber's ceiling lights danced over the jewel's facets like light dancing on the crests of ocean waves. She supposed that's what Caroline loved about it.

Who cares? Miranda threw her head back and laughed. "The keeper's ring is mine," she said with exaggerated drama.

Only Caroline isn't the keeper of the planet.

Because there was no keeper. Miranda had doubted Jovian lore and its so-called family prophecies her entire life. Caroline adored gemstones. That's why she treasured this ring. Most Jovians believed in the prophecies to some extent, so Miranda would feign belief too. She'd tell them Caroline was incapacitated, which they already knew, and that she had deemed Miranda the new keeper.

She stood, kicked the little chair to the wall, and exited the room, taking the tube to the entrance of Starbright's executive wing.

The once-bustling Starbright office met Miranda with silence. Had such a grand showcase of a building submitted to what smelled of death and despair? Illness and ammonia? She placed her hand over her smooth as ceramic face—as if it might be enough to spare her the aroma of doom—then proceeded to walk the carpeted floor, which suffered from what appeared to be dried blood stains and—could it be vomit?—not to mention the dirt from boots and who knew what else.

A battle had been fought, and it seemed as though Starbright had lost.

Glad to arrive in front of the laboratory door, Miranda barged through, entering with a bang.

Andy startled with a full-body shake. Clad in his white doctor's coat, he stared, holding a beaker of clear red liquid in one hand and a plastic tube that led to the neck of an unconscious Leonard in the other. Andy was the Jovian clone-turned-medical-practitioner who had rebuilt the lab into an infirmary.

Several beds, five in all, lined up in a row, each holding the well-muscled body of a Leonard, each with a clear plastic tube emerging from the Leonard's neck. Andy seemed to be ready to distribute the liquid. A cure for whatever ailed this once-elite security force?

"Miranda," Andy said, his eyes as wide as an owl's, "we weren't expecting you. Caroline's not—"

"I'm not here to see Caroline." She stood at attention with the intention of reaching full intimidation. "Are any of these men named Len?"

"Uh, yes," Andy said, still holding the beaker and the

plastic tube. He gestured with his elbow toward the bed beside the man he hovered over.

"Make him a priority," she said.

"Oh, all right, sure." Andy proceeded to pour the beaker of liquid into the tube he held. "How can I help you?"

"You can stop what you're doing this instant and make Len a priority," she said with unreserved authority.

He gazed at her, his mouth dropping open. "I didn't know you meant . . . immediately." Andy let go of the tube and stepped back.

"I say exactly what I mean," she said.

With beaker in hand, he moved to the adjacent bed and lifted the tube affixed to Len's neck. With trembling hands, he poured the liquid.

Miranda stepped forward, hovering over the patients the way herons round their necks over fish-filled lagoons. "Where's Head Leonard?" she asked, hoping the illness had already ended him.

"He's still functioning pretty well," Andy reported. "Not ready for a sick bed yet. He may even beat it on his own."

"Hm," she said. "Are the rest of them dying?"

Andy glanced over the men in their white hospital gowns. "Not if I can help it. They're under sedation because they're about to receive the treatment."

"And you think it will work?"

"Yes," he said. "I'm quite confident."

Impatience bubbled like boiling tar through her mind. "Caroline asked me to come," she said. "She is indisposed, as you know, and I am here to take over."

"I see," he said and slowly turned and placed the empty beaker on a metal tray. Then he faced her again.

"And because I am in charge, and because I will make all of the decisions henceforth, you must obey my commands." Miranda paused to let these statements sink in.

"Yes, ma'am," he said.

"My first command is for you to stop treating these Leonards—except for Len, who I insist you heal."

"They'll die without treatment," he said. "I've been working for days. The cure will likely restore them to full—"

"I don't want them at full capacity," she said.

"You . . . don't?"

"These Leonards are dedicated to Caroline, and she is no longer in charge. I require a new security detail that is dedicated to *me*. The one exception is Len, as I have already told you."

"May I ask why Len?" he said.

Miranda sensed Andy's fluttering, flip-flopping mind, his confusion flitting like an injured moth through the oneness.

"You may. He saved my life at the Mars launch. The day the Moon Children attacked."

"I see—"

"It's simple, Andy. Let these Leonards die, and when Head Leonard becomes too sick to stand, let him die as well. You will go down to the nursery today and ready the three-point-zeros in their nascent pods."

His jaw dropped. He seemed to want to speak but opted for the smarter choice of keeping his thoughts to himself.

"Clone three-point-zero is not viable," he finally said. "In countless tests, it has displayed an unacceptable tendency toward violence. I assume you are aware of this."

"You have no idea what I'm aware of." She straightened to her full, imposing stature. "Do not disobey me, or I'll replace you as well."

His hands dropped to his sides and facial features grew sharp with fear.

"Now, if you've finished giving Len the remedy, you may ready my new clones."

Andy stepped up to Len's unmoving body and carefully disconnected the tube, then placed it beside the empty beaker on the long metal table behind him. In silence he walked through the narrow space between patient beds and left through the laboratory door.

Chapter 21

Dmitri

Dmitri submitted to the virtual shove Miranda gave him when he approached her through the oneness. He may not have been able to enter the landscape of her mind, but he clearly saw everything that happened within Starbright's walls. He'd observed her intimidating Jovian form enter Great-grandmother's private chambers, open a drawer in the small desk, and remove the sapphire ring, the one Caroline received when she first arrived on this bright blue planet. He wasn't present when Great-grandmother received the ring, but he knew about it the same way he knew most things: via information he gathered "out there."

Miranda had laughed when she placed the ring on her finger, and that didn't make sense. She'd called it "the keeper's ring," but there was no such thing as a keeper's ring as far as Dmitri knew. Granted, he didn't yet know everything.

And now Miranda strode through the tube that led to the astronomical observatory. At any moment, she would enter his haven.

"Miranda is coming," he told Alexandria telepathically. "She will speak to you. Do not be afraid. Simply tell her I am in the 'out there,' though I will be right here, beside you, the whole time."

"Okay, Dmitri, but I can't help but be afraid," she told him.

Miranda slipped into the room as dark as shadow, the only sounds the closing door and the smooth taps of her graceful strides. Dmitri remained as still as can be upon his perch beneath the oculus. He moved the orbs of his eyes back and forth below his lids the way they did when he traveled. Beside him, he sensed Alexandria trembling, her pulse pounding. And why wouldn't it? Until now, the only Jovian she'd ever seen in Jovian form—Great-grandmother —had appeared safely inside the television screen.

"Wake him up," Miranda said rudely. "That is your job, is it not?"

Alexandria hesitated, unsure of how to answer.

"Tell her yes," Dmitri whispered into Alexandria's mind.

"Yes, that is my job, but I can't wake him at this time. He's too far out. Is there something I can help you with?"

Miranda lowered her chin as she appeared to size Alexandria up. In the silence that materialized, Alexandria shook more obviously than before. After a long moment, the extraterrestrial said, "You have the look and smell of an ordinary human."

Alexandria held her breath.

Angry, Dmitri's offense crossed internally from himself to Alexandria and back again, like two metal probes with a dangerous charge zapping between them. "She can't speak to you like that!" he said.

"I am Dmitri's cousin from Russia," she said with

pride. "I am his caregiver. Dmitri is here physically, but his mind is—"

"Yes, yes, I know how it works," Miranda snapped. "David was often unreachable—and look where that got him. Well, Alexandria, human from Russia, I have tasks to attend to, so I will give you a message and you can relay it to Dmitri later. I do not want either of you getting in my way. We must work together. Do you understand?"

"Why would we get in your way?" Alexandria asked.

"Because you're too childlike to know any better, and he's an uninformed half Jovian. Without that stool he sits upon, he's nothing but a boy."

"*Uninformed* is not a word that applies to Dmitri, ma'am." Alexandria feigned respect, though she kept her head down and her gaze averted.

"We'll see about that. I've taken over Starbright. It's your duty to make sure Dmitri works with me. I wear the ring." She held her smooth pitch-black hand under Alexandria's nose; the blue gemstone sparkled to life with light from the oculus. "You know what that means?"

Alexandria said, "No, I'm sorry I don't."

Miranda leaned forward, bringing her hairless oval head in line with Alexandria's human one. It was large, suited to her elongated body, and Alexandria made out the hint of facial features, some semblance of eye sockets and cheekbones.

Dmitri shared this moment with Alexandria, whispering, "Hold steady," in her mind.

"It's the keeper's ring," Miranda said. "Caroline is the keeper of this planet, but she is unwell. She has given me the ring, which means, very simply, that I am the new keeper."

Alexandria took a hunched step backward, unable to temper her fear any longer.

"It means I rule the Earth," Miranda declared. "The fact that I have to spell it out for you assures me that you and your cousin, here, are as uniformed as I surmised."

"She's lying," Dmitri told Alexandria, "but don't challenge her."

"If Caroline asked you to take over," Alexandria spoke out loud, "then I don't see why there would be a problem."

"I am here at Caroline's behest. She's not showing up in the oneness, so she may not have told Dmitri yet."

"I will be sure to let him know. Thank you, ma'am," Alexandria presented a halfhearted bow and backed up a step further, reaching the room's shadow.

Miranda continued to speak as she strode nimbly away: "Tell him we're going to do what should have been done a long time ago. Together he and I will set this planet straight. Humans had their chance and blew it. The Jovians always knew how the Earth should be treated, how it should be honored. Jovians live long lives because the universe deemed it that way. It's time we claimed responsibility for its leadership."

The door closed behind her, and Dmitri was thankful for her departure.

Alexandria let out a noisy exhale and resumed her place at Dmitri's side.

"Please don't worry," Dmitri said, placing his hand on her shoulder. "She needs me for something. Whatever plan she has won't work without me."

"What plan does she have?" Alexandria asked.

"I don't know yet. But I'll find out."

Chapter 22

Max

Max had never seen so many clones working diligently—and happily—alongside ordinary humans. And, most important, on equal ground. Before he left Earth, the Coalition had protested in the name of equal rights for clones. Original humans (those born in the traditional manner) had been treating clones as second-class citizens for over a decade—forcing them to work in security, soldiering, and policing—even if that's not what the clones wanted to do. It was good to see progress being made.

From the table at which he'd spent the entire afternoon, Max had a clear view of a meeting that included his parents, Connie, and some other Coalition members. His father's voice carried, so it was easy to hear when he said, "We better take a break to check on Caroline." That's when both he and Lisa left the pubspace.

Max had been waiting for a chance like this.

He stopped the first member of the Coalition to come near, a random original human or hybrid, carrying a tray of food. "Hey, anyone asks, I went up for some air, okay?" he said.

The guy nodded and continued to an empty table.

Max approached the staircase and climbed as noiselessly as possible. The less people who noticed, the better.

Sneaking out wasn't something he wanted to do after being away from his parents for years, but he couldn't admit to either of them how worried he was about Elara. He didn't dare tell them he intended to return to Starbright, to see if she waited for him to return to the *Orion Sparrow*.

He realized how ironic it seemed. Why would he care what happened to her when she killed members of the Coalition and could have murdered his family?

But they didn't know her like he knew her. They didn't know what it was like on Europa, or how it felt to be kicked off Io, double-crossed by the Jovians, made to live under a crust of ice.

He reached the bunker's metal door and undid its hefty lock. He pulled the door open and, with as little a thud as possible, closed it behind him. The late afternoon sun made him squint, but it also made him feel alive. The air still smelled terrible, so he took his NOxygen clip from his pocket and inserted it.

So many questions niggled at his brain. Where had Elara gone after she and her hive railroaded the bunker? Had she only pretended to want the seeds? Had Max been just another part of her strategy for revenge?

Somehow, he didn't think so.

First, she hadn't known he was going to land on Europa. Because, second, *he* hadn't even known he was going to Europa! And she hadn't multiplied when she first met him. So, what made her do it that day? Max didn't believe her intention was to attack him and his parents. He didn't think the attack was planned at all. She'd stood there and watched his family reunite—only transforming when his mother muttered something about Caroline.

Yes, Max remembered clearly. His mother said, "Caroline came up all those steps? And no one's helping her?" That's when it happened. That was the moment Elara changed.

Was it a coincidence?

Edmund thought the monarch had boarded his ship, but he'd been wrong. The monarch hadn't died with the *Regal Star*. If she had, the Moon Children would have vanished. His father must be right. Elara and the monarch were one and the same. She possessed the ability to become a thousand or a hundred thousand or even a million individuals. And she could change them all into vapor, liquid, or physical form.

Her defense mechanism in a nutshell.

As Max passed the pine grove, he searched for her in between the trunks of trees. He still believed she honestly wanted the pinecones. Could she be waiting beside the *Sparrow* right now, bag clutched in her hands, hoping Max would return so he could take her back to Europa? That would be the best for all involved. Max would convince her to take the Moon Children home so humanity could go back to living without fear of a gaseous death.

At a brisk jog, Max came to the forest adjacent to Starbright and ran as fast as he could until he reached the parking lot. He climbed the staircase to the back entrance, and the door popped open. "Thanks, Dmitri," he said, figuring that's the only way he could have gained such easy entrance.

The tube in the red room opened as well, and that thing didn't open for just anyone.

As he headed in, his comm buzzed, echoing against the

fluorescent-white walls. He pulled it from his thigh-side pocket. A phone call? From Natasha? But she always texted.

He touched the screen before the call went to messages.

"Hey," she said.

"Hey, what's going on?" He prayed she hadn't heard about the attack. His cheeks flushed at the thought.

"I'm on my way back to Kirksberg from visiting my mother in Russia," she said.

"Right now?" He sounded a lot more disappointed than he'd meant to.

Up ahead, a light flickered off the shiny white wall of the tube. For a second he thought it might be Elara, but then he found no evidence of her.

"That's not the response I expected," Natasha said.

"Oh, no, no. I'm just thinking you shouldn't be here right now because things are messed up. Dangerous, I mean."

"When aren't they? You sound sort of panicked. Did something happen?"

"Yeah," he said before he could stop himself. "I made a mistake. Again."

"What kind of mistake?"

"Ah, it's so embarrassing. I should have told you before, but—I don't know why I didn't."

"Tell me now."

He saw no way out of it at this point. She'd think him an idiot if he refused. "I found an unexpected passenger in my ship after I left Europa."

"You went to Europa?" She laughed. "What for?"

"It was a mistake. I was trying to get to Io and—"

"*You mistook* Europa for Io?"

"I landed there, just for a few—it doesn't matter," he

said. "As I was saying, on the way to Earth, I discovered a stowaway."

A wall of silence came between them.

Finally Natasha said, "Are you serious?"

"Yeah, and it gets even better," he added.

"I don't know if that's possible."

"It turned out to be the monarch. The Moon Children's leader."

"Oh no. Oh, Max."

"And she attacked the, uh, Coalition with a deadly gas cloud—and, um, killed several clones and—"

"Oh, Max," she said again. "I'm so—"

"Wait. I'm not finished." His voice trembled, which was embarrassing in its own right. "She also injured Caroline."

"Great-grandmother? Is she all right?"

"She's alive. Her injuries are pretty, um," he wouldn't describe them in detail, "serious, but she's recuperating in a pod."

"And she'll live?"

"I think so," he said. "I mean, I really hope so."

"Well, if she's in a pod, she should be okay."

"Is that right?" he asked.

"It's amazing what those things can do for a Jovian."

"Thanks, Natasha. I feel a lot better hearing you say that."

"Good. I wouldn't lie to you," she said.

He liked that. She wouldn't lie to him. That was nice.

"So," he said, "all of that is why I'm not sure you should come here. You're not feeling great as it is, and if the Moon Children catch up with you—"

"Too late," she said.

"Huh?"

"I just pulled into the docking station."

"Get out of here. Which one? Starbright's?"

"I think so, unless I made a wrong turn and ended up in Alaska."

"Ha ha," he said. "I'm heading your way right now. *Do not go anywhere.*"

WITH THE HELP of his comm, Max found the antiquated ship Natasha captained in an eastern part of the docking station. He waited at the bottom of the ramp for her to make her exit, nervously checking the area for Leonards. Soon her footsteps drew his attention, and she was strolling down the adjoining ramp.

Max did a double take. The teenaged girl he'd taken from Mintaka to Io had grown into a long-legged, very long-haired twentysomething—easily twenty-five. When she came near enough, he couldn't help himself, he reached out and hugged her.

"I'm so happy to see you," he said even though he knew she wasn't the kind of girl who showed much emotion.

Must have been too much too soon because she didn't return the gesture.

She may have placed her hand on his back for a second, he wasn't sure. He cursed his foolishness, knowing she'd never been emotionally "normal," never displayed her feelings like other humans he knew, even when she was a teen.

He let her go and stepped back.

Up close, he recognized Evander's blue-green eyes and Nadia's blonde hair, as well as a combination of their refined facial features: Evander's perfect symmetry, Nadia's clear skin and upturned nose. Damn, he wouldn't mind staring at her for a while, though obviously that would be rude. Natasha wasn't some poster he'd hung on the wall of his berth. Far from it, she was practically family.

"Sorry about the hug," he said. "I just feel like I've known you for a long time, and this is like a reunion."

"It's all right," she said. "I just don't—" She shook her head, as if she couldn't find the words to explain her odd behavior. "You've known me longer than most people. Since Mintaka. And you're the only person I know who has space traveled."

In the pause that followed, he didn't want to say it, but it needed to be said: "I'm *really* sorry about your dad."

"Thank you," she said, a flicker of a frown crossing her lips. "I was just with my mom for two days of mourning, but I'm fine now."

Fine? She was fine? Nope. I don't believe it.

He must have made a face or something because she followed with, "It's the Jovian in me. I can control my emotions. It's like I put them in a box in the center of my chest, and I only take them out when I am safe, and usually alone. Please don't think I'm cold. I'm not. I loved my father dearly."

"I don't think you're cold," he said in a hurry. "Not at all. I know you're special. And not only because you're Evander's daughter. I'm just so glad to see you again. You look . . . " He wanted to say "beautiful, fantastic, stunning," but went with the safer bet and said, "great."

She met his gaze and the air molecules between them dinged and zapped while they observed each other. A sudden spasm of shyness threatened to shake Max senseless, but he managed to hold her gaze. She reached out and touched his cheek, igniting a spark that warmed his whole face. As he wondered what the heck that was about, she tilted her head and blinked her thick-lashed lids, in no rush to move the conversation forward.

He swallowed, his chest rising and falling with amazing tension.

"So, what's going on with the monarch?" she finally asked.

Speaking on autopilot, he told her the important details while replaying the touch to his cheek in the background of his mind.

"You're convinced she came for the seeds?"

"I don't know," he said. "She may have wanted revenge from Edmund—or the Jovians in general. Edmund double-crossed her at least once. In the end, though, she just wants a safe place for her people to live, you know? I get that. Isn't that what we all want?"

"It is," Natasha said.

"I really miss your dad."

She bit her bottom lip. "So do I."

"How are we going to straighten out the world without him?" Max asked.

She started coughing. At first just a harmless tickle, but then her neck clenched into ropy vines, and she clutched her chest with both hands.

"It's nothing, nothing," she said once able to speak.

Snapping out of his lovelorn delirium, Max had started to reach for her but somehow managed to refrain. "That did not look like nothing," he said.

"Please don't tell anyone."

Something scared him about the way she said that. He held his breath, hoping she would elaborate.

A pall of shame seemed to have crept into her confident demeanor. "Earth is just not the best place for me to live. I should stay . . . out there." Her eyes reached for him, for some sign of understanding.

"I won't tell," he said quickly. "But say the word, and we'll leave this place. I'll take you wherever you want to go."

Evander would want him to watch over her. She was stubborn and tough, and that could be a deadly combination. Someone needed to keep an eye on her, to make sure she didn't push her new heart too far.

"Don't worry, I'm fine as long as I'm wearing my e-skin."

"Are you wearing it now?"

"Yes." She pointed to where it peeked out of the V-neck of her unitard, the e-skin a near-perfect match to the epidermis she was born in.

"I never noticed," he said.

"It's always there."

"Okay, I'll try not to worry. As long as you never take it off."

"I never do. Not even to shower, if you must know," she muttered under her breath.

"Oh, that must be . . . " He tried very hard not to picture her in the shower. "Tough."

"You have no idea. I miss the feeling of water so much. Sometimes I just want to tear this thing off and submerge myself. I mean, really actually submerge—" A growing look of embarrassment came over her.

He held back the desire to say, "Don't let me stop you."

He'd never seen her blush. Never saw her act any way except completely confident. He breathed the word *damn*, then said, "I can imagine how hard that is. But you're able to resist because it's important, right? You have to keep that e-skin on in order to stay healthy."

"Sometimes I wonder what difference it makes," she muttered. "I'm going to do something important with my life and then I'm going to die."

It was news he didn't want to hear, a bullet shattering the sunny windowpane of the future. "I'm sorry, what?"

"I shouldn't have said that. It's just something Uncle Jimmy told me. It's written in the stars."

"No, it isn't." Max's anger was a knee-jerk reaction, nothing more. He had no factual reason to deny what she'd been told.

"I guess you don't believe that sort of thing," she said. "You're right, anything can happen, as my father always reminded me. But, I mean, look at me. I was born with one foot in the—"

"If you're worried your body can't withstand Earth's atmosphere, I'll take you away right now," he said a bit too forcefully, but he couldn't help himself. He'd already appointed himself her protector.

She shook her head. "There's a reason I'm here. A reason my ship wouldn't let me take Svetlana back to her world. It has to do with Evan."

"Is she the Lost Sister? The one from the prophecy," he asked.

"Yes, that's right. And she just arrived, so please don't speak of whisking me away quite yet. I'm meant to be here, at least for a short time."

"Evander's sister," Max said, the sadness of Evander's passing floating back to him like a dark cloud.

Natasha coughed again, and Max prepared for the worst. He could lift her off her feet and run her to the *Sparrow*, if necessary. They'd be safely away from Earth and whatever caused her trouble in a matter of minutes.

"Yes, his sister," she said.

"You brought her here. Maybe that was the important thing you were meant to do."

Natasha pursed her lips in a doubtful manner. "No. I think there's more. I don't feel finished yet."

"Listen," he said, "the offer stands for me to take you away anytime, whenever you feel ready, wherever you want to go."

"That's really nice of you," she said, "but I'm a pilot too, so I can fly myself out of here. And the only place I can live is Mintaka, so . . . "

"I've been there a few times," he said. "Not only the time I picked you up. It's the coolest place I've been in the entire universe."

"Yes, I know it's beyond words. The problem isn't whether I want to live there or don't want to live there. The problem is my mother. She never wanted her family to leave Earth, but then Uncle Jimmy whisked me away, Dad left her to find me and never made it back home, and Dmitri ran away and has become a literal part of Starbright. When I told my mother the news about my father's death, she assumed I would stay with her. She thought I came back to her for good. When I told her I couldn't stay, she forbade me to leave—but here I am, as you can see. It wasn't hard to sneak away. Not physically, anyway."

She retained her stoic façade, but Max saw the emotion building underneath. It made the skin below her eyes tremble, her mouth quirk.

"I really don't want to talk about this anymore," she said.

"You're upset. Of course you are." The urge to hug her became overwhelming.

"My mother doesn't deserve to be alone. Let's leave it at that. But I had to leave her. Do you understand what it means to have something so important to do that you would defy every one of your loved ones?"

"Yes, I do. Of course I do," he said, planting his hands under his armpits as a way to resist temptation. "It's okay. I'm on your side. Just remember that. I want to help you.

Your father changed my life, he made it so much better, and I'll be grateful to him for as long as I live. I left my parents too. And I care about you. I want to help you any way I can."

She breathed in and nodded. "Thank you," she said.

"Besides, Mintaka is a beautiful place to live," he said. "They don't call it the innovation epicenter of the galaxy for nothing."

It truly was like no other place Max had ever visited, a loosely formed planet at the heart of a captivating nebula. Home to freethinkers, builders, teachers, creators of all kinds.

"One day it will be my honor to take you there," he said, "and find some real water for you to swim in."

"You think there's real water on Mintaka?" she said, her hope buoying her. "I've only been on the medical floors, so I don't know about any of the others."

"Oh, you're in for a treat," he said. "It's *incredible*. I can't believe Evander didn't tell you. On the Earth floors— you know, the spaces they designed to more or less replicate places on Earth—they have these real parks with gigantic trees and thick, green grass and even mostly real air that doesn't smell too weird. If Earth water exists anyplace outside of this planet, that would be it."

Chapter 23

Evan

In the observatory, Evan found both Dmitri and Alexandria in the midst of meditation. Dmitri sat with his spindly boy legs crossed on the stool, and Alexandria stood like a much-larger bodyguard posted beside him.

Is this what they do all day? How long have they been living like this?

Through the silence, Evan stepped closer. The sun hovered straight overhead, and the light poured upon them like a spotlight teeming with dancing dust motes. *Space dust, probably*, Evan joked with herself. But then she realized it actually could be space dust.

She gazed at the oculus, open at the top of the ceiling, the sun looming brilliantly beyond it. And oddly enough, when she did so, everything went dark. Black. Evan couldn't see anything at all. Was she blind?

Soon, her vision adjusted, and a few pinpricks of light shined through what appeared to be a black backdrop. *Are those stars?*

What she saw was similar to the night sky she'd viewed

from home, when she stood on the deck as she had a million times. At home, she spent many nights staring into the sky just because she felt—no, *she knew*—there was something out there for her. "The pull of the stars," she used to call it, but it was a term she kept to herself. She'd mentioned it to her mother once and was sorry afterward, when Svetlana chirped out a laugh and steered the conversation back to school or homework, or whatever she considered more important at the moment.

Only it was not nighttime now, so the fact that Evan saw the night sky proved both strange and exhilarating. Her skin came to life with pleasant goose bumps. An electric buzz entered through her eyes and seemed to connect her like a wire to the cosmos. Wouldn't her mother love to hear that!

Was this what Dmitri saw when he gazed through the oculus? Did all Jovians see it, or was it just for her? What did it mean?

She sensed something palpable then. Similar to the instinctive feeling of someone watching her from afar. Were Dmitri and Alexandria staring at her? Her skin warmed as she attempted to disconnect from the view, to return her focus to the room in which she stood. She closed her eyes and when she opened them again, the room's stone walls trickled back into focus.

She was right—both Dmitri and Alexandria stared upon her with uncomfortable intensity

"You have seen it," Dmitri said.

"Um, I don't know," Evan answered. "It was, like, pitch black. Is that what I was supposed to see?"

"But there were stars too," said Alexandria, eagerly. "Did you see the stars?"

"I did."

Alexandria and Dmitri turned to each other with

simultaneous precision. "She saw them," Alexandria said with a slight, somewhat-eerie smile.

Dmitri nodded. His dark-blue eyes caught a glint of light and flashed like little mirrors again. Evan hadn't imagined it the first time.

"There are messages sometimes," Dmitri told her. "In the stars."

"Are there?" Evan asked. "I don't know. I saw the stars in the night sky, like the ones I've seen at home."

"Yes," Dmitri said.

"If there are messages," she said, shrugging, "I can't decipher them."

"No, you can't," Alexandria said. "No one can."

"Oh. Uh-huh," she said because she didn't know what that meant.

"We're very glad you decided to return," Dmitri said. "You must travel with us."

"What, you mean right now?" Evan shifted back on her heels. She had assumed they would talk, that Dmitri would tell her what they wanted or needed her to do, why she was there. Maybe give her some direction. Some inkling of her purpose or mission, or whatever. "Where are we going?"

He pointed at the opening in the ceiling.

Should she be frightened? Maybe she should be leery of these two strange relatives. As she hesitated in indecision, the *welcome, welcome, welcome* chant came back to her like a song in her mind, a feeling of acceptance and gratitude flowing along with the words, and she wanted to know more. That's all. She wanted to know more.

"How do I travel with you?" she asked.

Alexandria offered her hand, and Dmitri offered his. "Just take our hands," they said.

And off they went.

It was what she imagined it would be like to become a shooting star—if shooting stars had consciousness. *And maybe they do.*

Together, the three of them floated down the river that is the Milky Way and swam in pools of bright green-blue nebulae. Traveling with Dmitri and Alexandria was by far the most amazing thing she'd ever done, even if it only worked because they escorted her. She was truly Jovian; her ability to accompany them on this journey proved it more so than her parentage, more than her acceptance into the oneness, more than the story of the Lost Sister.

In this universe, the opportunity to live a Jovian life included a mental connection to the cosmos, and that in itself, while mind-bendingly overwhelming, also brought Evan a great deal of contentment.

It didn't feel real, and yet, here she was, light-speeding toward the Jupiter System without a spaceship or gear.

The same interests that enticed her to spend nights gazing skyward in the universe she grew up in actually transported her to those places in the Jovian one. The same desire existed in both places, but in the Jovian world her curiosity actually went somewhere and became satiated, and back home, it remained far above her head, unfulfilled.

Dmitri wanted her to learn about their family and their history, their values, their moral code—and traveling was "the most efficient way to do it," he'd said.

He brought her to Jupiter, where she observed Io and its past, the knowledge entering her mind without effort. Like water filling a cup, she experienced Jovian memories not her own, knowledge not her own. Similar to the oneness, the information entered like a babbling brook, and instead of trying to stop it, Evan welcomed it in.

Jovian history brimmed with strong leaders—not only

Caroline and Edmund but older beings Evan had never heard of nor imagined. It was rich with peaceful proclamations and the desire to explore celestial bodies far outside their home. Jovians had discovered the bright blue planet millennia ago. They'd used their engineering genius to travel there, to explore and indulge themselves in its plentiful terra and atmosphere.

Like humans, they weren't perfect—they'd made mistakes along the way—but they generally meant well. They valued life in all its vast and numerous forms. They valued intelligence and knowledge. Progress. A placid existence for their people.

Only the unemotional aspect of their race struck Evan as decidedly foreign. Cold and hard to grasp, the way they lacked empathy and yet clearly admired nature and the universe as a whole jumbled up in her mind like a conundrum. And yet, in their own way, the Jovians cared. Though it was difficult to decipher, Evan sensed it was so.

And that was as fascinating as their sleek forms and strange, musical way of speaking, which she would describe to anyone who asked as similar in sound to synthesized violins.

Evan probably could have spent the next ten years delighting in such travels and indulging her Jovian consciousness in new experiences and information before she so much as yawned or batted a bored eyelash. But they hadn't the flexibility for that.

Her presence on Jovian Earth was needed. What for, she still didn't know.

She opened her eyes and realized at once that one of her hands held Dmitri's and the other held Alexandria's. Dmitri sat cross-legged on his stool and Alexandria stood loyally at his side. With synchronous precision, they released their hold and allowed their hands to fall at their sides.

"I feel like a new person," Evan told them because saying something like "that was amazing" just wouldn't cut it.

"You are the person you were always meant to be," Dmitri said, imparting the confidence Evan hoped to one day to possess. "You must go to the greenhouse and meet Dayana."

"Yes," Alexandria said with a nod. "It is time."

As Alexandria walked her to the door, Evan drew in a rigid breath. That she would play some part in the Jovian world was no longer a question. It was the reason Dmitri was sending her to Dayana. She had no choice but to follow his lead, to take her limited courage and stretch it as far as it would go.

INSIDE THE HARSHLY LIT TUBE, Evan started up the incline, which became steeper as she went. Faintly behind her, the sound of clacking metal materialized. She stopped and listened. Her mother had warned her about the Leonards, and it sounded like one of them neared. She began to run.

The Leonards were sick. Evan couldn't let him catch her and make her sick too. Svetlana would be livid, not to mention the illness could kill her.

She reached a doorway with an ocular detection screen to its left. Dmitri didn't tell her she'd be locked out. She banged on the door, then stepped back and faced the screen. When she leaned in for a closer look, the door slid open. She breathed the words, "Oh, thank goodness." Then, in her haste, she stumbled over her own foot and crashed into a small, brown-skinned woman.

Was this Dayana? Evan didn't have time for introductions.

"He's after me," she said in a panicked whisper. "I have to hide. He's sick, and he'll lock me up."

The woman calmly stepped aside as Evan bypassed a table of potted plants and squatted below it. A few larger trees in heavy pots set on the floor in front of her would hopefully obstruct the Leonard's view should he enter the room. Evan waited to see whether the secret of her presence would be safe.

For a few moments nothing happened. The woman in the wheat-gold dress stood in front of the table and faced the entrance while Evan took in the soothing sound of drizzling rain, breezes chattering through tree leaves, and the occasional birdsong. The scent of flower petals and mosses, water dripping on rocks, and the dampness of soil soothed her agitated disposition.

It's like being in the forest, she thought.

A sudden squeak marked the opening of the heavy sliding door, and the Leonard came in. With his strange half-robotic head, wearing his black uniform and heavy boots, he breathed in a labored way. He and his various paraphernalia clicked and clunked as he extended one arm, using the wall beside him for balance.

Evan wondered if he would fall over.

"Hello, Dayana," he said in a strained, raspy way, identifying the woman for her.

"My goodness, are you feeling all right, Leonard?" Dayana asked. Then she covered her mouth and coughed loudly before clearing her throat.

Is everyone at Starbright sick? Evan wondered.

"I might ask you the same thing," he said.

"Only it's not the same thing, as you well know," she said.

"Yes." He bowed his head with resign. "I know."

Evan thought about that. Whatever made Dayana sick was not what made the Leonards sick.

"I hope to be cured of what ails me soon," Head Leonard said. "Andy's come up with a treatment. He went against Miranda's orders not to administer the cure to me."

"Well, that is good news. I always liked Andy."

"I came as quickly as I could to tell you that she's back," Head Leonard said. "And she's threatening a violent takeover."

Dayana's demeanor sharpened. "I am not surprised. Are you?"

He wavered slightly. "What do you mean?"

"I mean that you reap what you sow," she answered with a clenched fist at her side.

Startled, Head Leonard hunched into a stance of protectiveness.

Dayana continued, her voice grating with subdued rage. "The Jovians knew this would happen if they resorted to violent measures of any sort—*weaponry* of any sort." She gestured to his body armor: the club he wore at his side.

"I agree it was a mistake," he said. "Over time Miranda influenced Caroline. I don't know what you want me to—"

"I want you to keep your war out of my garden!" Dayana spoke with such volcanic force it seemed as if the power of the entire planet spewed from her mouth. Through the clear glass ceiling above, Evan watched the clouds cover the sun, and a sudden crash of thunder boomed. A gust of wind carrying sheets of rain rattled the glass roof.

Alarms went off in Evan's head. *Did Dayana just make that happen?*

Head Leonard cowered. "I will certainly try, ma'am, but this is no fault of mine. They made me the weapon I am. And from what I've seen, there is no place in this universe that's free of violence of one kind or another."

Closing her trembling lids and taking an obvious, intentional step back, Dayana seemed intent on centering herself. The rain splatters ceased, and the clouds moved to reveal a bit of sun.

"You're not wrong," she said more gently. "But Starbright can be the safe place we need it to be—it was built to be that place—and I intend for it to remain so."

"My team and I will do our best to protect it—and you," he said with admiration. It was clear that he respected and maybe even cared for this woman. Evan wouldn't have thought him capable of either had she not witnessed it herself.

"Your team is not well, so I'm not sure how effective they'll be," Dayana said. "I can take care of myself, but Starbright will need your help if it is to survive—even with the supreme one in place."

"My team is not well because Miranda does not want them to be well. And Dmitri, while he may be the supreme one, is not strong," Head Leonard said. "It's only been a matter of days since he gave himself up to the sky."

Strange that he considers Dmitri "not strong," Evan thought. But perhaps he didn't know how truly powerful Dmitri was.

"How much time do we have before Miranda acts?" Dayana said.

"She already has. She's ordered Andy to wake the three-point-zeros. I'll send word covertly to the bunker to see if there's anything Caroline and the Coalition can do to thwart her."

"Caroline is still convalescing in a pod," Dayana said, "and I sense her growing stronger."

"All the more reason for me to send Len."

"Very well," she agreed.

Head Leonard turned to leave, then stopped and looked back over his shoulder. "I'm afraid the world as we know it may be slipping through our grasp."

"And we're going to hold onto to it with everything we've got," Dayana said, "the tips of our fingers, if we have to."

"Yes, ma'am." He nodded.

As soon as the door closed, Evan crawled out from her hiding place. Dayana continued to stare at the closed door, obviously preoccupied with the situation at hand.

Feeling awkward, Evan fidgeted in place. "I'm so sorry I barged in like that. Dmitri said I needed to come up here and meet someone named Dayana."

Dayana turned to her, the force of her presence like an invisible wave that nearly knocked Evan over. "And so you have," the woman said.

"I've never been in a greenhouse before. It's so fresh and alive—it smells like the ground after a drenching rain."

Dayana smiled and the light changed. Evan swore the surrounding plants leaned their thin branches toward her.

"This is a special place," Dayana said.

Suddenly the oneness reared up, the sound of a crowd taking note of something interesting. Evan's eyes bulged, and she grabbed her forehead.

"I'm fine," she said. "It's just a swell of . . . Jovian chatter in my mind. Like a large group of people talking at once in a gigantic building."

"The oneness." Dayana looked at her knowingly.

Evan tied up the distraction in her mind and pushed it aside. "Yes," she said. "I'm part Jovian. I only found out what that actually means today."

"You are Andrew's child."

Evan nodded. "I am. And Svetlana's. Do you know her?"

"I have never met her, but, yes, I know her. And Evander as well, your brother."

"Uh-huh." This conversation didn't seem to be going in a productive direction. Evan glanced around. "I've never seen so many different plants. Where are they from?"

"Earth. Jupiter. Io. Europa. Some of the other moons as well."

"And planets, like Mars and Venus?"

"Oh, no, unfortunately. Those planets died long before this collection began."

"And where are you from?"

"I am from Peru," she said. "But I have lived within these walls for some time now."

Evan nodded as she would have had this been an ordinary meet and greet. "I come from another, um . . . "

"Another universe," Dayana said without apology. "I know."

"It's weird. You obviously know me, and I feel like I know you too."

Dayana smiled, then covered her mouth as she coughed. She appeared sort of young and yet not young at all. Her skin was smooth, deep brown, her eyes, bright and kind and also knowingly tense. And that cough. Evan wondered if she had a cold—or was it something more serious that troubled her?

"There is a reason you are here," Dayana said.

"I think it's because we can't let Earth die. Or—that sounds so big and horrible."

"No, you're right. We cannot let it die." She brushed her hand over a rosebush with light-purple blooms.

"Because that would be awful on so many levels."

"Agreed."

"Miranda plans to take over from Caroline. That much I learned through the oneness," Evan said. "I think it may be about revenge."

"It's about hurt feelings," Dayana said. "Caroline made Miranda feel like she didn't matter. And both of them suffer from a thirst for power."

"That's pretty scary, considering who they are."

"It is."

"And on top of that, we have to get the Moon Children to stop annihilating everything," Evan added with new boldness.

"Yes, we do." Again, Dayana reached out and a tree limb reciprocated. She touched it tenderly.

"I'm wondering, does the Moon Children's monarch even understand what's happening? Does she realize she's killing the planet?"

"I think that when someone attacks your family, you're willing to do whatever you have to, to keep your loved ones safe."

Evan considered her own mother, how she left her comfortable universe for a hostile one just to make sure her daughter would be okay.

"Elara will visit when the time is right," Dayana said. "She can be reasoned with. We will talk to her."

"Oh—we?" Evan startled.

"I've been waiting for you. But you already knew that, didn't you?"

She did know. When she thought about it, she'd always known.

"Your brother, Evander, was equally attuned to the universe as you are. The way forward for this planet and all of the life it sustains does not involve Jovian royalty or leadership that favors one life form over another."

"Yes, I understand," Evan said. "When Evander explained what was going on with the Moon Children on Jovian Earth, I started thinking what a possible solution might look like. And I wondered . . . " She glanced away, suddenly unsure. "No, it's stupid. It would be too simple."

"The simplest ways are often the best—and the hardest to come by."

"Okay. I thought that instead of trying to eradicate the Moon Children or send the Jovians back to Jupiter or ship all of the humans and clones and hybrids to Mars, would it be possible for us to, I don't know, invite everyone to stay?"

Dayana's face beamed as brightly as the sun. Evan wouldn't have been surprised to learn that her insides had sprouted vines that budded and then blossomed throughout her body.

"Because, you know," Evan continued, drawing on the information she'd gathered with Dmitri and Alexandria, "the Moon Children want a better, more comfortable place to live than Europa's negative-260-degree habitat, so of course Earth would be a big improvement in that way. They're so different from Jovians and humans, so I can't see them socializing or becoming friends—they're not that kind of species, anyway—but they can withstand the cold, so what if we invited them to settle in the polar regions? Antarctica isn't hospitable for humans, hardly any of us want to live there, but it's also not all ice and ocean—and it's far warmer than the moon the Moon Children have been living on. And there are trees and sunlight. I wasn't eavesdropping, but through the oneness, I heard Max tell his parents that Elara came to Earth for the seeds of pine trees. Pinecones. She wants to grow trees, and I assume she hopes doing so will eventually result in land. A better place to live."

Dayana stood absolutely still.

"Is that . . . oh, I'm rambling, I'm sorry. It's probably a dumb idea."

"No," Dayana said sharply. "You are right. You are absolutely right."

Encouraged to continue, Evan said, "And Edmund, from what I've heard, is responsible for making their species miserable. They once lived happily on Io, and the Jovians forced them out. The way I see it, the royal family has an obligation to help them. How we'll make that happen, I have no idea."

"Anything is possible, especially for a person who can change minds the way Evander could."

"You mean me?" Evan laughed internally at the idea that she might be that convincing or powerful. "Oh, no, I'm sorry to say I don't have those gifts. I don't have any gifts that I can think of. I'm really not like Evander at all. I assumed you could do it?"

"You have empathy and an open mind," Dayana said. "Those two things can take you anywhere."

"Okay, but no, I'm not Evander. He was a beloved president. He gave speeches and stood up for the rights of all beings. I've never done any of that. I'm not a leader. Believe me, I'm much happier when no one notices I'm in the room."

"Oh, but you *are* very much like him. And you will do these things, in good time. I promise."

"Do what things?"

"Never mind that now," she said. "Nothing will happen

quite yet. Have you met Dana and John? They are Jovian, and you will like them. They, too, have open minds."

The answer popped directly into Evan's mind, without effort. She simply knew who they were. "They're the Jovian couple who lead the settlement project in Alaska," Evan said with growing enthusiasm. "And they're my mother's adoptive parents. That makes them . . . my grandparents!"

Dayana clapped her hands. "Serendipity is such a happy thing."

"Yes. But it doesn't feel like a coincidence."

"It never is," Dayana said.

Chapter 24

Dmitri

In the observatory, upon his stool, with Alexandria at his side to anchor him, Dmitri traveled deep into the "out there" in search of information about the keeper of the Earth.

Not far away, in the near past, he came to Great-grandmother and her belief that she held the position, and how Edmund agreed, and she was happy. Then Dmitri observed the conversation the two of them had just before Edmund died, when Great-grandfather admitted he had never believed Caroline was the keeper but couldn't tell her so, knowing how crestfallen she would be—and, he feared, angry.

Great-grandmother's disappointment picked Dmitri up like a child's doll and tossed him, propelling him backward in time. He found himself nearing a black hole, its force sucking him into the unknown as if he were a speck of dust being sucked into a vacuum. A body, had he had one, would have been destroyed, but he was just a mind out here, and as soon as he made it to the other side of the black hole, the universe began to guide his journey, nudging him all the way to Earth's infancy.

There Dmitri watched the sun plant a seed in Earth's molten core where like a cell splitting in its mother's womb Dayana would grow.

His next thought dawned on him like the first flickering ray of a new day: Dayana was immortal, or as immortal as any living thing could be. As long as Earth lived, so would she.

She was the keeper. The only one. She and the Earth were inseparable.

Did Miranda know? She seemed to think the keeper's position was nothing more than Jovian prophecy, a powerful role she could pretend to believe in and then seize for herself. Her goals converged in Dmitri's mind: The same way she'd decided to hold the keeper's position, she'd also decided to lead the planet by force, and to do away with Great-grandmother in the process.

She is the opposite of a keeper, Dmitri thought. *She intends to destroy everything, beginning with Edmund and Starbright.* Wait, how did he know that?

He just knew.

Miranda had killed Edmund.

But no, Dmitri needed to see the evidence. He needed to be sure.

Alexandria squeezed his hand.

Had he ventured too far? Had he been gone too long? His thoughts felt cold; his mind numb around the edges. But he couldn't return yet. He needed to see more.

A conversation between Miranda and Leo bloomed. Dmitri saw them sitting together in one of the habitable structures they'd built on Mars, a rectangular living area within a row of interconnected metal modules. The two

Jovians sat in too-small chairs for their Jovian forms, Miranda a head taller than Leo and a table for two between them. They spoke with their Jovian voices in the native language, and Dmitri understood what they said without trouble, thanks to his many trips through the oculus.

"It has to be done," Miranda told Leo. "You know it as well as I. Caroline is barely Jovian at this point, let alone royal. And Edmund is out of control."

"That may be," Leo said. "I'm only suggesting you speak to Constance or Jimmy before we go ahead with the rest of your plan."

"Honestly, I would happily take that advice, but you know how deaf those two are to our requests. Caroline's been begging Constance to return to Earth since she was stripped of her powers. I only wish I'd known sooner. I wouldn't have waited so long to act." She glided her left hand over her right forearm the way a human woman might caress a long satin glove.

"I realize all of that," Leo said, "but I implore you to wait just a little longer."

"Oh, now, you know I'm not one for waiting," she said, taking her usual casual air. "Besides, you've already done what I asked. You've built the beautiful machines that will give us a fresh start before matters become any worse. We can't have the Moon Children sending our bright blue planet into another ice age or, worse, a death spiral. I'm sorry Edmund will become collateral damage, but we can't risk losing the entire planet for the sake of one Jovian. You wouldn't want Earth to become the next Venus or Mars, would you?"

"Of course not. That's not what I'm saying," Leo said, rubbing his chin. He turned his head toward the window at the center of the room. The light that entered was dim and diffuse, evidence that Mars's dusty atmosphere produced a perpetually overcast day.

"Then what is it you are trying to say?" Miranda said with impatience. "Because I don't like what I've heard so far."

"It's true I've done what you asked," he said in a reluctant tone. "I've built the weapons you've requested."

"Yes, you have," she said, her delight shining like light from her words. "Please describe them for me again. I never tire of hearing about them."

Leo sighed, his body dripping with reluctance. For a moment, Dmitri thought he might refuse her, but then Leo began to speak: "The device that will destroy the *Regal Star* is an ordinary missile—nothing new there—but your ship, the *Umbra Alaris,* is fixed with a weapon that at the press of a button will combust, producing a giant balloon-like chemical cloud that reacts violently with Earth's atmosphere and pretty quickly—a matter of days really— dismantles the planet's underlying ecosystem. All the plants, animals, forests, habitats, air, water, etcetera, etcetera will slowly decay and ultimately expire." He paused to rub the top of his smooth, oval head. "This will cause the few humans who survive in their underground dwellings to eventually die of starvation."

Miranda eased into the support of her chair's backrest, then raised her chin toward the ceiling so that her head draped over in a graceful curve. "Wonderful."

How could she find this wonderful? Dmitri thought.

"You're fine with all of that? You've carefully thought it through?" Leo asked.

"When I said I wanted to take the planet back to square one, I meant square one. The *Umbra* and I can make that happen. You deserve a medal for your good work."

"I'm just . . . " He stopped short, placing his palms flat upon the tabletop.

"You're just what?" she asked with a sharp edge.

"Well, I'm having some trouble rationalizing . . . " He petered out again.

"Speak freely," Miranda demanded. She stood, the chair pushing back behind her.

"It's just . . . your plan is going to cause a lot of death and destruction. And Edmund? I mean, I never thought the day would come—"

"Forget about Edmund," she said, folding her arms over her flat chest. "As for the rest, it will only be temporary. We've been over this, Leo. Everything will grow back. Life on Earth will renew itself like it has many times before. Like I will as well. If I'm willing to sacrifice myself —my body—for a couple of centuries of intense healing, I don't see anything wrong with asking Earth to do the same."

"Yes, I know. That is very," Leo paused, "courageous of you."

"It is," she admitted. "And you have to be courageous as well. While I'm down and out, you must hold up your end of our agreement and diligently watch Earth from your perspective on Mars. Some of the Jovian clones surely will survive underground or in their nascent pods, and when the Earth has mended itself, you and I will reign over them together. We'll rebuild together. It will be a whole new, wonderful world just like we've discussed many times."

"Yes, yes, you're right," Leo said with more energy. "That's all very good. I just, well, sometimes I feel bad about going to such extremes. Sometimes it strikes me as unnecessary. And I don't want you or I to have any regrets."

"We'll still have to cleanse the oceans, of course," Miranda said, no longer listening to him. "But this time we'll take control of the planet from the start. We never should have let the humans run rampant as they have. Too much free will is not a good thing. Only clones will exist on the future Earth. Clones we can easily control through the oneness, as it was always meant to be."

"You're right," he said, sitting up as if he'd come upon some newfound respect for her.

"And if Caroline bows to me," Miranda said, "and the humans agree to allow me to reign supreme, I may not have to do it after all."

"Caroline is weak," Leo said. "I wouldn't be surprised if she bowed to you."

"Either way, she will certainly die soon."

These last words whirled through Dmitri's consciousness and left behind a cold shiver that spread through him like the promise of a deadly disease. *Is Great-grandmother near death?* The desire to hurry back to Earth and warn her, to tell her what he'd learned, flashed through him. When he attempted to make a return to the observatory and his physical form, however, his mind flopped, flimsy as wet paper. Alexandria had tried to call him back, and he'd put her off. She'd squeezed his hand, and he hadn't squeezed back. Had he ventured too far? Had his humanity siphoned out of him? Was he lost in the oneness?

He'd sought out this past moment and, it seemed, he'd become tangled up in it.

Is this how David had died?

If Dmitri had a heart, it would have been pounding through his ribcage in an attempt to draw his attention. But he didn't have a heart out here. He had nothing but his thoughts. A consciousness that lacked direction, an exhausted mind that moved this way and that, as if tangled in a net that threatened to pull him under.

Alexandria squeezed his hand, and, panic-stricken, he attempted but failed to gather the strength necessary to respond. She tried again, the human part of him aware of her touch but too weary and lost to move. He knew what he was supposed to do—to connect with her and return home—but like a fly caught in a spider's web, he continued to spin in place.

"What is happening to me?" he shouted to no one in particular. "Why can't I seem to—"

"Dmitri! Go home," Great-grandmother's voice crashed like thunder through his mind. The lightning in her urgency gave him the might necessary to let go of this time and space, to disengage from the moment and set off in a new direction.

This time when Alexandria applied pressure to his hand, she hooked him and began to pull him back. He was free. Light-speeding toward home. Passing stars and moons, sailing alongside asteroids. His panic subsided, and the ease of gratefulness saturated his being.

"Have you been listening, Great-grandmother?" Dmitri asked. "Have you seen what I've seen?"

"I have. Thank you, Dmitri."

"You are out of the pod, then?" he asked.

"Yes, I am awake."

"I've seen as well," Natasha said. "We must stop her."

"Stop her," a chorus of Jovians sang through the oneness, spreading across the darkness and entering the "out there." Evander, Edmund, Andrew, David, those who came before and who would come after, all chanted, "Stop her."

Chapter 25

Svetlana

Svetlana observed the workings of the Coalition from what had become her "usual" table in the pubspace, far from Connie and her computer, where the members received orders, shared important information, and brainstormed solutions and hopeful ways forward.

Hours passed and Svetlana didn't speak to anyone. When Lisa asked if she'd like to visit Caroline in the pod, Svetlana had turned her down. She tried not to feel bad for Caroline, but it was hard with her face burned so badly. She hated to see anyone suffer . . . and yet her empathy only went so far.

Out here in the pubspace, there was no one to talk to. No one hanging around with time on their hands after the latest Moon Children fiasco and all the Coalition did to prevent the world from falling into a downward spiral.

If she planned to make a life here, she would surely feel and act differently—as in wanting to do something to help—but that was not her plan. She intended only to let Evan carry out her Jovian duty, whatever that would be, and then convince her it was best to return to their "real" lives.

Svetlana twirled a spoon around her cup of black coffee and stared at the smooth, curved wall that passed behind her. Nothing interesting in her coffee or on the wall . . . except, what was this? A couple of yards away, some type of circular panel about three-feet tall began at the floor and rose to chair rail height. A decoration, she supposed, but her imagination told her it looked like an escape hatch.

Now that she had taken notice, she realized a panel like this one appeared every dozen feet or so, as far as she could see. So, yes, just a decoration she hadn't taken notice of before: a circular disk the size of a monster truck's wheel with carved hieroglyphs around its outer border, interesting in its own subtle, beige way.

She sat back and sipped her coffee. The spaceship that landed in Kirksberg in the 1960s had been decorated with a ring of hieroglyphs too, so she wasn't surprised to find something similar in the bunker. It made her wonder how ancient this place was. What kind of aliens had built it? Had Egyptians been here at one time, and if so why? The world was filled with mysteries. Mysteries she would never solve.

A flash of shame came over her and made her scowl. Why was she thinking about Egyptians and mysteries when her daughter was out there somewhere, doing who knew what?

It wasn't like Svetlana not to act or pursue when the safety of her child was involved.

When Evander went missing years ago, she'd run out of the house in Tula, Russia, and straight to the airport, barely a coat on her back. But this felt strangely different. Strange because she wasn't freaking out. On the contrary, she felt rather calm. And the voice inside her, the same one that had whispered the word *inevitable* when she'd first arrived at Starbright's docking station, that same voice convinced her to stay put, to let things be for once. Just wait it out.

She drew in a deep, somewhat tense breath and thought, *Yes, I'm going to let this be.*

Evan would come back to her. Or, if not, perhaps it was time for her daughter to leave the nest. Wait, did she just say those words to herself? Was it time to completely let go? To trust her daughter's judgment? Trusting a child's decision-making skills was part of being a mother. Was she willing to let her grown child make her own mistakes?

After all, it turned out to be a good thing Evan had left the bunker when she had because she'd missed the Moon Children's attack that morning. She could have been killed or badly injured like Caroline. But then again, she hadn't left the bunker to keep herself safe. She had abandoned a safe place most likely to go to a more dangerous one. That wasn't good.

Could Svetlana trust Evan's belief in Natasha, who claimed the Jovian world needed her—would actually *die* without her? Such grand statements! And what about the way they insisted Evan was the Lost Sister in a Jovian prophecy?

Svetlana raked her hair back. *I mean, what the hell?*

Believing in a story like that—especially one that claimed this supposed lost sister was the missing piece of such a worldly puzzle—was similar to believing the future was written in the stars, that everything happened for a preordained reason.

An ironic laugh escaped Svetlana's lips.

Despite her own better judgment, she often wondered if own life was written in the stars.

Thud.

Svetlana twitched out of her thoughts. If she wasn't mistaken, something had hit the wall to her left.

Thud. Thud.

There it was again. This time the sound was louder. Some force bumped the wall. Harder, more baritone. *Thump, thump.* She felt the vibration in her chest.

A twisting scratch, like a seal breaking, followed.

Svetlana glanced down. The wall decoration or panel, whatever it was, the thing with the hieroglyphs around the border had separated from its inlay in the wall. A half-inch space materialized on one side.

It *was* a door! She pushed her chair back with a sudden violent scrape against the floor and bent over for a better view.

Thump. Thump. Thump.

The panel came fully away, and a sizable boot-clad foot thrust through.

"Um . . . " Svetlana stood. "Fran, Lisa, you need to come over here."

A glance toward Connie's workspace revealed that Fran and Lisa weren't present.

"What is it?" Connie said, yet to rise from her stool.

"It's one of those huge men," Svetlana shouted and staggered back as the panel came fully away from the wall and fell to the floor. "I think it's a Leonard!" She'd screeched the name.

The man in black uniform crawled on all fours through the opening. He was thin for a Leonard, not nearly as wide as the others, and as soon as he emerged fully from the hole, his arms and legs collapsed. "Doe-n," he panted from where he lay, "beee . . . aff . . . " muttering something indecipherable.

By this time, Connie and three or four other members

of the Coalition stood with Svetlana. Connie instructed them to help her move the table.

"He's sick," Svetlana reminded them. "Maybe we shouldn't get too close."

"It's Len," Connie said, squatting next to him. She took hold of his shoulders and helped him turn over. "He's a good guy." Then she twisted around and gave orders: "Randi, Kyle, get the med kit and some water."

"I've . . . take en thik-yur," Len said, his chest heaving, head lulling to one side.

"Where did he come from?" Svetlana asked. "Why would he crawl through the wall like that?"

"I don't know," Connie said while studying Len's face. "The bunker has some secret passages, and one of them leads straight to Starbright, but no one has ever arrived through a panel. And believe me, we checked them when we moved in here." She placed her hand on Len's forehead. "He's pretty warm but that could be because he's been running."

"I veered uf . . . the passage and sot . . . unmarked enter-ance," he said, through heaving breaths. "Caroline banned Leonards from bunk-her, so I," he cleared his raspy throat, "had to caffel no one stupped me." His upper body collapsed as he coughed out something about Head Leonard having a map.

Are more Leonards on the way? Svetlana wondered.

"Okay, okay," Connie said. "I'm sure you're here for good reason. Just a take a minute to catch your breath."

Kyle arrived with the med kit, and Connie pressed a vitals checker to Len's wrist. "Good, your numbers aren't too bad. You can sit up, but take it slow." She helped him sit up and lean against the wall, then offered him an open bottle of water.

He drank. Some of the water spilled over the sides of

his mouth, which he wiped with the back of his hand. "Miranda has taken over Starbright," he said, breathing more naturally. "She's in her Jovian form and plans to use the three-point-ohs to take Caroline's place."

"What's a three-point-oh?" Svetlana asked as the hairs on the back of her neck rose to attention.

"It's a clone. An evolved one," Len explained. "Technically called a 'Leonard three-point-zero.' Highly skilled in security and programmed to use force. Violent. And Miranda knows this. She's letting the Leonards who are sick from the Moon Children disease die because their loyalty lies with Caroline."

"Letting them die?" Connie erupted.

"But you just said you took the cure," Svetlana said.

"I saved Miranda's life at the attack that occurred at a recent Mars launch. Andy said she demanded I receive it for that reason."

"You saved her life, so she saved yours," Svetlana said. "Where does your loyalty lie?"

"Head Leonard is my superior," he said in a solemn tone. "He sent me as soon as Andy told him Miranda's plan. None of us were able to reach Caroline through the oneness. My loyalty is and has always been with Caroline."

"He's basically programmed," Connie said, "so we can believe him."

Svetlana remained leery.

"The cure requires time to take effect," Len said, slumping with exhaustion. "It will be days before I'm back to my usual strength. I used every ounce I had to reach this place and warn all of you."

"Thank you," Connie said. "We appreciate that."

Svetlana didn't like what she was hearing. Problems never ceased in this place, and she just wanted to go home. She glared at Connie and said, "Why didn't you know about Miranda's plans? Why didn't you know she was here? You're Jovian. Isn't the oneness working?"

"Miranda must be manipulating it. The royals can keep their thoughts and actions to themselves."

Then Svetlana remembered: Evan most likely went to Starbright—my God, couldn't anything go smoothly?

"Len, did you see my daughter, Evan, at Starbright? She may have arrived yesterday morning."

He shook his head. "I've been bedridden for the past few days. Haven't seen anyone outside of Andy and Head Leonard."

Of course he hasn't, she thought.

"What about Caroline," he asked. "Is she any better? Can she stop Miranda?"

Svetlana wished he hadn't directed the question to her. She didn't know. She didn't care to know. All she wanted was to avoid this whole terrible mess and take Evan home.

"She's recuperating in a pod," she said. Then she peered through the open wall panel but saw only darkness.

Chapter 26

Caroline

Caroline didn't know where Fran and Lisa had found the cane they offered her, but she appreciated it very much. Made of wood, it curved naturally, much like her injured leg. Her movement down the corridor of the bunker sounded out a step-step-tap, step-step-tap, and made her feel even older than she was.

Weakness plagued her, though the pod had done its job of mending her cuts and burns as well as it could in a short time. Her face, tender with new skin, still wore scabs where the poison had done its worst. Her throbbing ankle and knee purpled beneath her clothes thanks to the awkward way they'd twisted under Van, the clone of her beloved grandson.

Van had only wanted to help—he hadn't meant to hurt her. She'd been stunned by the onslaught of poison, her confusion leaving her unsure of which way to turn. Van headed toward her and, overcome by the poison, fell upon her.

She accepted her injuries as if she deserved them.

When she'd climbed the bunker steps to see what all

the cheerful noise was about, she never expected to find Elara there. Why would she? Everyone had been shouting about the return of Fran's son. There had been no reason to suspect Elara might show up at the bunker's door.

But that's exactly what she'd done. And Caroline knew it the moment she'd stepped into the outdoors with its winter air and cold sunlight. She and Elara had locked eyes. And in that second, Elara transformed. Caroline remembered running toward Fran and Lisa and their son, Max. It had been a reflexive action. She wanted to warn them. To protect them.

Then Fran shouted, "To the bunker!" and suddenly bodies came rushing at her in a mad scramble to get away. She became confused, turned-around, *frightened*.

Van must have seen her distress and taken pity on her. But he'd been the only one who had. No one else tried to protect her, no one offered a hand to guide her back to the bunker. Svetlana screamed for Evan, who wasn't to be found, and Fran ordered Max to run.

Caroline was no one's priority. No one's concern.

With her free hand, she touched her sore, swollen cheek. It radiated warmth and made her feel sad. Like she'd been beaten down one too many times. Like she might not come back from this.

And now there was Miranda to contend with.

"You all right?" Fran asked. "We could look for a pair of crutches, if you think they would be more comfortable."

"No," she said. "The cane is perfect. Thank you, Fran."

She pressed on. Step-step-tap, step-step-tap, turning into the large, circular pubspace with the staff in hand. She greeted the others with an apprehensive countenance. Huddled at the far side of the room, several Coalition members seemed to have surrounded one of her Leonards.

The thin one. He had defied her command to stay away from the bunker? Why would he?

Svetlana wasted no time rushing toward them.

"Fran, Lisa," she said, "we have to do something. Miranda arrived at Starbright this morning. She's threatening a takeover."

Fran pressed a sigh through his lips. "The hits keep on hitting. She sure got here fast," he said to Caroline. "What's the plan?"

"I'll take care of Miranda," Caroline said.

Svetlana pulled a face. "You don't look like you can take care of . . . much."

"It is my duty," she said.

"I don't think you understand. Miranda is in her Jovian form," Svetlana said. "Len says she's ten feet tall."

"Yes," Caroline said without fluster, "I know her Jovian form quite well."

"Then am I missing something?" Svetlana asked. "Because Fran says that unlike Miranda, you *can't* take your true form. So, how will you stop her?"

Caroline tried to stand straight, which was difficult considering she needed the cane to achieve balance, and her knee had blown up to twice its normal size. "Head Leonard is still loyal to me."

"Head Leonard is sick," Svetlana said. "Is he powerful enough to put Miranda in her place even when he's well?"

"With some help from Len and the others," Caroline said, "I'm sure he—"

"There are no others," Svetlana interrupted. "While you were in the pod, most of the Leonards were left to die. And there's something else: Miranda has woken the three-point-zeros."

Caroline suffered a wave of dizziness. She didn't know

any of this. The cane slid over a smooth patch of flooring, and she lurched forward.

"Whoa, whoa . . . " Fran lunged at her, catching her before it was too late. "Easy there. You all right?"

"She's *not* all right," Svetlana said. "She can't even stand on her own two feet."

"Hey! Easy, Svetlana." Fran scowled.

"It's my responsibility to deal with Miranda," Caroline insisted. "It's my duty and my desire. I will talk to her."

"Good," Fran said as if the dilemma were settled. "You'll have to do it soon. We have to be proactive—"

"Or maybe we should leave," Svetlana said under her breath.

"Leave?" Fran crossed his arms over his wide chest.

"You don't have to stay here, on this Jovian planet. There is another option," she said.

Lisa eyed Svetlana angrily. "You can't be serious. This is our home. We're active leaders here, and we have no plans to abandon our posts." She turned to Caroline and said, "Don't worry. We're not going anywhere."

"I'm only pointing out that it's a viable option," Svetlana said. "Not all of us have a responsibility to this planet."

"You're right," Fran grumbled. "If you don't care what happens here, you're free to go. You certainly don't need our permission."

"Of course, I'm leaving," Svetlana said with a huff. "You knew that was my plan since day one. I didn't want to come here, and I will leave as soon as I find the means to do so. Hopefully with my daughter."

"Right," Fran said. "You've made it crystal clear that you don't care what happens here."

"But I care about *you*," she said, in a kind tone, "which is why I'm saying you and Lisa and Max should come with me. We can head over to Starbright now, I'll find Evan, and we'll get out of here together, even if I have to steal a spaceship and figure out how to fly it myself."

Fran shook his head, and Lisa muttered, "She doesn't get it" as she turned away.

A moment of anger lingered thick as humidity in the air.

Caroline had an idea. "You can have one of my ships," she said.

Svetlana paled as she turned her intense, blue eyes upon her. "I'm—what?"

"You are welcome to any one of my ships."

"Will it take me where I want to go? Do I even have permission to take a time trip?"

"Of course you do," Caroline said, "but I recommend that you have Natasha fly it."

Svetlana scoffed. "Well, she's in Russia, so—"

"No. She's back," Caroline said, averting her gaze.

"There you go, Svetlana," Fran said, placing his heavy hand on Caroline's shoulder. "Your ticket home."

Svetlana blinked. Overwhelmed into silence, Caroline supposed.

"Maybe you should thank Caroline," Fran said.

"Oh, I uh—" Svetlana's boldness had withered.

Through the oneness, Caroline heard Evan tell Dayana she didn't want to go home with Svetlana, but Caroline chose not to say anything. Best not to be the one to break the bad news.

"You don't have to say anything," Caroline said, and a sudden pain shot through her knee and radiated to her hip.

"We better get to Starbright then," Fran said, nudging Caroline forward. "We can't give Miranda too much time to work on whatever it is she plans to do."

Caroline slowly crossed the pubspace—step-step-tap—

and joined the group surrounding Len. Fran and Lisa would assist her on the journey, and Svetlana and Connie would take the lead. Members of the Coalition had already gathered water, power bars, a few survival tools like flashlights, matches, and survival gear into packs to wear on their backs.

"Randi, Len, I'm putting you in charge of the bunker," Fran told them. "How long is this tunnel, anyway?"

"A mile and a half or so," Len said. "Should take you about fifteen, twenty minutes."

Everyone glanced at Caroline and her cane.

"Probably a bit longer," he added.

"We got this," Lisa said, patting Caroline's shoulder. "Don't you worry about a thing."

Caroline held her head high, raw cheeks and all. "Len, I think you should spend some time in my pod," she said. "I sense you need rehabilitation."

"Thank you, ma'am."

"Where will the tunnel take us, exactly?" Fran asked.

"The docking station," Len said.

Fran gave him a curt nod. "Good to know."

As Caroline's gaze brushed over Fran, a moment of gratitude heated her already-warm interior. How lucky was she to be placed in this man's capable, caring hands? Her own daughter-in-law hated her—quite literally avoided her —and this man, this non-Jovian and his kind wife, watched over her and her sad, decrepit body as if they were family. Somehow their kindness broke her heart, and as they set out on what was sure to become a dangerous task, she hoped none of them would notice the weepy emotion in her eyes.

Chapter 27

Svetlana

Svetlana and Connie took the lead with Fran and Lisa helping Caroline several paces behind. Grateful as she was for Caroline's offer of a ship to take her home, Svetlana assured herself that nothing had changed between them. She did not have to forgive Caroline, or become the daughter-in-law who stood dutifully by her side. She wished the old lady had remained in the bunker, in the pod where she could continue to recuperate. But Svetlana also agreed the so-called queen needed to come with them to Starbright, that she should be the one who stood up to Miranda.

They'd moved at a quick pace for longer than twenty minutes, and all of them panted and strained, except for Connie, who seemed like she could easily continue for another ten miles. She was young, and a clone, of course. Strong. The only copy of Constance, which was strange. Why had Constance cloned herself, and why only once? And where was Constance now? Why weren't she and Uncle Jimmy here to help the humans and clones?

Shouldn't they be present in such a dire moment in history?

"I see the entrance," Connie said.

Svetlana squinted into the distance. "I don't see anything."

"You will."

"I guess you have better eyes than I do," Svetlana said, feeling suddenly on the long side of middle-aged.

"Of course I do. I'm a clone. I can see better than you, and I can also not be seen."

Connie often displayed the insensitive bluntness of a human twentysomething. "Right, I know that. You have camouflage abilities. That's cool."

Connie blended into the rough, rock-lined walls of the tunnel, and Svetlana broke into a startled laugh. "Wow, it's as easy as that?"

Connie began to reappear, at first just a shadow of herself, and then in full-blown color.

"It's as easy as concentrating," she said. "And I'm probably ten times stronger than you as well."

"Yes, I know all of this. I didn't mean to be rude . . . or condescending, if that's what you're implying."

"You're often rude *and* condescending, Svetlana. I'm used to it. Everyone is."

"I don't think that's fair," she said, suffering a stab wound similar to the kind her daughter often inflicted.

"It's obvious that all you care about is yourself and your kid. Which is understandable to some degree. But there are other people in the world. People who are in pain. You're not the only one who has problems or catastrophes to work out."

"I had no idea that's what you thought of me."

"Not just me. Everyone. Just about everyone, anyway," she said as if not caring an iota for Svetlana's feelings.

Slapped down by Constance's clone. How appropriate!

Ahead, the door came into view. "Ah, I see it now," Svetlana said, hoping to put an end to the conversation.

Behind them, Fran and Lisa ushered Caroline along, the three of them cringing in pain and breathing heavily.

"Everything okay?" Svetlana asked Fran, partly to prove to herself (and Connie) that she did care about other people.

"Give us a minute to catch our breath," Fran said while Lisa put a vitals checker to the underside of Caroline's wrist and asked her how she was feeling. Caroline whispered something Svetlana couldn't hear, and Lisa waited a moment before reading the device.

"I realized something on the way over here," Fran said.

"Sounds serious," Svetlana said. "What is it?"

"It's Max. He's not here."

"Where is he?"

"Lisa and I haven't seen him since breakfast."

"You think he left the bunker?" Svetlana asked.

What is with these kids going off on their own?

Then again, Max was thirty and space traveled for a living, so should they even be worried? Svetlana was sure he could handle himself.

Fran's eyelids trembled closed as he released a frustrated sigh. "He was upset about the Moon Children attack and said he needed some space, so we gave it to him."

"Maybe he was tired from his trip and decided to stay in his room," Svetlana said. "Connie, can you ask one of the clones—"

"Just did," she said from a few yards ahead. "Yesterday Max told one of the members that he was going up for air."

Fran nodded as if he could have predicted that Max would venture out on his own.

"It's okay," Lisa told her husband. "Going off on his own is just his way of dealing with things. You know that. I'm sure he's fine."

Fran took in a noisy breath and said, "Okay." Then he said, "How are Caroline's vitals?"

"Could be better," Lisa replied, "but not awful."

"Good." Fran said. "Are we ready?"

"As ready as we can be," Lisa said.

Connie pressed her cheek to the door like she was eavesdropping on a conversation on the other side. A click echoed against the walls, and a screen appeared in the stone panel to the left. Connie laid her hand on it, and the door slid open.

The tunnel flooded with the calming blue light from the adjoining docking station. That weird, lightheaded daze started to work on Svetlana's nerves right away. Her shoulders lowered as she imagined her heart rate did as well. Unlike the first time she saw these lights, when she'd time traveled out of Starbright, she knew the colored glow produced feelings of complacency. This time, she'd keep her guard up. As a matter of fact, she replayed her conversation with Connie and let it prickle across her mind. So what, if all she cared about was Evan? Didn't that make her a good mother and, in turn, a good person?

The docking station spread long and wide before them. It was as vast as a plowed field. The open, basement-like space in its middle hosted only three spaceships of different shapes and sizes. A small round saucer similar to the one that time traveled her and Evan here, a hexagonal block-like medium-size ship, and a tube-like giant much larger than both of the others. On the opposite side, a number of lit doorways gleamed. At least one of them, Svetlana knew, led to the tubes. To the right, the part that resembled a subway station with giant sliding doors every few feet, opened up to more ships.

"That's Miranda's there," Connie said, pointing to the small saucer in the middle.

"How do you know?" Svetlana said.

Connie glared at her as if she were stupid. "The oneness."

"Okay, so here's what's going to happen," Fran said, waving Svetlana and Connie closer to where he and Lisa huddled with Caroline. "Caroline will—"

A door on the opposite side of the room slid open, and all five of them hunched a little and turned in its direction. No one emerged. The door closed again.

Svetlana scanned the area for a place to hide. A wheeled vehicle sat parked like a small, metal tank to the right. "Let's go over there," she said pointing to it.

Caroline limped with Lisa at her side. Step-step-tap. Step-step-tap.

Something thunked in the distance.

"Someone is definitely here," Svetlana whispered. "Should we go through one of the docking doors and lay low for a few?"

"Yeah. Let's," Lisa said.

Connie seemed to be concentrating on something internal: her mouth pursed, eyes squeezed into slits. "I don't sense anyone, but I agree we should take cover."

"Through here." Fran gestured to the closest set of automatic doors. The group moved as soundlessly as possible.

The doors opened, and the five of them hurried through, leaving the calming blue basement lights behind.

The space they entered was not a place to stow just one ship, or even a few, but an entire second docking station spread before them, vehicle after vehicle lined up in wide berths. How many ships did Starbright harbor?

Suddenly the scrape of rushing footsteps approached.

Fran caught Svetlana's eye, and they shared a moment of concern.

Lighthearted chatter filled the air, and Natasha and Max came out from beside one of the ships. "Dad?" Max said. He and Natasha ran to them. "What are you doing here?"

The sight of the young couple broke some of the tension. The more the better, and Svetlana welcomed the prospect of two pilots who could possibly whisk her and Evan away—not to mention, they'd found Max.

"Where have you two been?" Lisa said. "Sorry, that came out wrong. I meant, where are you coming from?"

"Natasha got back from Russia a little while ago," Max said, "and she was showing me the old classic she flew there." He coughed in a self-conscious manner, Svetlana thought. "It's really cool. What are you all doing here?"

"Miranda's planning a hostile takeover," Fran said. "Caroline's going to talk some sense into her."

"Natasha was just telling me," Max said.

"I'm glad we ran into you," Fran said. "If things go south, get to your ship, and blast out of here."

"And bring me with you—but not until I get Evan," Svetlana spoke loudly, sure to be heard. "Have you two seen her?"

"Evan is staying," Natasha answered without apology.

Svetlana's defenses rose, her body taut with clenched fists and teeth. "We can't be sure of that until we see her and ask her. Have you asked her? Have you even seen her?"

"No. But I know that she's staying. She has to. She

wants to. We told you before, she's the lost sister from the prophecy. None of this works without her."

She wants to? Well, Evan wanted a lot of things growing up, too, and not all of them were good for her.

"What do you mean by *this*?" Svetlana said. "None of *what* works without her?"

Natasha stood straight like a soldier and used a voice of recitation when she said: "The lost one, like her brother before, possessed mettle and honor, and a heart worthy of lore. She laid to rest the resistance, sidestepped the queen's insistence, and rendered a solution for all mankind."

Svetlana stood there and blinked, a verbal response escaping her. *What does that mean?*

A door opening in the distance interrupted this exchange. Rays of blue light spilled into the room about a hundred yards away, and the brute with half a robotic head followed. His baton and whatever else he wore on his body clanked with every lengthy stride.

"She's coming," he shouted to them. "Take cover. I'll hold her off."

Svetlana bit her lip as she scoured the area for a place to hide. "There's a partial wall behind us," she said. "It will have to do."

"Move quickly, everyone," Fran said, practically lifting Caroline off her feet.

Svetlana wondered where Evan might be in this enormous building, and how she would manage to make her way upstairs. They reached the half-wall and squatted behind it. Svetlana peered through a crack in its middle.

Once again the heavy slide of a door opening sounded. Head Leonard took a fighting stance: legs apart, arms bent, one hand clutching his billy club.

Footsteps entered the room. Not heavy, thudding, harsh strides, but graceful ones. The air stood still as all ten towering feet of Miranda came into view. She was sleek as a knife blade, beautiful in all her glossy, menacing glory. Black and smooth like a brand-new car. Something about her—something intangible and otherworldly—felt horribly dangerous. She seemed to move in slow motion, and yet she covered the ground between herself and Head Leonard in just a few strides.

Svetlana's hair stood on end the way it used to when she'd first encountered the Jovians, when she was just twenty-three years old and knew nothing of this Earth's devastating future.

When Miranda reached Head Leonard, the ceiling lights reflected across her ebony arm as she carried out a smooth backhand that sent him soaring through the air.

His baton flew out of his grasp and bounced off the metal side of a parked ship as his body rose and then fell, landing flat on his back on the cement platform fifty feet away.

He staggered up, patting his chest before unzipping something to arm himself with, something that fit into the palm of his hand. He prepared to have another go or take another beating.

"Perhaps you should stay down," Miranda said, feigning empathy. "Those nasty Moon Children have given you one of their lethal diseases. No one expects you to beat me, and Caroline, I'm sure, would prefer to keep you alive. You were always her favorite pet."

"Hm," he grunted a deep baritone. "You sound jealous. We all knew how badly you wanted to be Caroline's number one."

"You're wrong about that," she said. "I didn't want to be her number one. I wanted *to be* number one. And that's what I am now."

He resumed the fighting stance. "I serve Caroline and always will."

"I was afraid you'd say that." Miranda checked her wrist as if there might be a watch there (there wasn't), and Svetlana noticed a large ring on one of her fingers sparkling in the dim lighting. "Where is that three-point-zero?" Miranda said. "It would be much more entertaining to watch him fight you than having to do it myself."

"Funny," Leonard said, "in all Caroline's time on Earth, she never raised a hand to anyone. Not even me. Not even when I deserved it. Every Leonard who ever passed through this building would have traded his life for hers."

Miranda took two steps closer. Her footsteps, while light, created vibrations that shook the platform floor. "I do believe you will serve her until your dying breath." She tilted her head, seemed to study him.

Leonard grasped what looked like pepper spray and something else—a knife?

"I bet you wish you had those laser guns I suggested we outfit the security squad with," she said.

Leonard raised his arm as she neared. A cloud of spray gathered in the air, but she stepped right through it and kicked him in the wide girth of his chest. The blow flung him into the air, and he toppled onto his back before skidding several feet. Miranda caught up to him easily and placed a foot at his center. Then she stomped on his chest, grounding him into the floor while he coughed out a few painful, thudding exhales. Svetlana was grateful not to hear the crack of broken bones.

The docking station shook, the connected ships creaking in their holds.

With her foot pinning Leonard down, Miranda said, "Stay. In. Your. Place."

Leonard didn't move. Whether he was alive or dead, Svetlana couldn't tell.

"Caroline!" Miranda called as she scanned the area. "Come out here. I traveled all the way from the red planet to see you, and I expect a face-to-face greeting, as is the Jovian custom. Is it not?"

She turned away from Head Leonard and began to walk toward the half-wall Svetlana and the others huddled behind. "It's important that we talk, or did you limp through that dank tunnel for the fun of it?"

"You'll have to face her, Caroline," Svetlana whispered. "You'll have to talk to her."

Caroline, barely able to stand, trembled; she seemed unable to focus on any one thing. "I must stop her," she said, sounding delirious.

Svetlana looked to Fran, their mutual concern coming together like grasping hands.

"Yes, that's right," he told Caroline. "Will you be able to do it?"

"Fran, come on, she's obviously not up for this," Lisa said.

"Miranda must be stopped," Caroline said in a light-headed voice. "There have been whispers of foul play."

Svetlana couldn't believe this. Why must things always go from bad to worse? "What are we going to do now?" she said.

"Caroline," Fran said louder, "she's in her Jovian form. You have to talk to her."

"No, she doesn't," Lisa said, placing her hand on Caroline's shoulder. "You don't have to do anything."

"She must be stopped." The words dribbled from Caroline's mouth.

"I'll do it," Natasha said.

Max whipped his head in her direction and mouthed the word, "What?"

No one else acknowledged her, and she didn't reply to Max.

Though Svetlana reminded herself this wasn't her planet, not her fight, she tried to encourage Caroline. "You can talk to her. You need to negotiate, to convince her not to do this. You were once good friends."

Caroline peered upon Svetlana with glassy eyes. The old woman's cheeks were so red and raw, and Svetlana couldn't help thinking she should be resting in her pod.

Fran sighed heavily. "This clearly is not a good time."

"Miranda's right there," Svetlana said. "If not now, when?"

"Caroline hardly knows where she is," he whispered.

"I agree," Lisa said. "And I'm not going to let you throw her to the sharks—"

While they spoke about her as if she weren't there, Caroline attempted to step out from behind the wall.

"What are you doing?" Svetlana pulled her back into the fold.

Meanwhile, Natasha said, "I'll go. I can stop Miranda. And it's my duty as well."

Connie stepped up beside her. "I'll come with you."

"We don't have to fight her," Natasha said. "We just have to distract her long enough for all of you to enter the next station and find a better place to hide."

Natasha pointed down the corridor that seemed to spread a mile behind them. "My ship is in the next quadrant. Worse comes to worst, find it and wait for us there. Do you remember what it looks like?"

Svetlana didn't see the door, but she did remember the ship. "I think so."

"And what about you," Max asked Natasha. "What if Miranda doesn't want to talk? What if she—"

"This is what I'm meant to do," Natasha said. "I'm Jovian. My father was a great negotiator, one of the world's best. If it's meant to be, I'll convince her to stand down."

"Fine. I'm coming with you," Max said.

"You can't," she said. "If something happens to me, you'll have to fly my grandmother and the others away from here. I promised I'd bring her back to Kecksburg, and I don't lie."

"Yeah, but, no . . . I made a vow to protect you," Max said, his voice cracking. "And I refuse to break it."

"No, you didn't," she said. "To whom?"

It struck Svetlana that Natasha and Max were a couple. They were in love.

"I just wish you wouldn't do this." Max groaned and started to walk away, then turned around and came right back.

"I agree you should do this," Fran told Natasha, "but, like you said, don't try to fight her. Just be really careful. Don't let Miranda get too close. If she starts anything, get out of there. Run. No one's gonna hold it against you."

Max and Natasha gazed into each other's eyes. "I'll see you in a few minutes," she said. "I promise."

He kissed her and then she moved out from their hiding place, Connie in camouflage following after.

All Svetlana could think was, *This better work.*

Chapter 28

Dmitri

Dmitri twitched and landed full weight upon the stool.

It was jarring, moving from a virtually bodiless form into an eighty-pound combination of flesh and bones.

"You're back, thank goodness," Alexandria said. "I squeezed your hand so many times, and when nothing happened, I thought I might have lost you."

"I'm sorry," he said, still feeling the relief of making it back. "I had much to learn."

"And did you?"

"I did."

"The others have arrived in the basement. Your great-gran. Natasha. Svetlana too. Miranda found them right away. What will happen?"

"I must close my eyes and see," he said. "Stay beside me."

"Of course," she answered.

The docking station came to mind. Head Leonard lay

motionless on the ground. Great-grandmother, as pale as quartz, grimaced due to the pain Dmitri sensed pulsing through her body. Natasha was there as well, and Connie, nearly invisible, beside her. Together, the two women approached the Jovian.

"Ah," Miranda said. "You're not Caroline. Is this the best the Coalition can do? A mostly human and the clone of the one who nullified Caroline's power? Don't I deserve a moment with the queen herself?"

"She can see you," Natasha told Connie in a whisper.

"Yes, I can see your friend," Miranda said. "She's just another clone."

"Just another clone?" Connie said. "You disrespect the one who made me."

"Do I?" Miranda said.

"And the one who made me can take away your powers, need I remind you?"

"Well, where is she, then?" Miranda said. "Constance hasn't shown her face around here in years."

"That doesn't mean she doesn't know or care about what happens here."

"Yes, I'm so sure she—"

"What do you want, Miranda?" Natasha said. "The world is in dire shape without your game playing, and we're not here to fight. We need solutions to the problem of the Moon Children and—"

Dmitri sensed it before it happened: In the blink of an eye, Miranda was on his sister. The alien's smooth-as-ice hands gripped Natasha along both sides of her neck and lifted her off her feet with the grasp of a giant.

"Someone with such thin skin should not attempt to lead the planet, let alone protect it," Miranda seethed. "You can't win without a strong heart."

The sound of breaking threads ripped through the air.

"Stop!" Natasha shouted, clawing at Miranda's hands to no avail.

Miranda tore Natasha's e-skin from neck to collar bone, then shoved Natasha away, sending her back-first into the wall. Natasha slid to the ground as she grasped at the two flaps of e-skin, her eyes bulging at the sight.

In the quiet seconds that followed, Miranda stretched her long neck toward Natasha, as if admiring her work. She tilted her oval head and said, "You appear to be done. Where's number two?"

Still in camouflage, Connie leaped upon Miranda's back as if she were a pole to climb. With her legs wrapped around her sleek, black chest, and arms encircling Miranda's neck and head, Connie reached for the alien's smooth face and pressed her fingers into the subtle welts that were her eyes.

Dmitri concentrated, sending Connie sparks of strength.

Miranda howled and lurched forward, attempting to fling Connie from her back. But Connie withstood, wrapping her arms around the alien's neck and jaw, determined to twist her head.

"My people are not yours to use," Connie said in a low growl. "We will have our freedom from the Jovian royalty whether you like it or not."

She held Miranda in a headlock while Max, who had until now remained hidden behind the half-wall, raced down the corridor to Natasha and gathered her up. He guided her toward safety, checking for blood and injuries along the way.

When they caught up to Caroline and the others, a terrible, metal crash rang out.

Miranda had launched Connie into the exterior wall of a parked spaceship. She lay unmoving on the ground.

Dmitri spoke to Connie in her mind: "You will be all right. Stay down," and sent her healing energy.

And then he told Natasha, "You must go. Leave us. Get to your ship."

"We will," Natasha answered him internally as she and the others broke into a run. She was panting profusely when she told them: "Dmitri will take care of Connie. We have to get out of here."

"Go, go, go!" Dmitri shouted to her.

Miranda pursued them, striding on her long legs. "Why are you running from me, Caroline?" she said. "Is it because you're not Jovian anymore? You've become one of them, haven't you? Vulnerable and weak. A mere human, the thing you most despise. I can't even imagine how terrible that is for you. How pathetic you are!"

"And what have you become?" Caroline choked out dry, splintered words. "Have you asked yourself?"

"I am the true leader of this planet," Miranda said and Dmitri worried she could bring the walls down with the volume of her voice alone. "I will do what the Jovians should have done ages ago."

Caroline's knees buckled, and she collapsed into Fran and Lisa's grip. "You're a monster. The last thing the planet needs is your violence."

"She's fading," Fran said as they ushered her forward.

Dmitri concentrated on giving Great-grandmother healing energy, but it didn't seem to help.

The group continued clumsily toward the exit: Natasha limping with Max's support, her chest heaving each difficult breath. Would she die because her e-skin had ripped? Dmitri didn't know. All he knew was that she wanted to live!

Beside her, Svetlana wondered where Evan was, if she could reach her daughter in time to take Natasha's ship home. If she left the planet now, would she ever see Evan again?

Dmitri threw open the door, and the five of them and all of their worries stumbled through.

He slammed it closed just as Miranda was upon them.

Chapter 29

Evan

Evan carried out whatever orders Dayana gave her: Move these plants to that table. Place the cacti on the floor. Spread this sandy, sparkly substance—an element found only on Jupiter, apparently—upon the bottoms of each glass wall.

"It will strengthen them," Dayana told her.

Miranda had entered the building in her Jovian form, which meant they had to prepare for the possibility of battle.

Dayana hummed as she worked. Occasionally, she paled and slowed and limped a bit. Other times, she lifted and moved trees that looked to be three times her weight. All Evan wanted to do was help, so she continued to ask, "What else? What else? What else?"

As they shoved one of the heavy potting tables in front of the entrance, Dayana suddenly covered her mouth and cried, "The child! I nearly forgot the child."

"Where is it? I'll go get it. Is it a baby?"

"No, no, no. It's here. With the conifers and nearly frozen water. In the cold room."

"The cold room?" Evan said, thinking a cold room would not be a good place for an infant.

"Come. We will go together."

Dayana walked very fast for a small woman. Though youthful in her energy and strength, she seemed too old for childbearing. Subtly wrinkled around her eyes and forehead. Still, Evan wanted to know: "Who is the child, and um, is it yours?"

"It is one of Elara's," Dayana said without offense. "A long time ago, she brought him to Peru and asked me to watch over him. He was just a tiny seedling, not much of anything at all, and far too young to visit a severe climate like Europa's. So of course I said I would. When she didn't return and I traveled to Starbright, I brought him and many other individuals that you see here." She gestured to surrounding potted plants and trees. "I believe Elara is coming for him soon. He woke this morning. He wouldn't have woken if she wasn't near."

"The monarch *gave* you her baby?" Evan stepped more slowly as this information sunk in.

"Yes, that's right," Dayana said, nodding Evan forward. "Come."

They reached a space in which the temperature dropped, raising the hairs on Evan's arms though her unitard was long-sleeved.

"This is where I keep the specimens from Jupiter's moons," Dayana explained.

Evan ducked under the long, lean arm of a pine in her path. "There are pine trees in the Jupiter System?"

"Not anymore," Dayana said. "When the sun was younger and stronger, both Europa and Io were different. Life was by no means plentiful, but there were some trees." She continued past another table crowded with strange, bushy creatures that expanded and contracted as if breathing.

"Quiet now," Dayana said, "we're nearly there."

Evan tripped on a root and splashed into a stream that numbed her foot, though the water had not penetrated her boot. "An actual stream?"

"Shh," Dayana said. "There, on the potting table. In the basket. Go look."

Evan hurried toward the table that held a group of leggy succulents, some of them like seaweed with trailing octopus arms. Nestled in the center of them rested a light-colored basket, woven of twigs and some type of tree bark.

Evan peered inside: A dark-brown blob the size of a loaf of bread sat at the bottom of a pot.

"That's him," Dayana said.

Evan sank with disappointment. It didn't look like much of anything. Just a rock-shape blob of clay resting on some peat. "I thought it would be more—"

The top of the blob moved, and two little slits opened like eyes and blinked at her.

"Oh my gosh." Evan's jaw dropped. "Is that—its head?"

It opened a pea-sized mouth and squawked.

Dayana joined Evan in front of the table and patted the little thing. "Mommy is coming, sweet one," she cooed. "Don't fret." She picked a tiny piece of peat from his plump body.

"Lift the pot out of the basket," Dayana said. "We must comfort him."

Slowly, Evan reached for it, offering her hand to the babe's tepid face. It rubbed its surprisingly smooth cheek into her palm and gurgled.

"He looks so . . . cute and helpless," Evan said, and he

squawked gently in reply. "Mommy is coming, she'll be here soon."

"He is nearly helpless. And will be for years. It's our duty to watch over him. To keep this place safe for him, and everything else in the garden."

"Don't worry, little guy," Evan said, "you can trust us to care for you until your mother comes. We'll watch over you and make sure no harm comes to you." For the first time ever, Evan experienced the serious weight of maternal responsibility. "We will take care of this planet for you," she vowed.

"He will be the monarch one day," Dayana said. "After Elara passes, he will carry on the hive."

"And he is why Elara will be willing to negotiate?" Evan asked.

"She is his mother. She wants him to develop and grow. Our children are why all of us do what we do, isn't it?" Dayana said. "We negotiate, we advocate, we fight for what we need as a people, if we have to. But most of all, we protect. We make sure there is a safe place for our children to thrive. If we don't, who will?"

"Is that why you're here? To protect the children?"

"My children are the trees and the animals," she said. "The water, the land, the air—"

"*Life*," Evan whispered. "That's the reason for all of it."

"Yes, that is right."

"Life in all its many varied forms."

The air surrounding them seemed to sparkle. Not just like dust motes in a ray of sunshine, but actual sparkles. Glittering air. Whether Dayana noticed, Evan didn't know.

"Life is rare and beautiful and truly precious," Dayana said. "Do you know how vast the universe is?"

Evan thought of her travels with Dmitri and Alexandria. She could honestly say that it was "unthinkably so."

"And how many places, do you believe, sustain life?"

"My guess would be not many," Evan said. "Earth and maybe Jupiter seem to be the only ones in this solar system, so I'm sure it's just as rare in the other galaxies."

"You're right."

The babe closed his tiny eyes, and Dayana placed him back in the basket with its moss bedding. He turned over in his pot and settled peacefully.

"Elara will come," Dayana said, "and she will desire a solution for herself, her people, and her child."

"But will she like our ideas for the future?" Evan asked.

"All we can do is hope," Dayana said, and then she gasped and called out, "Elara! You made it."

Evan followed Dayana's gaze across the room and caught sight of a bright silver creature who presence turned her skin to gooseflesh.

Chapter 30

Dmitri

Bright afternoon sun poured through the oculus and Dmitri gazed wide-eyed upon it. "I only make her stronger," he said through a mental haze of deep contemplation.

Alexandria turned toward him. "Who do you make stronger?"

"Miranda. And I know what I have to do," he said. "I must tell her that if she doesn't stand down, I will break the oneness. I must convince her I will disconnect."

"But how will that help?"

"She's not like Caroline. She cannot create the oneness in her true form. If I extricate myself, the oneness will end. Miranda will have no means of commanding the clones. She can proclaim leadership, but the clones won't obey her."

"Tell her," Alexandria said. "You must tell her."

Her adamance surprised him. He turned to her with a questioning squint. "You would be happy for me to extricate myself?"

"I'm sorry, Dmitri," she said, her cheeks brightening

red with shame, "but you almost didn't come back from the 'out there.' I know what happened to David, and I don't want it to happen to you."

She was right. He'd been stuck. What happened to David could happen to him. It nearly *did* happen to him.

"Do you remember what it felt like to be ordinary?" she said.

He thought of his mother first, then their Russian home and how he sometimes used his human mind to shoot paper balls across Alexandria's bedroom. He remembered days in the park and talking to Aunt Helena and Uncle Ivan, and nights when he and Mother watched movies together, staying up late into the night. "I do remember," he said.

"I miss it," Alexandria said. "I miss home."

He took her hand. "We have to finish this."

She squeezed his fingers. The familiar gesture meant everything to him.

"Yes. Finish it, Dmitri, please let's finish it."

He straightened his back and took his cross-legged stance upon the stool. "Miranda!" he called internally. "Leave Great-grandmother and her people alone."

In a nanosecond, he'd located her through the oneness and pictured the scene: Miranda stood on one side of a door, with Great-grandmother, Natasha, and the others on the opposite side.

"There you are," Miranda said with a droll smile. "Where have you been? I need your help."

"I can see that," Dmitri said.

"Well then, open the door to this docking station. I don't want to have to kick it down."

She spoke in a calm way, but he sensed her frustration.

"I don't feel that you are in a position to make demands," Dmitri said.

"I don't care what you *feel*, child. I wear the keeper's ring, and you will obey me."

"Caroline can work the oneness simply by taking her Jovian form, but you cannot," he continued. "You and she do not have the same abilities."

"Every royal has different abilities. There's no need to state the obvious."

"You need me to create the oneness for you," he said.

"Not true. Any Jovian can fulfill your role."

That, he suspected, was a lie meant to hurt him. David had chosen him because of his telepathic abilities. Not every Jovian excelled in the oneness. Like Miranda had said a moment before, every royal has different abilities.

"Is that so?" Dmitri asked.

"That is *not* so," Caroline's voice cut straight through the oneness.

His father's voice followed: "Stop her. She must be stopped."

After that, a chorus of Jovians called to him, chanting, "Stop her. Stop her. She must be stopped."

Dmitri, resting in his usual pose upon the stool, uncrossed his legs and let them hang down. As he swung his limbs back and forth, the oneness glitched. Sparks crossed the oculus overhead.

"I am the one who connects with the oneness so that you, too, can connect with the oneness. It's your only way to communicate with the clones. What good will it be to take this world down to the bare bones and not be able to control those who remain?"

Miranda didn't answer.

"That is your plan, isn't it?" he said.

In his mind, he watched Miranda turn away from the locked door, to stride down the corridor. "You vowed to work with me," she said.

"No, I did not. And you lied. You said you were the keeper at Caroline's behest. But Caroline isn't the keeper, and you knew that. You have never believed in the keeper."

"Dmitri, please," she said in a much friendlier tone. "I have a plan for the Jovians, for a renewed Earth. One that's better than before. We can build the new world together, if you'll just remain loyal to me. If you'll just . . . trust me."

"Trust must come from within. It cannot be forced upon a person. And I was never loyal to you. The oneness isn't meant to be used as a tool of manipulation or destruction. It is meant to bring beings together, to share information and education, to warn others of potential hazards."

"I'm warning you now," she said. "Join me or there will be repercussions."

He was ready to stand. For the first time since he arrived at this place, he would release the oneness, neglect his responsibility. This would not be easy. Forces would act against him, try to stop him. When he took David's place, the stool and his body snapped together like two parts of a Neodymium magnet, and now that he contemplated severing those parts, the stool beneath him vibrated at a higher frequency, intent on keeping him there.

He moved his foot toward the ground, and an invisible power drove him back. His skinny leg shook with the effort. *I will do this.*

The Jovians called to him: "Stop her. She must be stopped."

As he continued to press, he began to grow warm, then to sweat. *I must do this.*

His strength persevered, and the chant in his mind grew louder—he sensed the energy of others joining him, nurturing his efforts. He concentrated on the task at hand, knowing what he had to do, knowing there was no other way.

The force began to recede. Just a little bit at first, just enough to make him believe stepping down was possible.

"Stop her. Stop her. She must be stopped," the Jovians cried, and his foot stomped the floor as if it weighed as much as a boulder.

Dmitri was standing on one leg. The majority of his weight remained balanced on the seat; the second leg, still suspended from the stool. He breathed heavily, and the knee he relied on to hold up his body buckled then straightened, then buckled again. It required all of his concentration to force it straight. His body trembled, and when he went to wipe the sweat upon his lip, his arm flew up like a misdirected airplane and crashed into his cheek.

The misdirection was all too familiar, and he smiled. *My old body is coming back.*

"Dmitri, stop," Miranda begged. "Can't you see? The universe wants you on that stool. That's where you're meant to be. Do you dare go against the desires of the universe?"

"The oneness was never supposed to be used the way Great-grandmother used it, and it's not meant to be used the way you want to use it, either," he told her.

"You're shaking and sweating," Alexandria said. "Are you all right? Maybe you shouldn't—"

"Listen to your caregiver!" Miranda said. "Don't disconnect. You're reverting to your original form. Becoming an ordinary human. If you put that second foot on the ground, there will be no turning back. You'll spend the rest of your life in a wheelchair. Is that what you want?"

What Dmitri wanted was to be himself again.

He fought to get his suspended leg to obey, to reach for the ground. He wanted to break the oneness, and he wanted his body back, both in equal measures.

"I will kill your family if you do this," Miranda shouted. "I will go to your mother's house in Russia, and I will track down your caregiver, who could never protect you against someone like me."

Alexandria said, "Don't listen to her!"

Dmitri continued to fight the force that defied him. Streams of sweat rode the sides of his face, his muscles jerking and jumping and reclaiming lives of their own. He moved his leg inch by inch, begging the stool, and the universe that guided it, to let him go.

"I can be your protector, if you'll let me," Miranda promised. "Please, Dmitri, I want to take care of you!"

His foot reached the floor, and the stool fell backward. He stood four and a half feet tall. But it wasn't over, he knew. The hot, prickling energy David had given him trickled downward and began to pool at his feet. It rose slowly into his ankles. Soon it reached his knees and then his thighs. It passed through his middle, moving beyond his liver and stomach, up into his chest, swelling and growing in pressure. He wondered if he was about to burst.

The energy stretched through his neck and moved like a shadow into his skull, hovering at first, then circling like a raptor. Everything he could see—the observatory walls, Alexandria in his peripheral vision, Miranda frightening his family and friends in the docking station—donned a neon-green tinge that grew more brilliant by the second. So bright and powerful, it surely would not remain put for much longer.

All at once, his head snapped backward as if something pulled him by his hair, and a bright bolt of glowing-green electricity shot out of his eyes. Like a loosed arrow, it threaded through the center of the oculus and whistled its way into the clouds. Thunder cracked and sparks rained down.

Alexandria gasped, and he sensed her jump back, out of harm's way. "Dmitri!" she screamed.

The projectile of energy continued to flow out of him, seeking the deep reaches of the universe. He didn't know when it would stop, or *if* it ever would. With each exhale, he thought it was nearly there, wherever *there* might be—but the green light continued to flow, seeking whatever it sought, traveling to wherever it needed to go.

And then it happened: The oneness heaved. He saw it in his mind. The pointed head of the green energy sliced through the threads that anchored the oneness. The threads came apart, allowing others to loosen. And the fabric of the oneness, once taut and vivacious and filled with all of the varied parts of the cosmos, took a staggering breath as if it had been stabbed.

At first it hurt Dmitri the same way it hurt to have the wind knocked out of him. There was a surprise to it, and a suddenness, a gasping for breath followed by a subtle righting of the situation. He was still alive, still breathing, still standing on his two feet, though he was not the same person he'd been a few moments before.

The oneness would not be the same, either. It may have bore the wound and continued to hold for now, but it had suffered a fatal blow. Dmitri sensed it would not survive for long.

His consciousness pulled back, retreating from the "out there," returning to him, finding its way into his mind. It trickled like water. Gently, humanly.

It was done.

Dmitri slouched with exhaustion. "I'm going to step out of the circle now," he said breathily.

In his mind, the family called to him, "Stop her. Stop her. She must be stopped."

With bile in her voice, Miranda continued to command

him: "Get back on that chair and undo what you've done. You cannot leave your post! Do not do this, or I'll blow up this entire place. I have the means, and I swear I will do it, starting with Starbright and ending with the rest of the world. I'm coming up there, Dmitri. Do not leave your post!"

He let that sit for a moment, his thoughts afloat in the silence. He had disconnected. All he could do now was rely on the goodness of the universe to pull through.

"I-ah hope that you won't," he said, and he stepped out of the circle.

Chapter 31

Fran

This was good. They were getting away. Dmitri secured the door behind them, and Miranda wasn't coming through, which Fran had to assume meant she wasn't able.

Caroline, however, did not look good. Hardly conscious at this point, she'd said her piece to Miranda, loud and firm, and it had taken just about everything she had left to give. With her eyes closed and the stress of pain and injury pulling her face long, he worried she was coming to her end.

Death was not an option for Caroline.

He needed her to stay alive for more reasons than one. For many millions of reasons: First and foremost, the survival of the entire planet might depend on it. No, she wasn't the keeper, but her connection to Earth was undeniable. Fran wouldn't let her die. She once told him that if she died, so would Earth, and there was no way in hell he was going to chance it.

They needed to get away now.

Natasha limped ahead, with Max at her side. She

didn't look much better than Caroline at this point. Another battered soldier in need of safe haven.

No one spoke as they walked the never-ending corridor. Fran hoped they'd come upon Natasha's spaceship soon. All of them stumbled now and again because they were worn out, the lack of conversation a product of their exhaustion.

Wait. Where was Svetlana?

He turned as much as he could without throwing Caroline off balance. Svetlana lagged several steps behind. Her face said it all: the wheels of her mind spinning behind a frowning veil of distress.

"What are you thinking back there?"

With a small shudder, she popped out of her thoughts. "What am I always thinking?" she said. "Evan, of course."

"Catch up and come talk to me." He passed Caroline to Lisa and allowed them to move ahead, then joined Svetlana and her slow pace.

"We're heading for the ship that can take me back home, and now I don't want to leave. I can't abandon her, Fran."

"Have you considered that Natasha might be right? That maybe Evan wants to stay."

"Of course I have. The last time I saw Evan, she told me she needed to stay. But does that mean it's what she should do?"

"I don't know," he said. "It's been my experience that Jovians have really good intuition. So, if she feels she's meant to be here, I think we can probably trust that."

"*Probably*," Svetlana said with a huff. "I don't like *probablies*, Fran."

"Well, sometimes they're all we've got."

"It's not good enough," she said.

"Look, Evander was a natural born leader. Maybe

Evan is too. Yes, they grew up in different worlds, but they have a lot in common—most notably their parents. Face it, your children are special. It's impossible for you and Andrew not to produce a special kid."

The thought seemed to hit her with the delight of surprise, and she laughed a little. That laugh. Seemed he hadn't heard it in ages.

"Lucky me," she said.

"We're gonna be okay. No matter what. You and I always figure things out eventually, right?"

She didn't say anything in response, and he sensed her reluctance to give in.

"And what about Caroline?" she said. "What are we going to do with her?"

"What do you mean?"

"She can't travel to my world."

"Why not?"

"There are no Jovians where I live. It's a universe without Jovians."

He leaned in close to her and whispered: "I'm not sure whether you've noticed but she's pretty human right now."

"Is she?" Svetlana raised her brows.

"Have you not seen her?"

"Even if she is, she doesn't deserve a second chance. Besides, she's supposed to stand up for the planet. Like a captain who goes down with the ship. She's not supposed to duck her head and run."

A rumbling sound in the distance caused the structure above their heads to vibrate and shudder. Flashing lights bounced across the walls and raced to unknown destinations.

"What is that?" Svetlana shouted. "What's happening?"

The others had moved significantly ahead by now, and

Fran started to jog, pulling Svetlana along with him to make sure she followed. "Whatever it is, we don't have time to argue."

"You're saying I have to leave Evan here, but Caroline is allowed to come?"

He didn't know how to answer. There was little logic in the question.

"I'm saying we have to go now, or Miranda will find a way to enter this place, and I'm not going to leave you to fend for yourself," he said. "Andrew's been gone a long time, but when he died, I vowed to help you out any way I could, and I don't know if you remember this about me, but I keep all my vows."

Up ahead, one of the ship's doors rose. Natasha and Max slowed to a stop in front of it. Natasha stumbled inside; Max followed a step behind her.

"I can take care of myself," Svetlana said. "I'm going to get Evan." She pulled back and slipped out of Fran's grasp. "Leave without me if you have to."

"No." He lunged at her. "Not this time."

He grabbed her by the arm. She twisted in an attempt to free herself. When he didn't let go, she stopped struggling, and they stared at one another. Her Baltic Sea blue eyes brimmed with coldhearted determination; they were downright icy, full of steel. As he held her angry gaze, something soft crept in, something vulnerable and sad. She was scared.

"I know you're right," she said, her voice quivering. "I don't know why I'm still fighting."

"Get on the ship, Svetlana," Natasha said from inside. "You're meant to leave."

Svetlana nodded with a couple of angry jerks of her head. "Fine. I'll come," she said. Then she turned to Fran and whispered "Thanks."

He didn't know if she wanted it to sound sarcastic, but it did.

"Uh, one problem, guys," Lisa said. She still had a good part of Caroline's body weight draped across her shoulders. "There are only three pods."

Shit. Fran entered the ship and saw for himself.

"Double up," Natasha said with a worrisome cough as she staggered into the pilot's seat.

Chapter 32

Evan

The strange silvery being walked in without making a sound, and shivers sprang up all over Evan's skin. Evan bowed her head, as if her body recognized this as the proper thing to do when in the presence of royalty, even if Evan didn't.

So this was a Moon Child, up close and in person. Evan could barely see her, she shined so bright . . . and blurry.

"Welcome," Dayana said. "We are delighted to have you."

Elara placed one three-fingered hand on her chest and extended the other, first touching Dayana's shoulder and then Evan's.

The child in the basket at Evan's feet stirred underneath its blanket of moss. Evan lifted the basket and offered it to Elara. It was hard to believe the little bark-colored blob would one day glow the way its mother did.

Elara pulled the child from the basket and petted its head. Then she proceeded to make clicking sounds of the sort Evan had never heard. It was all so surreal, and she wondered how she came to be in this place, at this time. With all the happenings that happened every day, how was it that she became involved in these otherworldly circumstances?

After a moment, Elara replaced the babe to the basket and put the basket on one of the potting tables. She then approached Dayana. The two of them stood at about the same height. Evan didn't know if Dayana observed the same way ordinary humans did, but when Evan looked at Elara, her eyes clouded up in a sort of numb and watery way.

The two stood like that, face-to-face, not speaking out loud, not doing anything that Evan could see. They might have been meeting on another plane, for all Evan knew.

After what stretched into a long moment, Evan sensed a change in the air and soon after that, Dayana spoke: "Elara has agreed."

Evan, afraid to show emotion or any response that might sway this fragile moment, said only, "That is wonderful." Meanwhile, her insides tingled with elation.

"Elara and her hive will inhabit Antarctica. She is grateful. She has plans to raise pine forests and possibly some plants native to Europa."

"More trees for the planet. That's great," Evan said, smiling in Elara's direction.

"Max said I could have the seeds," Elara said.

A breeze could have blown Evan over at that moment. *Elara speaks!* Evan's scalp buzzed in a not unpleasant (not exactly pleasant) way. She wasn't sure how to respond but felt she had to say something. "I know Max. He's Fran and Lisa's son."

At the same moment, Dayana stepped back and dropped her head in her hands. "Oh no. No, no, no!"

"What is it," Evan said. "What happened?"

"Miranda has a device—" she said, as if watching a scene in her mind play out. "Your mother and Natasha are nearby with some of the others. Caroline is there," she said with urgency.

"Maybe they're taking Mom back home," Evan said. "She didn't want to come here in the first place. She only did it for me."

"I'm not sure there's time."

"Time for what? For them to get away?" Evan asked.

"You'll have to tell them to go now, tell them to hurry."

Evan raced across the room. "I don't know my way. Do I just follow the tube?" She waited for Dayana to open the door.

"Not like that," Dayana said. "Use the oneness."

"Mom's not in the oneness."

"But *you* are. You have the skills. You can do it," Dayana said. "Just try."

"But I've never spoken to my mother this way. I don't think it will work."

It had taken Evan days to bring the oneness under control, for it to ramble like a docile stream through her mind instead of a steady brook of chaos. She feared that if she opened it up again, it would overwhelm her, drop her back into that horrible, uncomfortable state, and ruin her chance to speak to her mother.

"This is important, Evan. Tell them to leave—and tell your mother goodbye. I'm sorry, but it may be your last chance."

A hot shiver raised Evan's hair. "To talk to her? Like, ever?" Her heart pounded as a surge of adrenaline swept her into overdrive. She had to do this now. Evan calmed herself as much as she could and listened for the oneness, lugging it to the forefront of her mind.

"Mom," she said, as if speaking into a void. "Mom, are

you there? Please answer. Mom!" She waited a second, then shouted, "This isn't working. I have to go down there."

Dayana patted the air with her hands and stepped in front of Evan. Her understanding aura seemed to penetrate Evan's skin and embrace her. *It's all right, it's all right.*

"You are the future, my dear," Dayana told her gently. "This is an uncertain moment. You must stay here with me. Together, in this sacred space, we will hope that the danger shall pass."

With that, Evan's overzealousness fell back to Earth and the responsibility she owed this place, this planet, grounded her. She trusted Dayana, the keeper of the greenhouse and all of its trees—of Elara's child—and all of Earth's many forms of life. *This* was the most important role Evan would ever play. She was more than a daughter, more than a child, more than a person who wanted to do good. *This* moment was why the cosmos had called to her.

"I understand," she said.

"Talk to your mom through the oneness," Dayana said, nodding as she spoke. "You have the skills."

"What if she doesn't respond?"

"She will receive the message, I promise."

Chapter 33

Dmitri

Dmitri stepped out of the light and collapsed into Alexandria's arms, his limbs jerking, his mind flooding with happiness and love and thoughts of returning home from a very long journey.

"I've got you," Alexandria said as the two of them sank to the floor. "I've got you."

He lay down, twitching and jerking, while he caught his breath. He struggled to sit up with her help. "We-ah have to go now. Do you know where my wheelchair is?"

"No idea," she said, with a crazy laugh. "I feel like we've been released from mind prison, don't you? And I'm hungry. So hungry!"

"We have not eaten in a long time," he said.

"We haven't done a lot of things in a long time," she said. "How are we even alive right now?"

"We have no time to talk," he said. "Miranda has a plan, a very bad plan."

"Don't tell me. I don't want to know." She squatted in front of him and tipped her head in a gesture toward her back. "I'll carry you away from this place the same way I brought you to it."

"On piggyback," he said with a giggle. It felt so good to smile. "Yes."

He still sensed the oneness hovering. Waning but still there. He could see Miranda racing through the docking station. She was coming for him and Alexandria, and her anger burned red hot.

He climbed onto Alexandria's back, wrapped his arms around her shoulders and squeezed as best he could with his skinny legs.

"Good?" she asked.

"Go-ah!" he said. "Please be fast."

"I will try," Alexandria said, grunting as she stood. In a few quick steps, she'd exited the door to the tube.

Dmitri's throat constricted with regret. He would miss the observatory's light most of all. The light and the energy and the "out there," all of which were already fading from his mind, becoming a fuzzy memory. Like dreams so glorious in sleep that disappear with the morning light, the "out there" was siphoning away, impossible to draw back.

The door closed behind them, and the tube's fluorescent light made him squint.

"It will-ah be okay," he said, and Alexandria answered with "I hope so."

"Hurry," he said again. They had to make it through the tube before Miranda caught up.

Chapter 34

Svetlana

The spaceship's door closed with a metal clack, then sealed with a high-pitched squeal. The air pressure rose, making Svetlana's ears pop, then settled. Regulated, she supposed.

"This is Natasha's ship, the one that refused to work last time," Svetlana said, still feeling like she was betraying Evan by leaving.

"It'll be fine, Grandmother," Natasha said with a cough as she busily worked from her captain's chair.

She'd been coughing on and off since her e-skin tore, and Svetlana found it more than a little worrisome. If they made it home, they'd have to figure out a way to fix it.

How can I leave without saying goodbye to Evan? I'm so sorry, sweetheart, but this is what you wanted, she thought.

"I don't see why it'll be any different today," Svetlana muttered, half hoping the ship *wouldn't* work and they'd be stuck there. But Miranda was out there, so no, she couldn't hope for that.

"Just stay in your pod," Fran said from the one beside hers. "Are you two okay, Lisa?"

"As much as we can be," she answered. "Are we sure it will sustain two of us?" Lisa had been the last to climb into the pod she'd share with Caroline. She and Fran had laid Caroline, mostly nonresponsive, to one side, with enough room for Lisa to lay on the other.

"Yes, it definitely will, Mom." Max stood in between the pods and the cockpit, looking as fidgety as a teenager. If anyone looked worried, Svetlana thought, he did. "The covers of the pods will come down automatically," he said. "You don't have to do anything. Just stay in place."

Then he returned to Natasha and, grabbing the back of her chair, observed the flight controls over her shoulder. Svetlana could still see them from where she lay.

"Have you primed the thrusters?" he asked.

"Yes."

"What about the sensors, did you check the—"

"Do we have permission?" Svetlana shouted the second she thought of it.

Natasha said, "We have Caroline. She's the one who grants permission. And, yes, I've checked everything." She pressed her hand into the middle of her chest and pulled the two ripped sides of her e-skin together as she concentrated on the screen in front of her.

Max watched Natasha closely, that familiar blend of love and worry tensing the muscles in his jaw. "Let me think." He plunked into the chair beside hers.

"Helmets!" he said.

"Not needed for a time trip—but feel free if you want to."

"But then why the pods?"

"Just buckle in," she said. "The pods are a precaution."

"Oh, right. Good. You know I've never done this before." He settled in the chair and clipped the sides of the harness together in several places.

The sound of the clicking keyboard continued. Then Natasha took a shaky breath and angrily shook her head.

"We'll figure it out," Max said. "Time trips are tricky. Sometimes it has nothing to do with the ship. Or the pilot. I mean, from what I've heard."

"I know. That's true," Natasha said. "When Evan and I tried to time-trip here, we needed Svetlana to join us before it would work. It's completely . . . unpredictable."

"Yeah," Max said. "I've heard stories from other pilots."

He reached out and took Natasha's hand in his own, and that was it: A forceful thrust emerged out of nowhere and pressed Svetlana and the others through time.

Chapter 35

Evan

Below their feet, the floor of the greenhouse seemed to come alive, shuddering and groaning. "What's happening? Why is the floor shaking?" Evan asked. At the same time, the oneness amped up in her mind, the stream of voices grew louder, individual cries rising up from the general din.

"Stop her!" they said. "We must stop her."

"Quickly!" Dayana clapped her hands twice. "Evan, go to the central wall. Elara, take the one opposite."

While Evan headed for her assigned place, Elara went to the basket that held the babe. A group of plants surrounded it like loosely spaced hedges. Elara paused for a few seconds to observe before adjusting his moss blanket.

"Yes, yes," Dayana told her, "he'll be safe there."

Elara stepped away and stood beside the wall in which Dayana had instructed her to stand.

"Press one palm to the glass," Dayana said.

All three of them did so, and right away Evan felt something like electricity snapping and beaming between them. They were connected, like a closed circuit.

The vibration in the floor ramped up. It tingled the bottom of Evan's feet and her ankles, then creeped up her calves as it grew in strength. She assumed one of the ship's engines geared up for liftoff. Maybe it was Natasha's. Maybe her mom and the others were getting away.

Hope shined a light through her dark, worried thoughts.

A deep hum filled her ears. The sun became covered in cloud and the room darkened; the vibe became unbearably ominous. "Stop her," the chorus in Evan's mind sang. "She must be stopped."

"Is it Miranda?" Evan asked. "Is she doing this? Or are the others—"

The babe cried out.

Elara removed her hand from the wall. The circuit broke, and Evan stifled the "No!" that attempted to leap from her mouth. Elara went to her crying child. She hovered over him. Bent to kiss him.

Please come back, please come back, Evan internally begged.

Or was this okay? Would the greenhouse be safe without Elara's input? Why didn't Dayana call Elara back?

Across the room, Dayana appeared to be in a trance. Hadn't she realized the circuit had been broken?

The sight of the mother bobbing her child conjured Evan's thoughts of her own mother, her earliest memories. Playing in the backyard. At the beach. Being dropped off at school the very first day. Svetlana's presence was a constant in her life, always so caring and strong. And at the moment, it broke her heart. Evan prayed Svetlana received the message she'd sent through the oneness. Her mother hadn't responded, but that didn't mean she didn't get it.

Elara continued to comfort her child.

The humming atmosphere grew in intensity. The

vibration below Evan's feet rattled her eardrums and threatened to become overbearing.

"Have they gone yet?" Evan cried out. "Is this the sound of their ship? My mother, Natasha, the others?"

"Stay put, Evan," Dayana said in an unwavering tone. "We must save the greenhouse. The trees. The *life*."

"I know. I'm here. I'm staying."

The voices in the oneness continued to chant, "Stop her. She must be stopped."

The babe cried out, and Evan began to cry as well, tears riding the slopes of her cheeks. Was this it? The end of her life? The end of the world?

Elara turned to her. Her body, a gentle, watery glow. She looked upon Evan with the same kindness and attention she offered her own child, a kindness Evan swore she could feel inside her body as if Elara's light penetrated her skin and took the raw redness out of her frightened feelings.

Evan removed her palm from the wall and then replaced it.

Something happened.

When she replaced her hand to the wall, she felt a connection occur. Energy snapped and beamed between herself and Dayana.

She was about to shout, "It's back," but when she looked up, Elara was no longer there. The babe lay in his basket on the table. In her peripheral vision, Evan saw a ray of light flash across the room and pass through the door.

"She's gone," Evan whispered, mortified. "Elara is gone. She left the babe."

"Take her place at the wall opposite," Dayana commanded. "We will have to do it without her. Trust in the universe."

Evan did as she was told.

She raised her palm to the glass wall and hoped for the best.

Chapter 36

Miranda

Miranda strode through the tube, all the while grumbling to herself. "Did he dare leave his post? But how can that be when he's the supreme one?"

And then she remembered, this particular supreme being was half human. Unpredictable and bubbling with free will.

The oneness was waning. It felt like a bloodletting. Her life force, pouring out. Her power dwindling.

In a panic, she burst through the observatory door and froze at the sight of the empty stool. The lack of light. Rock walls steeped in dark, unwelcoming gray. Damp and cool. Already growing mold. Dmitri's absence lurked in the shadows.

He was gone. He and his human protector. But how? Where did they go? She never imagined he would actually do this. Become human again. *Why would he do this?*

She attempted to use the oneness to reach Caroline, to demand she call Dmitri back to his post. This was Caroline's doing, no doubt. "You haven't won," Miranda said, but the message went nowhere. To no one.

Caroline had escaped to another universe. Dmitri had extricated himself. The oneness was as good as dead. No one could hear her.

No one was listening.

She was losing. But did that matter? She could still do what she set out to do.

She stood in the center of the room and gazed up at the clouded oculus—it had seemed so glittering and alive when the boy and his guardian were there. Now it felt like nothing.

The quiet persisted. And then a voice reached out to her. It was Leo.

"Oh, Leo, they've gone."

"Don't do this, Miranda. We were wrong. I'm sorry, but we were wrong."

"The only one who was wrong was you!" she shouted as she sped out of the room and barred him from her mind. Reentering the tube, she strode back to the docking station. The door opened to an array of ships. Natasha's was once one of them. But now its berth lay empty.

With a braid of anger, frustration, and fear tightening her chest, she reentered the blue light of Starbright's base-ment. *It doesn't matter*, she told herself. *Caroline has escaped, but she is human and will die. Dmitri is gone, but one day yet another supreme being will rise. I am meant to be the leader of this planet. I will return it to Jovian rule no matter how long it takes.*

She crossed the wide, mostly empty space and reached the saucer-shaped vehicle sitting pretty in the middle.

Upon her touch, its door raised open.

She climbed in. Took the captain's chair. Eyed the shiny black button she would soon press to activate the device. *I am willing to sacrifice hundreds of years. That's how much*

I love the Earth. One day, Jovians everywhere will call me a hero. And where will Caroline be? Dead, like the rest of humanity.

The door closed, and she stared out the viewport. From the corner of her eye, she saw something transparent and shiny—like crystal—floating in the air. Was it a winged thing? Something . . . shimmering. Like a cluster of gnats swarming in sunlight. Or rays of moonlight. Yes, silvery, sparkling moonlight.

A Moon Child, it occurred to her.

Could it be Elara?

The lighted swarm moved closer to the ship, and as it did, it took on the shape of a body, a body with a telltale oval head and thin, glistening limbs. This glittery being came very close to the *Umbra*'s viewport and peered inside. Miranda sat perfectly still as the two of them studied each other through the pane that divided them.

She flushed with the warmth of satisfaction. "Eliminating you will be easier than I thought," she said and reached for the deadly black button.

Chapter 37

Dmitri

Dmitri and Alexandria came to the end of the tube and entered the big, mostly empty red-glowing room.

"Ugh, I hate these lights," Alexandria complained. "My eyes don't want to stay open."

Dmitri knew what she meant. But his eyes were open, and he saw oxygen tanks and medical kits. Boxes of bandages and NOxygen clips.

A man stood beside the far wall. He wore a red doctor's jacket—or maybe, with normal lighting, the jacket would be white.

"Wait, Alexandria," Dmitri said. "Someone is here."

"Where?" She turned too quickly, jostling Dmitri, who clung to her back.

The man raised his forearm and gave a little wave.

"Hello?" Dmitri said.

"Yes, hello. I-I'm here for you, I think," the man said. "I sensed something. It wasn't the oneness exactly, but something else. An 'intuition,' I believe it's called. I felt I needed to come here and wait."

"And what are you waiting for?" Dmitri said.

"You are Dmitri, correct?"

"Yes."

The man nodded. "I'm not sure exactly why I'm here. I just spent the past several days trying to save the last of the Leonards, but Miranda interfered, and I just—"

"You are Andy," Dmitri said. "The doctor."

The man nodded. His shoulders rounded over with sadness and exhaustion, Dmitri assumed. "Anyway, I brought this wheelchair," Andy said, gesturing behind himself. "Can you use one of these?"

"Thank goodness," Alexandria said. "Yes, we can."

"Good, good," Andy said. "If you're leaving now, I can bring it down the stairs for you."

"That would be great." Alexandria readjusted Dmitri's weight on her back.

"Just one more thing," Andy said. "Have you seen Miranda? I know it's strange for me to ask, but she wanted me to wake the three-point-zeros, and I—I don't know why I'm telling you this, but for some reason, I think it's important for you to know."

"Oh." Dmitri paused as a surge of nerves set his limbs in jerky motion. "Did you wake them?"

"I didn't," Andy said. "I couldn't get myself to do it. They aren't, um, well, no one wanted—"

"It's okay," Dmitri said. "You-ah did the right thing."

"I put them to rest." Andy averted his eyes as if he expected to be punished for it.

"Good. We have to go," Dmitri said.

"Oh, okay, yes." Andy turned and reached for the wheelchair. "Go ahead and I'll follow."

"Thank you so much," Alexandria said. "Lugging Dmitri around is not as easy as it looks. Please hurry."

She rushed out the exit door and took the cement set of stairs too quickly for Dmitri's liking.

The doctor followed. When he reached the bottom of the staircase, he unfolded the chair and placed it in front of them.

Sweat already dampened Alexandria's hairline as she helped Dmitri transfer from her back to the chair.

"You look like an Andy," Dmitri said, his noodly lips attempting a smile. "And that makes you-ah part of my family, doesn't it?"

"*Your* side of the family, not mine," Alexandria specified.

Andy smiled. "I'm a clone of your grandfather. Obviously."

"You realize you have to come with us," Dmitri said. "It's not safe here. We must leave right now."

Andy gazed sadly at the building beside them. "She's going to destroy this place, isn't she?"

"Yes, Andy, and we must-ah run."

"This way," Alexandria said, pushing Dmitri across the parking lot.

The three of them raced into the safety of the forest.

Chapter 38

Miranda

With the button of the device depressed, Miranda leaned into the back of the pilot's seat and waited for it to build power and detonate. "Only a minute," Leo had told her. "Sixty seconds. That's all it takes."

The mechanism buzzed at first, then made a deeper sound, lower in tone. An ominous drone.

It's working. Miranda closed her eyes.

She would gladly sacrifice hundreds of years. Hundreds of years of recovery to wake as queen. She opened her eyes and gazed down at her hand. Caroline's ring, the blue sapphire, was hers. And when she woke, all would bow to her. The survivors. The strong. The Jovians.

Through the window, the monarch continued to watch Miranda with eerie silence. Soon, though, she backed away and then raised both of her bright arms to shoulder height. Immediately, to either side of her, a line of Moon Children appeared at least fifty beings long. It spanned the center of the station, all silvery and light. And Miranda admitted they made a beautiful sight, one that couldn't hurt her as long as she stayed put, even if they were to transform into poison gas.

Instead of transforming, though, the Moon Children duplicated. And then duplicated again. And again, and again.

"What are you doing?" Miranda whispered.

In no time, there were hundreds of them crowded into the vast room, all of them surrounding her ship. Not as a vapor or fog, but as bodies lined up side to side. Thousands of duplicates duplicating over and over and over again, until Miranda couldn't see through them and their blurry, silvery, mind-numbing light.

They were as thick as a blizzard, like a wall of snow.

More and more and more. Their replication seemed infinite.

Fascinating, Miranda thought. And for one second, she was sorry she'd be incapacitated for so long. She'd miss this place. Miss the many wonders of this world.

The Moon Children and their glittering monarch would die, and that was not a shame. If the planet was to survive, they had to go.

Only seconds now, she thought, *until the new day begins*.

The droning device became so loud, it made static of Miranda's ears and crowded out the thoughts that occupied her mind.

And then there was a brilliant flash.

Chapter 39

Luna Liberi

Elara summoned her hive.

They arrived at the speed of thought.

A dense army of beings. Her protectors. Her bodies. Her tribe.

On this day, they would lend their protection to something else. Their new home. The Earth.

As the explosion occurred, the many layers of the hive materialized to stop it. The device incinerated the hive layer by layer by layer. There was no pain. Just loss followed by gain followed by loss. As long as Elara evaded the violence, the layers of the hive came back and back and back, duplicating again and again until they'd smothered the power of the decimating device.

There would be no sky-high explosion.

No killer cloud to starve the surviving human population.

Just a long, rumbling quake, terrible in scope.

Starbright would suffer a shaken foundation and cracked walls, but it would remain standing. Observatory connected; greenhouse intact; plants very much alive.

Only the *Umbra Alaris* and its pilot annihilated.

Chapter 40

Natasha

Natasha had never woken in the midst of a time trip before, but this one proved different. Perhaps because no one had ever tried to speak to her while she traveled before. To her surprise, it was Evan's voice that woke her sleeping mind. "We survived," she said. "The greenhouse and the babe and the Moon Children and the trees, we all survived.

"It was Elara," Evan said. "She and her hive. They saved us."

She mentioned the plan for all to coexist, and how Dana and John would lead the charge, teaching nonviolence and empathy. How the Coalition would join them as world leaders, along with President Abela. How they would start anew as a people and a planet once again.

Natasha wanted to respond, to tell her how wonderful all of this was, but like a dream switching to the next scene, Evan's presence faded, and Dmitri's emerged.

"Alexandria and I have left the observatory," he said. "The oneness is waning. I'm going back to Mother. I will live the life of an ordinary boy in Russia. You must live as well, Natasha. I feel you are ailing, and you must find a place where you can be happy. I'm sorry it can't be Earth."

She can't tell him the truth, can't tell him her e-skin has ripped and she knows she will not live. Her duties have been fulfilled. Her life will end prematurely as she always knew it would.

But her family was safe, so it was all right. She could let go.

She sank into the bodiless whoosh of time-tripping across the universe.

"You must live," Dmitri said, waking her once more.

"I love you," she answered, but she doubted he heard her. She couldn't breathe. A terrible pain had crept into the center of her chest, and the sweet swell of blackness was welcoming her in.

Chapter 41

Svetlana

"Get up, get up, hurry!" Fran's voice boomed with panic in her ears.

Svetlana blinked. Something hard and white surrounded her. A bathtub? She lay on her side. Where was she? Oh, the traveling pod. Her memory came back like the wind. She pressed up on both arms and found Fran and Lisa standing nearby in the cramped quarters of Natasha's spaceship. The time trip back to the universe without Jovians had worked!

Lisa and Fran gazed into the pod closest to the exit, their expressions dire. "We'll have to carry her," Fran said. "But her vitals are mostly good?"

"Considering what she's been through," Lisa said. "Grab her legs."

"Who is it?" Svetlana said. "Is it Evan?"

"Caroline," Fran answered. "You don't remember?"

Where was Evan? She wasn't there, unless she already —Svetlana grabbed her forehead and remembered with dizzying certainty that Evan hadn't returned with them.

In front of her, Max struggled to rouse Natasha, limp with unconsciousness, her head lulling toward the floor.

"What happened?" Svetlana asked. *My God, had they crashed? Was everyone dying?* "Is Natasha all right?"

"She's barely conscious," Max grumbled as he struggled to steady her. "I'm sure she'll be fine. You hear that, Natasha? You're going to be fine."

Natasha's e-skin hung open with ragged, thready edges, and Svetlana remembered how Miranda had ripped it before they ran for their lives. Svetlana climbed out of the pod and suffered a spin. She grabbed the co-pilot's chair for stability, then doubled over and gagged.

"I can help," she said as soon as she could speak.

Max said, "You sure?" Before he slung one of Natasha's listless arms over Svetlana's shoulder.

Svetlana patted Natasha's colorless cheek. Her beautiful face had the pallor of a sick person much older than the years she'd been alive. She'd aged again on this trip, maybe as much as ten years, and with her e-skin flapped open at the neck, Svetlana glimpsed her real skin, the pale, powder-pink of her chest—and a ruler-straight seam line. *Her surgery.* Did she have a mechanical heart? For a moment, Svetlana couldn't look away.

"Take her arm and hold it over your back so she balances out," Max said.

Svetlana did so, whispering, "I've got you," in Natasha's ear.

"You guys ready? Zero time to spare." Fran sounded like his old FBI agent self.

"Natasha, can you hear me?" Svetlana spoke into her ear. "Don't worry. We'll fix your e-skin. I can sew it. It'll be good as new."

"Open the door, Max," Fran said.

Max pressed a button on the control panel. The door

raised like a metal arm, inviting in the chill night air, which smelled like pine and chimney smoke and earthy, mulchy ground. *Home*, Svetlana realized. It smelled like home.

"Where are we, do we know?" she asked.

"The woods on the outskirts of town," Fran said. "I saw it coming up fast when we came in for a landing."

"You were awake for the landing?" Svetlana asked.

"Yeah, I was," he said. "Weren't you?"

"No," she said. "I have never been awake when I've traveled."

Fran shrugged. "Come on, guys. Let's move. I'm sure somebody saw this thing come down, and they'll be here any minute."

He and Lisa, with Caroline wobbling unconscious between them, stepped out. "Careful," Lisa said. "It's dark but the moon is out. Our sight will adjust quickly."

"All clear," Fran shouted. "Come on, Max."

"I thought we'd wake up on my deck at home," Svetlana muttered. "That would have made more sense."

Once outside the ship, she and Max stumbled over a few raised tree roots as they towed their unconscious cargo. The cool night air felt wonderful on her overexerted body.

Max looked back, unintentionally pulling Natasha off balance so that Svetlana almost lost hold of her.

"That's *not* Natasha's ship," he said. "It's not the ship we boarded at Starbright. What the hell?"

The light-russet-brown capsule left behind several yards of skid marks on the forest floor and had landed upright, like an acorn fallen from a tree. It was rounded on top and flat across its wider bottom, scribed with a ring of elongated hieroglyphs.

Svetlana knew this ship, had seen photos of it many times.

"It's exactly like the UFO that landed in Kecksburg,

the one from the 1960s," she said. "The famous Kecksburg UFO. Do you think—no, it couldn't be."

Fran waved them on. "Less talking, more walking, guys," he said. "When we get to the top of the hill, we can take a second to rest. Right now we have to keep moving."

They powered up the hill, slipping on pine straw and rocks until they reached the top. Svetlana left Natasha in Max's arms, so she could double over and catch her breath.

"Could it be that the beings who landed in the 1960s were actually us?" she asked Fran and Lisa as she struggled for breath.

"That's probably a good question for Caroline," Lisa said. "'Cause it's too weird for me."

"And me," Fran said. "But who knows? We'll find out what year it is sooner or later."

"But it wasn't us," Svetlana said, remembering the photos Andrew had shown her. "The beings on that ship were aliens. I saw pictures of them."

"I really don't know," Fran said. "This is a different universe, right? So anything is possible. What I do know is that we need to get out of here or a truckload of scientists in white coveralls are going to take us to a lab and study us."

In the distance, the headlights of cars flickered across the farm fields that led to the forest.

"There they are now," he said.

Lisa had already continued down the hill with Caroline. And Max lifted Natasha from the ground like a newlywed intent on crossing the threshold. With her gaze fixed on the spaceship, Svetlana couldn't convince herself to move on.

"Is this how it ends?" she implored Fran for an answer. "At the very beginning?"

Fran shrugged, raking his hand through his hair. "The important thing is we made it. We're alive. Two of us are sick, and I really hope they pull through, but the hows and whys of everything? All I can say is that strange things have been known to happen."

"Yes," Svetlana said. "If nothing else, that is true."

In the distance, a man shouted, "Over here. I found it!"

Svetlana sought out the sky and its knowing, twinkling stars, and shook her head. "What a crazy world we live in!"

"Yeah. Let's go see if you still have a house," Fran said.

"Oh no, I hadn't thought of that."

"It should be there," he added. "The neighborhood was built in the 1940s."

"You're right," she said, thankful for the reminder. "When Andrew first showed me the house, he said it was old but that it had good bones. That's why we remodeled it."

"That makes sense," Fran said.

She hoped so. She was so grateful to be there, grateful to be alive, to be away from Miranda and the Jovian ways, the world that teetered on disaster. Evan remained behind, and Svetlana wouldn't think about that just yet. For now, she would trust—trust that everything would be all right and she would be able to handle whatever came next— trust that some occurrences were inevitable and that some- times things actually did work out for the best.

Svetlana and the others continued down the hill and slowly crossed town, each of them lost in their own thoughts. The sun painted the horizon in pink and gray satin as it rose like a blazing beacon of hope showing them the way.

Epilogue 1

One Month Later
Natasha

Still in bed.

So tired of staring at the ceiling and the walls in Evan's teenaged room. After thirty days, Natasha had memorized every little piece of Evan's childhood from her white-painted furnishings to her school-age artwork to the crowded shelves and closet. Evan had posters of the moon and something called *Star Trek*—a popular television show, Max explained—some small handheld toys with screens of lighted blips that supposedly played games. Football? Baseball? Something like that. There were books, too, with covers featuring girls who rode horses, astronauts who ventured to Mars, aliens who took over the world. Natasha and Max shared a good laugh when they came across that one.

Observing Evan's things was about all Natasha had the energy for. Whenever she tried to leave the bed or put some of Evan's old clothing on, or even if she headed into the kitchen to get her own snack, Max spewed every reason known to man why she should stay put. The truth was, her heart pounded if she walked unassisted across the room, and that's why any doctor (human or Mintakan) would have prescribed bed rest—and she knew it.

Max often kept her company, entertaining her with books and news clippings and card games.

She'd told him she was prepared to die. Her life and death were written in the stars, just like everyone else's were, just like Uncle Jimmy had told her years ago, when he'd taken her to Mintaka for her heart surgery.

She would do something important and selfless—such as delivering Evan to the Jovian Earth, negotiating with Miranda (or trying to), and flying her grandmother home from another point in time—and that would be it.

Her heart. Her poor, old-beyond-her-years heart. . . . Once Miranda had ripped her e-skin, it didn't have a chance. It was only time before it rested in peace.

A couple of days after they landed, Grandmother had tried to fix the e-skin. She unburied her sewing kit from the closet in the hall and selected thread of a color that could only be described as an "imperfect match" but would have to do. Svetlana put on her reading glasses and sat on the sofa under the brightest light in the living room with Natasha draped across her lap. "This won't hurt a bit," she promised.

And she began to stitch together the six-inch gash.

As she did so, Natasha realized that Svetlana must have seen at least part of the scar the Mintakan doctors left behind—but she didn't say a word. And Natasha was grateful for that. She'd never seen the work they'd done, never had the courage to look.

Natasha had let Svetlana mend the e-skin, though she knew the repair would have no impact, good or bad, but when she'd seen the desperation in Svetlana's soulful eyes, when those eyes touched her with their solemn yearning to help, she knew just how badly Svetlana wanted to heal her.

Evan had stayed behind in the other world, just like she'd promised she would, and Natasha had helped make it happen.

A little guilt goes a long way, she thought.

The day after the sewing of the e-skin, when Natasha lay in Evan's bed staring at the ceiling, a letter from Evan arrived. A letter meant for Svetlana. It came not in the traditional, non-Jovian way, but via Natasha's mind. She wasn't sure how or why it happened. Natasha supposed it had been sent while she remained attached to the oneness —but either way there it was, in her mind, waiting for delivery.

It wasn't easy, reading that letter in her grandmother's presence. Though, in the midst of mourning Evan's absence, Svetlana had eagerly taken the chair beside Natasha's bed and listened.

Natasha began: "Hi, Mom, Dayana says you'll get my message even if you don't hear me as I speak. So here I go, using my new telepathic skills, though I have no idea what I'm doing. Starbright is under attack, and you are in the basement with Natasha and Caroline, and the Vasquezes. I wish I could come down there and be with all of you, but I can't. The future of the world is calling me, and I have to stay.

"I can't believe I'm saying these things, that this is even happening. But it is. It really is. Please know that I love you, Mom, and that I always have. In spite of our arguments, I've always felt like we were so close. I only hope that I can be as good a person as you are one day. As soon as I am able, I will visit you in your world, in *our* world, the same way Evander did.

"We will be okay, Mom. *I* will be okay, so, if it's at all possible, please don't worry about me. One day I will find my way back to you, I promise. Love, Evan."

When she had finished reading, Natasha hadn't known what to say. The letter's honesty had brought a quiver to her voice, but the words seemed to have given Svetlana some solace. She calmly nodded and thanked Natasha as she stood, then went straight to her room.

That had been three and a half weeks ago. And Natasha was still in bed.

She rubbed her head. Her scalp itched. Probably because she'd been taking long, hot baths every afternoon, her only activity outside of lying in bed and memorizing Evan's things. The water would have consoled her if only she could remove her e-skin and actually feel it. What she wouldn't do to submerge herself —but if she was going to submerge herself, let it be in the ocean or, better yet, a natural pool. Crystal clear and cold to the touch. She would float and dive and swim to her heart's content. Doing so wouldn't heal her, she knew, but maybe it would fill the emptiness of knowing what was to come.

She would soon die.

It didn't feel like the end of her life, but it was.

Max, on the other hand, refused to accept what she knew to be true. Over and over, he promised to find a way they could travel to Mintaka together, where the doctors could restore her to health, and her heart would beat freely in the proper way. This he pledged even though they lived in a universe without Jovians, in a place where Jovian technology did not exist and humankind did not travel to destinations located trillions of miles away.

Still, Max maintained his position. They would go "even if he had to build his own spaceship from scratch."

Ah. Here he was now. Handsome in his very ordinary blue jeans and cotton T-shirt. With his wide chest and healthy gait. She envied him. He looked like he could run a marathon and lift a sofa. Him and his smooth-as-silk complexion and glowing vibrance in his mocha cheeks. She wasn't afraid to admit how fond of him she'd become. And his fondness for her could not have been plainer.

It was nice, having someone who cared, feeling like she had a partner in this vast, mostly empty universe.

"Hey, guess what?" he said, entering the room a bit too cheerfully, the positivity a bit overdone.

"What," Natasha said without changing her flat-on-her-back position.

"Caroline spoke."

This was great news.

"Really," she said, her lack of energy reminding her she was not in the right mindset, or body-set, for celebration.

"My mother is ecstatic, you know, considering things seemed so touch-and-go for a while."

"Leave it to Great-grandmother to make yet another comeback," Natasha murmured with more humor in her voice than she actually felt.

"Just goes to show," Max said, arching his brows in a pushy manner, "you never know what can happen."

"Uh-huh," Natasha said, receiving his message loud and clear. "Except sometimes you do." She probably shouldn't have let that last part dribble out of her mouth.

Max dragged the wooden chair that he'd pushed into the corner of the room the prior night as close to the bedside as possible, and sat.

Natasha nudged the pillows against the headboard and

made the extra effort to be upright, her shoulders and back strained, as if her vitality had leaked out drop by precious drop the prior night. She wondered how gray her complexion might be at the moment. How sickly.

Max held her hand. His warmth—his life force—so evident when pressed up against her lack of it. "So, how are you feeling today?" he said, eyeing the stitches in her e-skin.

She turned her head away and grimaced. "Please don't ask."

"Do you want to play a game or maybe we could read some more of Evan's diary?"

He meant the notebook labeled "Evan's PRIVATE Thoughts." Written with old-fashioned handwriting. "Script," Max had called it. Entries that said things like "January 8: Tonight I went into the backyard and Dad brought his telescope into the sacred circle, and we scouted comets. Of course he had to point out Orion's belt for the millionth time. . . . "

Nosing into a thirteen-year-old's diary was not what Natasha wanted to do that day. She didn't want to play games or read, either. What she wanted to do was to face her truth. She was never going to get better. She'd spend the last days of her life in this bed, and Max needed to accept that.

"Sometimes when I go to sleep," she said, "my body becomes so heavy, like there are forces pressing down on me. One day it will push me so far that I won't—"

"Nope," he said with a curt shake of his head. "Not gonna let that happen."

She pursed her lips and beamed a Jovian stare at him. "Max," she said.

"I'm not kidding. I will find a way off this planet. You have to trust me. I've been working on it. We won't stay here. You will *not* die in this bed." The red of fierce determination rouged his cheeks.

"It's the 1960s," she said. "We need the technology of, I don't know, 2900, probably. Human progress does not move at the speed of light."

Max stood with a groan and headed for the door. She waited for him to pass through it, but instead he stopped. She heard him sigh before he backtracked to her bedside. He took her hand and squeezed it firmly. Tears glistened in his eyes. "I. Love. You." He spoke through a clenched jaw. Tears gathered and dropped upon his cheeks, but he didn't move to erase them, leaving them there for her to see.

His love felt like a raw, pulsing stab wound. Her whole body clenched around it, tried to fend off the damage it wielded. To hold it back. But she wanted it. She wanted to dive in and swim in it.

But the pain. She didn't want the pain that comes with loving.

Max lowered carefully onto the bed, lying beside her. He wrapped his arms around her, holding her with gentleness. It hurt so much to have her defenses breached. She imagined her soul, long guarded, oozing from the scars at the center of her chest, reaching out to him, touching him, connecting the two of them in spite of her self-inflicted cautiousness.

"I won't let you die," he whispered. "Not when you don't have to. We know you can live on Mintaka. We just have to find a way to get there."

"Okay," she answered. "But it may not be your choice to make."

He said nothing. Just stayed there with his arms firmly around her.

The satisfaction of being held, of connecting with him,

of settling into warmth and calm and quiet brought on drowsiness, and soon she drifted to sleep.

Dreams came. A blue-sky day. The sound of lapping water. Sun on her skin. Her *real* skin.

And then that familiar force arrived, the one that pushed her down. It pressed her underwater this time.

She was not afraid. She loved the water. It was so peaceful, so pure. If she could live anywhere, she would choose to live there. But being there meant holding her breath, which she did for as long as she could. And when her brain realized what was happening, that no breath had entered her body for some time, it woke her from the dream so that she would continue to live.

With a gasp, she pulled the air inside of her, startling Max, who had dozed off as well. He asked if she was all right, and she said, "Tomorrow I want to swim."

***

IN THE MORNING, Max arrived with a gentle tap at her bedroom door before dawn as planned. He had with him a stuffed canvas bag filled with, he said, "Everything we could possibly need."

"I'm still not sure about this," he whispered. "When you say you want to swim, you mean, like, float around a little, right? Cause if you're planning to scuba dive or do laps in a pool—"

"You told me we would go to the springs," she said, giving him a funny look. "I assume there will be no lanes for taking laps, no room for oxygen tanks. Just a stream and one tidy swimming hole."

"Yes, yes. You're right. I just don't want you to be disappointed."

She enjoyed his protectiveness and was grateful for the

steadfast way he remained forever on duty. She had the universe to thank for bringing them together.

"I want to float," she said soberly. "That's all I want to do."

"Are you sure you have the strength for all of it? You have to get in the car, take a short hike, put the swimsuit on."

"I don't need a suit. I have an e-skin."

"Oh, yeah. That's right."

"I'm sure I'll be exhausted when it's all done," she assured him, "but it'll be worth it."

***

THEY FOUND A VERY rectangular-shaped car in the garage (Impala, its silver nameplate said). Max drove. Natasha viewed the town of Kecksburg as if seeing it for the first time. Early risers walking their dogs. Pretty colored houses with their wood fences and tended lawns. Spring's warmth encouraging buds to show up on the trees as the scent of new life flowered the air.

The sun was just rising by the time Max pulled into a park and drove a few miles in. "No one ever comes this far," he said. They parked and entered a path into the forest that easily could have been missed. Gentle breezes chimed through the tall trees.

"Are you sure this is correct?" she said.

"Yes, this is it. You okay so far?"

"I'm fine," she said and put on a tranquil smile.

They held hands as they walked. The sun filtered through the branches and touched the top of her head.

"It's not too far?" she asked, already winded.

"No, just up ahead. I can carry you, if you want."

"No, not yet," she said.

They left the path and carefully stepped over branches that had fallen during winter storms, and the shoots of ferns peering up like little green heads from spring's muddy ground.

The burbling of a stream purred in the distance. The trees parted and Max stepped through, guiding her forward. Soon they came to a pool, about two body lengths across and almost perfectly round. It was surrounded by boulders plenty large to sit on, and a mellow stream fed it like a faucet set on low.

"How did these rocks get here?" she asked.

Max shrugged. "I have no idea. They were always here. Sort of like Stonehenge, I guess."

She lifted her brow in a humorous way.

"The *aliens* brought them," he said in a pseudo-spooky voice, then stuck out his tongue, which made them both laugh.

"Honestly, I love this place," Max said. "I used to spend a lot of time out here, in these woods. I didn't have any real friends. I'd just sit and, you know, throw pebbles, stare at the sky. Think about being an astronaut." He gazed at her coyly, checking her reaction, to see if she'd laugh at him, she supposed.

"Nobody else ever came, so it always felt like it was mine."

"Lucky you," she said. "This is beautiful."

"Yeah."

After Max helped her take a seat on one of the larger rocks, she kicked off the hiking boots she'd borrowed from Evan's closet. She was breathing a bit harder than she would have liked, but there was nothing she could do about it. Max would notice and he would worry. He sat on the rock beside hers. The walk had left her warm, and she removed her jacket, letting it fall to the ground.

"I'm so glad it's a warm day," she said.

"Yeah, are you sure you want to get in? It's still gonna be chilly."

"I'm counting on it," she said.

She removed her shirt, and Max whipped his head in the opposite direction.

"I have an e-skin, don't forget," she told him.

"I know," he said, "it's just I thought, you know, *privacy.*"

"You're so sweet. You really, really are."

"Yup, I know," he said with a sigh. "Everybody who knows me, calls me the sweet guy."

"Ha ha," she said.

Then she removed her pants, not standing up to do so, but struggling out of them from a seated position. She dropped them on top of her shoes and other clothes.

Max turned back and smiled at her, trying not to feel, she could tell, whatever mix of emotions made him clutch his hands together in desperation.

"I was thinking that I want you to see something."

A scared, semi-paralyzed expression settled upon Max's face.

"All right," he said.

"Don't worry," she told him. "Just . . . I need to do this."

"Okay, okay, show me."

"Not yet. Don't look just yet."

He closed his eyes and bowed his head.

"Did you get me a present, or something? Is it my birthday?"

"No, not exactly," she said.

"Tell me when I can open my eyes."

Natasha pulled at the neckline of her e-skin and easily undid the stitches her grandmother had made. Then she peeled back the skin over one shoulder and, with a bit of difficulty, did the same on the other side.

In front of her, Max grew still. His cheeks lost their cheerful softness and grew flat and pensive; Natasha could tell he suspected what she'd done. What she was doing.

He took a big, shuddering inhale and whispered, "Natasha, please—"

"Shh, quiet," she told him. "I *have* to."

She removed one arm of the e-skin at a time and left the top half bunched around her waist.

The air touched her in ways it never had before. She tipped back her head and basked in the tender rays that reached her real skin. The cool air breezed over her and made the hairs on her arms stretch upward to meet it. Her breath drew in that fresh air, and she imagined it healthful and nurturing.

She couldn't remember ever feeling so alive, so human and free.

Her heart stumbled, tumbling into an erratic beat.

Don't you dare quit on me now, she told it.

She had not yet looked down. Had never seen her chest and the evidence of what the doctors had done.

"Max, hold my hand."

He stuck out his arm, his eyes still closed. She took his hand, and he gently squeezed her fingers.

"I've never seen it," she said softly. "My own body without the e-skin on top. I never saw what they did to me."

"I'm here for you," he said. "I got you."

"I'm going to look, and I want you to look as well."

"Okay." His voice trembled. "I will."

Her heart pounded as she lowered her chin and gazed upon herself. The smooth, fair skin appeared untouched by the sun or even the air—like baby skin over her adult flesh.

The rise of her breasts led to a small, precisely sealed compartment in the center of her chest. It was more technological than human, but certainly not frightening or ugly.

Her heart skipped as relief washed over her.

Max was still squeezing her fingers. He hadn't yet opened his eyes.

"Are you okay?" he asked. "Have you seen it?"

"Yes," she said as she cupped her breasts with her hands. "You can look, it's not bad."

He met her gaze first, lingering for a silent moment, before his eyes traveled down her neck to her chest. He stared, his countenance growing soft. He didn't say anything. Didn't move.

"You're beautiful," he said. "All of you."

Then he raised his chin and leaned toward her. His lips met hers, and his breath spilled over her face. They shared a kiss that warmed her body and made her heart thump like feet running across pavement, threatening to take her away forever.

"Thank you," she said. "I'd never seen it before, and I needed you to be with me when I did."

"Anything else you want me to look at?" he asked with a humorous edge that made them both chuckle.

"Actually," she said, and she began to remove the rest of the e-skin.

Max turned away again, laughing and shaking his head in an amused way.

She was glad that she amused him.

"You know I'm not going in that water," he said.

"Yes, I know. I'll be careful not to splash you."

"Good. And you promise you know how to swim?"

"Do I know how to swim!" she shouted gleefully before plunking into the swimming hole like a giant drop of dew.

The cool, clean water surrounded her with goodness, and for one second, she wondered if it might heal her. She bobbed up to the top, fluttered her arms and kicked her legs, treading water, as she became accustomed to the frigid shock of it. Her breaths rose sharply from her throat, a slight wheeze she hoped Max wouldn't notice.

He watched her diligently for a few moments, standing guard, as if ready to jump in and rescue her should the need arise, but she proved she could swim, so he soon sat upon one of the larger boulders and reclined.

Natasha tossed back her head and dunked her hair. The water rolled over her cheeks and lips and entered her mouth. It cascaded down her chin and rode the length of her neck, drenched her brow and slipped into her eyes. The cold temperature energized her, made her feel as if she were brimming with life. This was what she'd dreamed of for years—and it was almost too much for her body to bear.

If she died in this beautiful place, she decided she'd be okay with it.

She submerged herself, feeling weightless. Practically bodiless. The pool was divine, delicious. She swam up and broke the surface. Then eased onto her back, the water lapping at her ears as she floated. She took in the long, sky-bound trunks of nearby trees and their high-reaching canopy of branches. The pure blue backdrop of the sky seemed no more than an arm's length away. She gazed at it to her sorry heart's content, knowing it was probably the last time she'd ever be able.

She decided to dive to the bottom. She glanced at Max, who lay back in the sun, one arm draped lazily over the side so that his fingers dipped into the water.

Then she dove.

The pool was deep, deeper than she'd expected.

She propelled herself downward, her arms making wide, sweeping outward arcs, her legs kicking determinedly behind. She set her resolve on reaching the bottom; she wouldn't worry about whether she could make it, whether she possessed the energy that was necessary, whether her heart would hold out. She would do it. Experience the quiet calm one could only find under the water. Or she would die.

She came to the pool's bottom, the place where plants wavered like reedy grasses in the breeze. She reached for them and petted their leaves. Beside them she eyed something that glowed. Two somethings, actually. Stones?

Two stones of the sort that seemed to vibrate with life.

She had seen stones like this before!

She reached out and plucked them from the bottom, then raced toward the surface. Her lungs burned as she kicked with all her might. No longer would it be okay to die, to lose her breath or allow her heart to stop beating.

She burst through the surface of the water, panting, heart pumping with abandon.

She splashed Max as she raised her arm and commanded him to "Look!"

"Do you know what these are?" she shouted through gulping, panting breaths.

"No," he said, the hopefulness spilling out of his wide and curious eyes.

"They're traveling stones. My father found some in his pocket when we visited Svetlana. He said that sometimes what you need comes to you. Evan and Svetlana and I used his to get back to Jovian Earth." She paused to see if Max understood.

"Okay," he said. "But—"

"They're what we need, Max. A trip out of here. A trip to Mintaka!"

He grabbed her up out of the water, and they rolled in a clumsy, urgent, bumping collision, laughing and wet and freezing, onto the forest floor.

"Can we go now?" he asked. "Can we please leave today?"

She required no time to consider her answer. "There's nothing I'd like more in this world," she said.

Epilogue 2

That first night, when they'd arrived to find Svetlana's house without one light shining either outside or inside, Svetlana's nerves began to roil. Was this even the right place? It *looked* like her house, more or less, though it wore a light-gray layer of paint instead of white. They paused as a group on the sidewalk directly across the street and contemplated the next move.

Svetlana had never lived in Kecksburg in the 1960s, wasn't even born in that decade, if this was the 1960s. So, why would this be her house? When she'd brought this up to Fran, he shook his head and said, "We have to try, right? I mean, what other options do we have?"

They had no other options. Both Natasha and Caroline remained unconscious, and everyone else was tired from hefting them through the woods and across town. They all needed to rest. If the house wasn't Svetlana's—

"Hey, the ship brought us here," Fran interrupted her thoughts. "Had to be for a reason, right?"

"That's true," Lisa said. "I mean, it didn't dump us in China or something. We're in Kirksberg."

"Kecksburg," Svetlana corrected her. "In this universe, it's called 'Kecksburg.' But, yes, what you're saying makes sense."

"You said there's a multiverse," Fran said, "so maybe this is yet another one? One where you were alive in the 1960s and you owned this house?" He raised his upturned palms in question.

Svetlana felt her brow lift. Any of these ideas could be true—or not. Who knew where or when the time trip had taken them.

"I hope you're right," she said. "And you might just be brilliant if you are."

They headed as a group down the driveway and entered the backyard through a wooden gate. Not the same gate Svetlana had at her house in the 2020s, but a weathered one with pointed tops. Svetlana entered the yard first, and the others limped in carrying Natasha and Caroline behind her.

She recognized the apple tree whose leaves fluttered as if welcoming her home. Amazingly, she found her house key under a clay pot she recognized: the one stained black and white, with moon and star decorations. She'd always kept that pot beside the back entrance.

Svetlana unlocked the door, and she and Fran entered with caution.

Lisa stayed back with Caroline, whom they'd deposited on a plastic lounge chair on the deck, and Max lay Natasha on another beside her.

Fran switched on his comm's flashlight, and Svetlana used the small but potent light on her wristcomm. They entered the kitchen quiet as thieves. Svetlana recognized the scent right away. Every home had a particular scent, and she'd never forget this one. The sweetness of apple and cinnamon, the salty, buttery hint of popcorn. While Fran shined his light into cabinets and the pantry, she pointed hers at the refrigerator, which was white, and boxier than she remembered. Not sleek or new. Its top third displayed a few sepia-toned photographs. Evan as a toddler on the swing, another of her holding a dozen brightly colored balloons, and one more of mother and child blowing out birthday candles.

The last one was a closeup of Andrew. Handsome and —gosh, she forgot how wholesome and vivacious he was— with his sand-colored hair and blue-green eyes, that unadulterated smile she could never get enough of.

"Bingo." Fran had been peering over her shoulder at the photos. "I guess I *am* brilliant." He chuckled, then said, "Your words, not mine."

After that, he left the kitchen and entered the living area. Svetlana followed him into the hall, and together they checked out the rest of the house, room by room. When they came back, Fran opened the back door and welcomed the others inside with an, "All clear."

They had a house. A place to live. A place for Caroline and Natasha to rest and recuperate (though Svetlana wasn't confident either of them would).

They all agreed the master suite would be the best place to situate Caroline. Lisa said she would need a hospital bed outfitted with an IV line, and, if they could get their hands on one, a blood pressure machine and heart monitor.

Svetlana readily gave up her claim on the spacious room she once—twice—shared with her husband. Which was for the best. This was the start of yet another life. This time, one without her daughter or husband or son. She was on her own. She would sleep in the guest room next door to Evan's bedroom, the room Natasha would occupy. Fran and Lisa took the bedroom down the hall from the master, the one Drew, the clone, once lived in, and Max would take the living room couch. He was used to the berth on his ship, so this would not be a problem.

***

IT HAD BEEN A MONTH SINCE their mysterious spaceship had crash-landed in Kecksburg, and Svetlana still didn't like the way Caroline had somehow ended up living under her roof, and Evan sadly had not. It didn't seem right. It didn't seem fair.

But Svetlana was used to unfair.

That morning, she made a pot of coffee as the clock neared seven, the sun sending warmth through the living room windows and into the kitchen it opened up to. Max was not on the couch. As a matter of fact, she couldn't remember a night or a morning when she'd found him sleeping there. None of the adults in the room wanted to overtly acknowledge the Max-and-Natasha situation— Max claimed his attention to her came from his duty to protect and care for her in tribute to Evander's memory— but the adoration between them might as well have been painted in bright purple.

They loved each other. Fran's son and her granddaughter. How wonderful was that?

Fran joined her in the kitchen, his face puffy from lack of sleep—no one had been sleeping much. "I'm glad you're up before me," he said, taking a seat at the table. "Your coffee is so much better than mine."

"I'm always up before you," she said passing him a steaming cup. "And my coffee and your coffee are exactly the same."

He smiled. "You seem cheerful. Any reason?"

"I guess I'm getting used to the idea of being here, in our new living situation."

He rubbed his scruffy chin. He didn't shave very often in this world. "Yeah. I get that."

"You know . . . without my daughter and with my—" she hesitated, "with the queen living in my master bedroom."

"Have you even seen the room since me and Lisa set it up?"

Svetlana brought her mug of coffee to her lips and turned away. No, she had not visited Caroline. Not once the entire month. "I'm thinking pancakes this morning," she said, pushing her seat back and standing. "Sound good?"

She could feel his eyes reaching for hers, but hers remained conveniently out of reach.

"No," he said sternly. "There's a reason I got up at early this morning and pancakes isn't it."

"Oh." She dropped back into the chair.

"I need to talk to you."

"Well, good. I always enjoy your company."

The impending moment hung in the air between them.

"What is it?" she finally asked. "Do you have something bad to tell me? Are you leaving me alone with Caroline?"

"Where would I go?"

She shrugged. "Back to your world."

"Oh, well, yeah. We will go back, and I think you already know that. But not right away. Among other things, we have to figure out how we're going to get there."

They shared a knowing smile.

"We also want to see Caroline to her end," he said.

"Oh, uh-huh," Svetlana said, grateful they wouldn't ask her to do it.

"Caroline wants to speak with you," he said, brusquely.

Svetlana's defenses rose. "Does she?"

"I know you don't want to hear it, don't want to deal with it, but Caroline feels she has something important to say to you."

"Really?" she said, the word carrying her usual sarcasm. "Something important. Hm."

He shook his head, the disappointment evident in his angry frown. "You know, Caroline spends each day in bed, under an electric blanket with the heat turned up because her body temperature . . . " His words petered out. "Stop looking so pissed off."

Svetlana bowed her head. "I'm sorry. Go on."

"Lisa checks to make sure she's comfortable throughout the day. Lisa brushes her hair and washes her and takes care of everything. And I'm not telling you this because Lisa or I think it should be some other way. Lisa and Caroline are close—"

"Close?" Svetlana hadn't expected that.

"Yes, Svetlana. They're close. And Lisa doesn't mind, you know, taking her into her final days."

It probably shouldn't have surprised Svetlana. She'd watched Lisa tend to Caroline through some difficult situations. Obviously Lisa respected and maybe even liked her.

"Okay, well, then good. I'm glad she feels that way."

"You don't feel any responsibility to Caroline at all, do you?"

"I mean . . . " All the reasons she didn't care for Caroline rose with her clenched shoulders. "I guess it's hard for you to understand, but I don't."

Fran drew in a slow breath. "Okay, well, late last night Caroline mentioned some things she'd like to say to you.

And I think you should hear her out," Fran said. "While it's still possible."

"Before she dies, you mean."

"Yeah. Before she dies."

"And you don't understand that I don't care if I don't hear it," Svetlana said, tempering her urge to lash out. "Not hearing what she wants to say sounds like a good punishment, if you ask me."

"For you or for her?" he said before sighing out a curse. "You've always been stubborn, Svetlana, and usually it's turned out to be a good thing that you are, but I'm not so sure this time around."

"Why do you want to help her? Just because she's old and sick? She's the same woman who used me and Andrew, and Evander, for that matter. Why do you care so much about her?"

"I want to help *you*," he said. "I care about *you*."

"I don't need this kind of help."

How could she make him believe it?

They retreated to their corners of the ring for the moment, but it wasn't over. Svetlana sensed Fran had more to say.

"Look, I know you don't need my help," he said, staring into his coffee cup. "You never need anyone's help. Except," his mouth drew together in a pinch, "sometimes you do. You're human. You have feelings. I wish you'd stop denying them." He paused, moved his coffee from one place to another. "Caroline is part of your family. She's a part of Andrew and Evander and . . . she's part of Evan too. She isn't all bad. No one is. And she's lost everything. She's not even Jovian anymore. Just an old woman who wants to make amends at the end of her days."

"Ugh," Svetlana groaned.

"Ugh," he groaned right back at her.

She couldn't help but smile at him. "You are so annoying, you know that?"

"Good friends usually are," he said.

"I mean," she scoffed, "must I always do the right thing?"

"Yes," he said, sitting back and imparting a touch of smugness. "Because that's who you are. The kind of person who does the right thing. For her friends, and her children, and her *family*. Caroline wants to make amends. I think it's time you let her."

Svetlana bowed her head and rubbed her forehead. "She can't change the awful things she's already done."

"Maybe, or . . . maybe not. In this strange world that we live in, everything is possible," Fran said. "It's possible for you to one day get back to Evan, and it's possible for you to talk to Andrew, who's not even a person anymore, and it's possible for you to forgive Caroline.

"All of these things can happen in this crazy, vast, mysterious . . . " He shook his head, overwhelmed, "place that we live in. It's possible that you're human in this world but you're Jovian somewhere else. That you're alive here and dead on another version of Earth or Jupiter or some black hole out there that's sucking the life out of a star that unknowingly ventured too close. Don't you see? Anything, *everything* is possible. More than once, I thought I'd never see you again. I thought it was impossible, that you were as good as dead to me—and then you showed up at the bunker. And I have to tell you, knowing that you lived and had been living all the time that had passed since our last meeting . . . that you'd made it back to Andrew and had another child, this time a daughter . . . it gave me a new kind of trust and understanding of the world.

"All of this stuff we call life," he gestured to what was around them, "is only the surface, only what we can see.

And there's so much more. More than we will ever know." He pinched the bridge of his nose and squeezed his eyes closed as if this statement, this *revelation*, were almost too much to bear.

She'd never seen him so thoughtful, so enlightened.

Would he be surprised to learn that she agreed with him?

She'd experienced similar ideas and feelings, and now, when she thought of them, she went limp and vulnerable. It was a moment before she realized there were tears in her eyes. She didn't want to cry, but it happened. Because some part of her knew he was right, knew she might speak to Andrew again, and see her daughter again. No matter what she did to protect herself from her own strong feelings, the truth would remain the truth. The world and all of its happenings would play out.

"Life is precious and rare," Fran said. "Our own solar system teaches us that. Earth is the only planet plentiful with life. And what we do while we're alive matters."

Svetlana used her napkin to wipe her face and blot her nose. "Fine. I'll talk to Caroline."

"Good," he said. He made a fist and gently struck the tabletop.

Then Svetlana went to him, took his hands, and pulled him to a stand. She opened her arms and hugged him. "Thank you for being my friend," she said. "Andrew always loved you, and so do I." Her words muffled into his broad shoulder.

"Back at you," he said in his usual manner.

Her smile lingered on him for a moment longer before fading as she turned away, ready to take a slow walk down the hall.

***

Svetlana reached the door that opened to the master. The place she'd mourned her husband and also went into labor with Evan. She remembered hiding from David with the toddler who was Evander and speaking to Uncle Jimmy through the window before he escaped into the night. The room was still painted blue with white trim. Still with a walk-in closet (though not quite so big as the one she remembered) and a dresser for two on the opposite wall.

The person reclined in the hospital bed hardly resembled the larger-than-life Queen Jovian that once ruled the land. Lisa drowsed in a chair beside the bed and its metal poles and wires, a tube draped neatly out of the way and ending under the skin of Caroline's small, curled hand. One of the pods from the ship may have been better for a former Jovian, Svetlana realized, but there had been no time to remove anything as large as a bathtub when they'd landed in the middle of the forest. Instead, Lisa had called the local hospice for what they needed.

The room smelled of antiseptic. A purifier hummed in the corner, and the beeping of a machine set a somber tone. Svetlana's gaze lingered on Caroline's face. The old woman's strong eyes shrouded behind thin, purplish lids; her proportional classic features caught in a net of wrinkles and hollows. Her body looked so gaunt under the blanket, the arms resting on top, veined and spotted and bony.

Lisa roused in the chair, breathing out an early-morning groan.

"Fran said she wanted to speak to me," Svetlana whispered. "Is it all right if I wake her?"

"I'm not sure she ever sleeps," Lisa said, "not the way we do. If you say her name, she'll answer."

With closed eyes and from a slightly raised pillow, Caroline said, "I am here."

Lisa retied her robe around her middle and stood. "I'll give you two some privacy," she said, squeezing Svetlana's arm as she passed on the way out.

"Svetlana," Caroline said and then pressed her lips together, as if speaking caused her severe discomfort—or maybe just being alive did. "I'm grateful you've come."

Svetlana didn't know what to do with her hands. Should she balance her forearms over the side of the metal guardrail, maybe touch Caroline's sad little hand? But no, she wasn't ready for that.

"Yes. Well, um, Fran told me—" Svetlana cleared her throat. "You wished to see me."

"Thank you." Caroline opened her eyes. They were smaller than they once appeared, watery, a bit cloudy. Not the beautiful brown with the gold flecks Svetlana remembered. Certainly no longer Jovian and fierce. On the contrary, Svetlana sensed remorse in their infirmity.

"I have some regrets," Caroline said as if able to read Svetlana's mind.

Svetlana nodded but would not reply. Not yet.

"I was never fair to the human race." Caroline spoke in a forthright manner in spite of her weakened state. "I understand that now. You and Evander both tried to tell me, to make me see, but I didn't. I couldn't."

"I remember," Svetlana said.

"I have learned a lot during my . . . physical transformation." Her eyes flicked guiltily up to meet Svetlana's, then darted away.

"I imagine you have," Svetlana said.

"Most important, perhaps, I learned that there is a gene for empathy," Caroline said. "Many humans have it, *most* do, I think. But it doesn't come naturally to Jovians."

"Dana has it," Svetlana said. "And John. Evan and Evander—"

Caroline attempted a smile but couldn't seem to make it happen. A slight tremor shook her head. "They are . . . the lucky ones."

The old Caroline would not have said such a thing.

"Until I began to transform," her voice rattled in her throat, "I had no understanding of human emotion. No way to know how it shaped their lives. And then it began to shape my own, and I saw the world in an entirely new way." She shook her head slightly.

Now that she knows what it means to feel, now that she has suffered, she can empathize. But it's too late for that.

"I'll be honest with you, Caroline. The only reason I can speak plainly with you is because you have lost. You have no power. If it's forgiveness you want, then maybe I can one day forgive you—but in another world, if you were still in power—"

"Why wonder what it would be like if things were different?" she asked in a surprisingly clear voice. "We are in this world. Only this one. This is the world that matters in this moment. And I haven't lost."

"You've lost the planet you loved, your true Jovian self, your grandson, your clones, your entire family—"

"I have only done what I was meant to do," she said. "The planet was never mine, and the lives of others take their own courses. What happened to them was not up to me. Just like the lives of your children are not up to you. Humans offer their children guidance, and they hope for the best. To do more is to interfere."

To some extent, Svetlana agreed.

"There is a natural path for each individual, and sometimes the only thing parents can, or should, do is get out of its way. These are all truths I've learned from you."

"Oh," Svetlana said, thinking of Evan, and how she

had to set her free so Evan could see where life would take her.

"I was cold to you and to Andrew, and most regretfully, to Evander," Caroline said. "I seemed uncaring, and I must accept the pain and guilt that comes with my new understanding. My only defense is that I thought with all my being that I was doing the right thing."

Caroline reached for Svetlana with her sad, clouded eyes before raising a shaking hand from the bed. The confession seemed to have required the last of her waking energy, and she sank deeper into the fibers of the mattress. Her body may have become even thinner than when Svetlana had first entered the room.

This would be Caroline's end. Maybe not this moment, but this time, this world. There would be no fanfare for this royal being from another planet, no desperate pleas for her to live. Just a quiet place with a handful of humans to see her off.

"I think I can understand," Svetlana said.

Caroline seemed to relax then, her expression easing into a more restful place of comfort. "Thank you for speaking with me," she said in not much more than a whisper.

Svetlana reached for Caroline's cold, dry hand. "I promise that I will try to forgive you."

In the silence that followed, a weight lifted from Svetlana's shoulders. Her mind was freed from the restraints of bitterness and smoothed over with new clarity.

"There's something else," Caroline said, and Svetlana leaned in closer to hear. "Andrew is waiting. Go outside, and you'll find him."

"On the deck, you mean? In the sacred circle?"

Svetlana didn't wait for an answer. She let go of Caroline's hand and sped out of the room. She passed Lisa and

Fran in the kitchen, smiling with abandon when she said, "I'll be outside talking to Andrew!"

"Oh, my goodness!" Lisa laughed. "That's crazy . . . and wonderful."

"Tell him not to be a stranger," Fran said as Svetlana slid the glass door closed behind her.

She stood on the deck, in the center of the sacred circle, the place Andrew had always set his telescope. "I'm here, Andrew. I'm here."

Nothing in the yard moved. Not the bushes or trees or even the air. The birds did not sing, the neighbors did not open or close doors or start the engines of their cars. It was as if the moment in time had come to a halt.

"Andrew?" she said.

"You made it home," he answered.

She looked all around, then up at the gray-blue sky emerging with the morning.

"I don't see you. Where are you?"

"I'm where I always am," he said, and she detected a smile bobbing on his lips. "We can talk here."

"Oh," she deflated. "I thought you might actually *be* here."

"I have news about Evan. She's been working with your parents, Dana and John."

"Really!" Svetlana said, her relief catching in her throat. "That's—oh my gosh—that makes me feel so much better."

"Together they're leading the way for all who remain on Earth. Human, clone, hybrid, Moon Child, animal, tree, whale, penguin . . . "

He told her about Dana and John's plan for the new settlements and harmonizing with the earth and the Jovians' nonviolent influence. Also Leo's new way forward for Mars. And Evan's idea for the Moon Children to stay. And how amazing that was.

"She really is the right person for the job," he said.

"Oh, Andrew, I can't tell you how happy this makes me. Dana and John and Evan, living and working together. Will I ever see her again?"

"Never say never."

"You know I hate when you talk like Uncle Jimmy. Or if you do, please let me know if seeing my daughter is written in the stars."

"Mm," he said. "She'll be busy for many years, you know. It's not easy to be a world leader, negotiating with extraterrestrials and rebuilding civilization."

"I'm sure. She probably wishes she stayed home like I told her to."

Andrew didn't reply. Svetlana knew why, and it was okay. *Evan wants to stay on Jovian Earth.*

She looked at the planks that formed a circle in the otherwise ordinary deck. "Does this thing still work as a portal? After we left the Jovian world, I wondered if it would close up."

"When it's needed, it works. In all the universes. Natasha and Max passed through a little while ago. They're traveling to Mintaka."

"Those little sneaks. Is that where they went? I'll tell Fran and Lisa. They'll be happy for them. They're in love, you know."

"Yes, I know."

"So, wait, that means this circle can take me back to Jovian Earth?"

"Yes, but you're not scheduled for a trip until the year—"

"Don't tell me," she said, stopping him. "It's better that I don't know."

"You're probably right about that."

"Did you know this was a portal when you built it?" she asked.

"I had a strong desire to bang some nails into wood. That's all," he said in his familiar, forthright way.

"You're all intuition," she said. "I love that about you. But what you're saying is that Evan, technically, can get back home again."

"Yes, she can. Rest easy, my love. All is as it should be."

"It's been a long time since I've rested easy. You know that."

"Try it now," he said. "I hear it's good for the soul."

"But will I lose our connection if I leave the circle?"

"No. The circle makes the connection, and the connection has already been made."

She walked to one of the aluminum lounge chairs, plopped down, kicked up her feet, eased her head back and moaned. "Oh, Andrew, it hurts. Losing people—and then finding them only to lose them all over again."

"I know," he said. "It's a lot for anyone to take. Even extraordinary people like you."

"Thank you, kind sir. I've always appreciated your flattery."

"And I've always appreciated your . . . everything."

As she lay in the quiet, the morning sounds rose from obscurity. Birds chirped and called to one another in song, a nearby car grinded to life, someone let a porch door slap closed. High up in the trees, the air whistled through branches.

"Remember that what you see, what you experience, is only one small part," he said. "There are other worlds, other dimensions, constant movement. Constant change."

"You know what's strange?" Svetlana said. "I wouldn't change any of it. Not one thing that happened. Because this is my life, whether it was destiny or fate or the universe setting my course, or me just doing my best to muddle through. What difference does it make, really? Of all the things that could have happened, you and I met and fell in love, and that love changed the course of our lives—and the lives of many others."

"What were the odds?" he said, musing.

"Probably about a trillion to one."

"Something like that. And yet it happened."

She gazed at the sliver of moon fading into the new blue of the sky. A few stars persisted as well. She may have been looking at Orion's belt and the cluster of specks near Callisto. Or maybe not. "Love is the one thing that remains constant across time and space," she said, believing it wholeheartedly.

"Yes," Andrew agreed. "You can trust love. You can trust it with all your heart."

"I do," she said. "I really do."

Epilogue 3

The Jovian Universe
2101

Lagging several steps behind the group of tourists and their guide, three very old, very wise individuals strolled the long corridor the Jovian family once called "the executive wing." One of these individuals, a man with a pot belly and partial crown of hair, oh'ed and ah'ed at every little detail and sight there was to see—the building's faceted glass walls, the spiral staircase that connected first and second floors, the mysterious red-lighted room that many people theorized about but no one understood—as if he'd never before set foot within its walls.

He found the cracks in the basement floor, which their tour guide surmised occurred during an Earthquake in the year 2051, especially fascinating.

But the truth was all three of these elderly individuals, James (aka Uncle Jimmy) and the two women who accompanied him (Constance, also known as Aunt Constance, and Ida Moore), knew the venue well.

Uncle Jimmy and Aunt Constance once posed as Jovians themselves, though they did not originate on Jupiter or Mintaka or anywhere else "ordinary" individuals like their friend Ida came from. Ida began life as a human, but she spent so much time with Jimmy and Constance over the years that some of their immortality had rubbed off on her. At this point, Ida was well over two hundred Earth years old.

Ida hadn't visited this particular version of Earth in over one hundred years, and she found the field trip fascinating. "Who would have thought Starbright International would one day reopen as a museum?" she said, drawing the attention of the tourists within earshot. Dressed in her usual hooded cloak, Ida failed to remember that others would find her strange and maybe even suspicious.

"Isn't this universe wonderful?" she said, lowering her voice. "I love this one. It deserves a gold star."

"Agreed," Jimmy said. "Then again, they all deserve a gold star in their own way."

"I'm not sure that's true," Constance said with a frown.

"Well, this one got it right," Jimmy said. "It's something they can be proud of."

"Only took them twenty-one hundred years," Constance reminded him.

"The important thing is that they got there," he insisted. "They made it work."

"True," she said. "They got it right . . . for now."

"Yes, for now," he said. "The kid came through, just like I said she would. Evan Peterman with her grandparents, Dana and John. Don't you just love the name Peterman? It's so earthy and human. They're my favorites, you know," Jimmy said.

"All the humans are your favorites," Constance said.

The tour had reached the conference room. The guide

said something about Caroline Jovian, a six-story-tall alien in her natural form, who led with few words and a chilling demeanor.

"I won't deny it," Jimmy said. "I have a soft spot for humans, always have, always will."

The leader of the tour, a pretty auburn-haired woman, had left the conference room, taking the group into the part of the tube that led to the astronomical observatory. Captivated by the tube's very secretive, fluorescent-bright interior, they gawked and chattered.

"I never understood something about you two," Ida said. "How is it you obviously care so much for humanity but always manage to disappear during a crisis of dire proportion?"

Constance gazed into the distance as if turning the question over in her mind.

Jimmy offered: "I think you know the answer to that, Ida."

The ancient woman pressed her thin lips into her mouth. "No, I really don't. I was once human, lest you forget. I know what's it like to face a problem so big or so many-headed that you feel absolutely helpless to do anything about it."

"We could never forget your origins," Jimmy said. "You are also one of my favorite humans. Or, more-than-humans, as it turns out."

Determined to have her answer, Ida said, "I remember when I was a young woman and I wished something bigger than myself was out there, watching over the world, making sure fairness and some kind of balance ruled the universe. I was desperate for reassurance, for some evidence that life had a point. That there were guardrails, a reason or a plan for everything . . . or at least some things."

"That's very human of you," Constance said. "But we

don't interfere because we feel that humanity should work it out for themselves. That's what it means to be human. To rise to the occasion. It's no good for us to fix every little problem that comes along."

"And yet it hasn't stopped him," Ida cocked her head in Jimmy's direction, "from interfering every now and again."

"I'm not sure I follow," Jimmy said. "Would you like to share whatever it is you are talking about specifically?"

Ida didn't answer right away. Perhaps unsure she should say it out loud.

"Speak freely," he told her.

They'd reached the observatory and filed in with the others, then found a vacant area to stand a distance away. The cool air smelled earthy and fresh.

"I'm talking about sharing the secret to cloning humans and, even more specifically, making Svetlana pregnant," Ida said. "We all know that missing one birth control pill does not a baby make 99.9 percent of the time. And your own fertilization of Caroline's human egg, for goodness's sake, which led to Andrew Jovian's existence. That kind of interference."

"Oh, well, that's just—" Jimmy stammered, though the hint of a grin plumped his cheeks.

Constance shook her head, a thin layer of disgust veiling her grandmotherly demeanor. "Some of us can't help ourselves."

Jimmy chuckled. "We're nothing if not, uh, mysterious. And I only help things along every millennium or so."

"Forget I asked," Ida said. "It's just something I ponder from time to time."

The sun cast a dazzling conical ray in the center of the room, and the three of them stared up at the oculus.

"Ah," Constance said, her arm moving toward the light as if she couldn't suppress her desire to touch it.

"This place is as beautiful as I remember," Jimmy whispered. "How did Dmitri manage to extricate himself?"

"Sheer moral strength," Constance said.

"While I have you both here," Ida interrupted, "can you please, please, please answer this age-old question: Is the future written in the stars, or is it not? You've never provided a firm answer, and I'll promise not to tell anyone, if that makes any difference. I just really want to know."

Jimmy turned to Constance and said, "Speaking of starlight, I need a vacation. What do you say?"

"I could use a rest, for sure. Where to this time?"

"I was thinking, the Sun," he said, jiggling with delight.

"You want to go home?" Constance said, thrilled by the idea if the crinkles around her smiling eyes were any indication.

"It would be nice to recharge our batteries, you know?" he said. "Warm up, burn off the lethargy that follows a hard century's work."

He reached for her hand just as she reached for his. Then they turned to face Ida, and Constance said, "Hold down the fort, my dear."

"I'll be happy to," Ida said, "but don't stay for too long, okay?"

A sudden flash rendered all present—the tour guide, group of tourists, and Ida as well—stunned. The gathering let out a unified gasp as they succumbed to momentary blindness. Even before the light faded from her eyes, Ida was sure Jimmy and Constance were gone.

"You never know what's going to happen," she muttered to herself.

<u>Prophecy of the Lost Sister</u>

The leadership's mother,
sent across time,
had with her a child,
who crossed the sublime.

Soon came the destruction
through moonlight and hive
of Earth's peaceful presence
where royalty thrived.

The lost one,
like her brother before,
possessed mettle and honor,
her heart worthy of lore.

She laid to rest the resistance,
sidestepped the queen's insistence,
and rendered a solution
for all mankind.

Look to the stars
and you shall see
where the cold light of fate
marks her destiny.

A Note from the Author

Dear Readers,

I can't thank you enough for joining the Jovian Universe cast of characters on this epic journey. I hope you've enjoyed following them through the highs and lows, the expected and the unexpected.

This novel marks the final installment of the five-book series. Moving forward, I'm going to miss engaging with this world and all who populate it! If you are too, please reach out to me and let me know. I may decide to write some supporting pieces down the road.

If you've enjoyed this book, I hope you'll leave a review (or just a rating) wherever you like to write book reviews. I appreciate and send good vibes in response to every kind review I receive. Thank you in advance for taking the time to type a few sentences worthy of your thoughts!

To reach out to me, subscribe to my newsletter, or read my blog, visit AuthorKimCatanzarite.com. I love to hear from readers and always reply to messages.

Acknowledgments

When I set out to publish my first novel, I did not fathom that it would become a five-part sci-fi series. I'd written several novels before, those that taught me the writing craft, but five parts of one whole had never crossed my mind.

They Will Be Coming for Us, about a young Russian woman who falls in love with a charismatic astronomer from a very special family was different. It would not be a "one and done." It had legs and those legs would walk and then jog and, finally, run.

I finished the first draft of *The Jovian Line* (working title) in 2018 and didn't publish it until 2021. After that, I was off to the races, publishing one book every nine months or so. This surprises some people. How can you write so much so fast? The answer is that I love to write novels, plain and simple. I've practiced my craft and have been steeped in the editorial world for decades. I'm driven to do what I love to do.

The other part of the answer is that the characters motivated me: I couldn't wait to find out what would happen to them and their world. From one book to the next, I needed to know.

None of the books in the Jovian Universe pentalogy would have been possible without my supporters. My beta readers, editors, proofreading pools, ARC readers, and reviewers (especially BlueInk Review). My cover designer (Damonza.com) and subscribers to my newsletter and blog.

My friends, family, Bookstagram peers, and all the lovely people I've met through my Writer's Digest classes. Each one of you has helped me produce this series, and I am very grateful.

In no particular order, thank you to Ron Skelton, Breanna Teramoto, Patricia Olson, Annette Masters, Anne Slater, Debra Dynes, Zoe Routh, Michael Solis, and Jay Fraser. Also, my mentors and teachers Daphne Du Maurier, E. M. Forster, Elizabeth Gilbert, Helena Bonham Carter, Mary Oliver, Ralph Waldo Emerson, Lucy Maud Montgomery, and every book I ever read.

Special thanks go to Joan, Ben, and Jennifer Kerrigone, Carol Catanzarite, Sienna Catanzarite, and my wonderful husband, Joe Catanzarite.

Thank you most of all to my readers. Without you, it's all just words on a page.

Into a book I go, to lose my mind and find my soul.

About the Author

Kim Catanzarite writes character-driven science fiction and dark fantasy novels. Her books are a mix of heartfelt family and friendship drama, fast-paced adventure, engaging plot twists, and unique imagination. She is the author of the Jovian Universe series and the Angel of Death series. Kim lives in New Jersey with her husband and daughter.

instagram.com/author_kim_catanzarite

www.ingramcontent.com/pod-product-compliance
Lightning Source LLC
Chambersburg PA
CBHW032339310726
48973CB00007B/1777